MW01702290

FIRST BORN

A FIRST BORN BOOK

FROM

THE GUARDIANS OF DARE CHRONICLES

Janelle Gabay

ISBN: 978-0-9961588-2-4

FIRST BORN

FIRST AWAKENED

LAST CHANCE

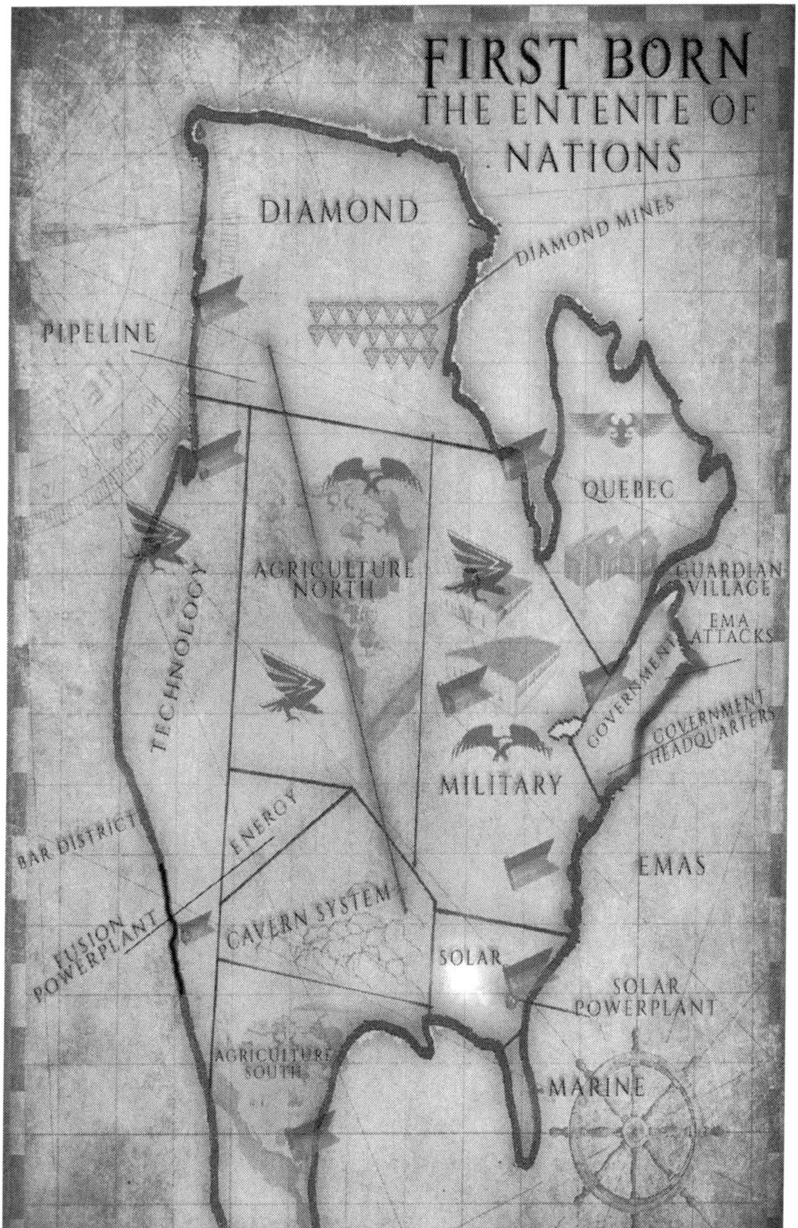
FIRST BORN
THE ENTENTE OF NATIONS
DIAMOND
DIAMOND MINES
PIPELINE
QUEBEC
AGRICULTURE NORTH
TECHNOLOGY
GUARDIAN VILLAGE
EMA ATTACKS
GOVERNMENT
GOVERNMENT HEADQUARTERS
MILITARY
BAR DISTRICT
ENERGY
EMAS
CAVERN SYSTEM
FUSION POWERPLANT
SOLAR
SOLAR POWERPLANT
AGRICULTURE SOUTH
MARINE

THE ENTENTE OF NATIONS

On July 11, 2045, after six years of deadly combat, the Entente War ended. The world divided, or as the elderly recall the world shrank. The bloodiest and most destructive battles were fought across the oceans. Many of these countries disintegrated, became known as the Wastelands, and soon forgotten. The countries that didn't rot away built walls and hid behind them. The grandest of these walls surrounded the entirety of the North American continent, which became known as The Entente of Nations.

To my mom and dad, who taught me how to love and filled my life with laughter.

To my husband, who always believed in my ability and encouraged my strength.

To my children, who never cease to amaze me every day. Without them there would be no stories!

LONE SURVIVOR

DECEMBER 20, 2110

Joe Prescott opened the door leading into his son's hospital room. His wife, Carolyn, reluctantly lifted her head from their son's bed. Tears drenched her face, and her arms stretched across Tarian's sleeping body. She smiled when their eyes met.

"He's alive, Joe. Our baby is alive." Her voice sounded hoarse and dry, but she continued, "It's a miracle. His friends … all the other kids on the bus … died and—" The grief strangled her silent.

She fought to keep the tears from forming, but they didn't obey and fell from her eyes. She didn't wipe them away because she wouldn't remove her arms from Tarian's body. Would she ever let him go?

"That horrible black ice on that stupid bridge! They should've canceled the field trip. I told Mrs. Middleton. Oh God, she's gone too. And I let him go!" She sobbed.

"I know honey. I know."

He wanted to silence her, to stop her pain, but the words

spilled uncontrollably from her mouth.

"The bus skidded … the poor children … drowned in that icy pond. It's awful Joe … just … just … just not right." Her voice had gained strength but gave out once more.

Joe walked over to stand behind his wife. He kissed the top of her head, caressed her hair, and gazed down at his second born son. His small chest rose and fell. The minor movement filled Joe's heart with relief.

Joe had endured death's sting for centuries, but tonight he had been spared. He thought about the many parents who had not been spared. Those parents suffered the most painful of all losses, the death of a child.

Joe grabbed the plump hand of his nine-year-old boy and felt the undeniable warmth of life on his skin. He knew what his son truly was.

This would be the most difficult of all the secrets he kept from Carolyn.

ONE

ENTENTE MILITARY ACADEMY (EMA)

DECEMBER 20, 2120

Tarian Prescott studied his class notes on the *History of the Entente Reconstruction.* He wasn't worried about the mid-year exam. He merely passed time since he couldn't sleep. He had an A in the class. He enjoyed learning about the aftermath of the Great Entente War. The details of reshaping North America into one, united, closed-bordered nation intrigued him. Outdated practices of international trading fascinated him. It boggled his mind to think of his homeland, the Entente, relying on any outside nation for resources. But the clock struck one o'clock in the morning, and he had to get some rest.

He rose from his desk, rubbed a kink out of his neck and collapsed onto his bed. With one and a half years of intense physical training, Tarian had gone from a gangly, boney-shouldered, first-year to a strong, muscular, second-year, and his body ached all over. His six-foot-two of newly acquired height consumed the length of his modest twin mattress. His long legs stretched outright, and his toes reached past the end railing. With his head resting on the palms of his hands, fingers laced, and his well-defined biceps spread triangular shaped on his pillow, he stared at the ceiling in anticipation. Tomorrow, his Cadet Sergeant had promised she'd tell him the truth about his father's death.

For the past two months, the secret had chiseled away at his psyche in painful sharp cuts. Insomnia began when he'd accidentally overheard the word 'murder' during a private conversation between his Cadet Sergeant, Audrey Gualtiero, and his dad's best friend, Senator Zachary Eastwood. The Senator was like a second father to him. He'd lived with the Senator the year before he began the Entente Military Academy, the year after his father's heart attack, so it surprised him that the Senator had never mentioned knowing Gualtiero, his classmate.

Gualtiero was the head of his company in rank and one year ahead of him in school. She ruined his life daily with her constant orders and demands for perfection. She was a walking megaphone. She expected nothing less than first, from bed making to underwater training drills. If her company came in second for anything, they suffered for it. Needless to say, Tarian made sure they never came in second.

"Why did the Senator kiss her on the forehead?" he asked himself as he had several times before. The Senator rarely kissed his daughter.

More questions. *How does she know my dad? Why would she call his death a murder? I know that's what I overheard unless I'm going crazy!*

He shut his eyes tight, exhaled and replayed the conversation inside his head but still had no answers. The word murder stuck. His father had died of natural causes due to a heart attack, so the mention of him being murdered struck hard. *Who'd want to murder an estate lawyer from the Government District?*

Tarian slipped into fitful sleep. As the bloody knife in his dream jammed its blade into his dad's chest cavity, cracking bone and gouging organs, he jumped awake with beads of sweat rolling down his neck. Anger burned through him. *How dare someone kill Dad!*

Shaking his head and rolling over onto his right side, he forced the vivid images out of his mind. He wrapped his body in the cotton sheet and willed his brain to be still. He needed sleep. He hadn't been able to let his father's memory rest in peace since the horrid day he overheard their conversation, but tonight was the final night of his ignorance. Gualtiero had promised she'd tell him the truth once off campus and on their way back to Salem for Holiday Break. No matter what transpired between now and then, he'd hold her accountable to that promise.

TWO

THE ATTACK

"Get up!"

Tarian vaguely heard Gualtiero's barking orders. Annoyance saturated every layer of his skin. The urge to wrap the pillow around his head, cover his ears, and go back to sleep nearly overtook him, but he couldn't disobey a superior officer.

"Now! Get up!"

Having finally slipped into a deep sleep, her shrill voice echoed and grated on his nerves, but EMA soldiers followed orders. He attempted to sit up, but sleep lingered inside him. Slowly his eyes focused. She rushed toward his bed with fatigues and combat boots in her arms. She threw them. The sharp heel of the boot hit his bare chest like a solid punch. Now, he was pissed. She'd gone too far with her superiority complex. He opened his mouth, the yell ready on his tongue then he caught himself. She held rank. Then he heard the ear-piercing fire alarm.

"Don't ask questions, just do as I say. Get dressed. Hurry!" Gualtiero's icy blue eyes stretched wide.

She didn't leave the room or turn around to give him privacy. Instead, she released weapons and a gas mask from her belt. Her usual steeliness had vanished. She looked frantic. When he glanced out the window, he saw flames of fire devouring the grass of The Plain. The alarm was not a drill. Then he heard something. *Gunshots?*

"What's going on?" Tarian threw on his uniform and yanked on his boots.

"The Prevallers are attacking the academy. They've found you. Hide this just in case." She shoved the hand-cannon into his belt. She handed him another weapon, a bigger arm that could easily blast three rounds in a split second.

"Did you say found *me*?" He stood in front of her dressed, armed, and ready.

"Come on!"

She pulled him out of his room and into the hall. Smoke rushed into his nostrils and clouded his eyes. He hurriedly slipped on the gas mask. His thoughts shot straight to his two best friends. He fought against Gualtiero's hold as he turned back to check two rooms. Empty. His two best friends, Gabe and Maria, must've heard the alarm and already fled the building. They'd left without alerting him. His heart sank with relief and betrayal.

Gualtiero clamped down on his elbow and dragged him toward the exit. Her strength amazed him. A flammable substance covered the doorway causing thick flames. They leaped through the vicious wall of red, fell to the ground, and rolled.

Back on her feet, Gualtiero tugged him up to his. They ran.

He followed her not knowing at first what direction she was taking him. The dim early morning sunlight veiled everything in a color-blending, fuzzy haze, but he could see more cadets running with guns. Vermilion trails streaked the skies. Black smoke crept around corners. Patton's statue twisted into an unrecognizable heaping mess of bronze alloy. Thick, rich dust and scorching fire were everywhere. The Entente Military Academy was under full attack.

"Someone is following us," he told her.

Another cadet with a rifle ran after them. Gualtiero turned and shot the cadet dead without hesitation. Astonished, Tarian stopped running. *What the hell is going on?*

"Move!" She shoved him.

He stared at Ian Khan's motionless body. "You killed Ian!"

"Yes, he was going to kill us. I'll explain later. We have to get to the boat!"

The sincerity in her silvery-blue eyes begged him to keep moving. He took one last scan of the magnificent yet formidable calamity surrounding him then ran. Buildings exploded behind him. Solid stone of impressive monuments tumbled into nothing but shimmery dust. He smelled the distinct odor of wood burning pleasant like a campfire, but the dangerous flames were only yards away from his flesh.

They ran alone now. They'd escaped the crowd of cadets, but not the echo of pain-infused voices. The screams reminded him of Ian's face, haunted by the fear of death in his eyes when the bullet pierced his skin. He remembered when Ian had provoked a fistfight and Tarian had been foolish enough to throw the first punch, an act that Ian could have easily used to get him expelled, but he hadn't. Tarian thought the two of them had come to an understanding. He was clearly wrong about that.

Gualtiero and Tarian charged across Thayer Road and then Williams Road. She took him up a dirt road that ran along the shoreline to the south dock where a bearded man in an interceptor craft waited for them. Tarian jumped into the boat first, followed by Gualtiero. Tarian thought he recognized the man, but on second glance decided he didn't. Yet, the man nodded at Tarian as if he knew him.

"Sit down," the man said before hitting the throttle. The boat sped away instantly at thirty-five knots, thrusting Tarian backward into his seat.

"Wait!" Tarian yelled to Gualtiero over the roaring motor. "We have to go back."

"We can't!" she demanded.

"I mean, Maria and Gabe. We have to find them.

"They're okay," she said then added, "I saw them. They escaped in a vehicle with Colonel Rigby."

He fixed his eyes on hers, and although she didn't look away, he didn't believe her. He almost jumped off the speeding boat and into the freezing river, but she held his secret. She'd promised him the truth, and that promise compelled him to stay with her. He was uninformed, and she was obviously very clear on the situation at hand.

He glanced down at the lethal weapon he held in his hand. He could aim it at her. He could force the promised information out of her right now. He began to lift the weapon but hesitated. He watched the man driving the boat as he dodged scattered debris in the river and falling from the sky. This man was no ordinary man. He was a trained soldier.

Tarian assessed Gualtiero. Her eyes alert like a watchdog, her stance athletic and her weapon ready. These two people were keeping him safe and alive. Slowly he accepted the fact that he had to trust them. The decision was made and hopefully it was the right one.

Tarian recalled the day he woke up and saw Gualtiero's face in the hospital. He had lost consciousness after taking the developmental drug, Sanoxine. EMA had given it to all the new cadets to build up their immune systems to fight advanced bioweapons the government feared were being produced in the Wastelands. He'd been the only person to have an adverse reaction to it. When he awoke dazed and disoriented in a hospital bed she'd spoken to him as a colleague. For the first time, her voice had been soft and caring, and he knew she was more than his superior officer. He sensed she had a special interest in him that went beyond the academy, a connection.

Twenty minutes later they were exiting the craft at Tomkins Cove and boarding a sleek, black tiltrotor. The man abandoned his boat and jumped urgently into the aircraft with them. Sitting in the pilot's seat was yet another impatient and angry man, another stranger Tarian was supposed to trust with his life—a young, twenty-something-year-old with large arms. The man aviated the tiltrotor the instant Tarian's feet left the dirt. Tarian stumbled to his seat as the aircraft took off. He sat in the back, balling his hands into fists desperately wanting to punch something; but instead, he took a deep breath and kept a keen eye on every person inside the aircraft.

After a seemingly endless flight, the pull of the descent stirred his empty stomach. As the tiltrotor lowered the last few feet to the ground, acid crawled up his throat, but he managed to control it. He'd mastered self-control over his emotions since his father's death.

The tiltrotor lowered onto a plain of snow in Battlefields Park in the Quebec District. The peaceful, pure white snow contrasted with the chaotic grounds at EMA. A narrow road set in position by the sharp blade of time cut through the dense snow. It wound out of the park and into the city.

An unmarked, dark green sedan sat covered in white flakes at the beginning of the road. The subarctic air inside the vacant car engulfed the foursome as they slid inside.

"Piece of shit car! Dammit, Eleanor! Invest in today's technology," the pilot, now driver, yelled as he attempted to turn the frozen ignition.

"Who's Eleanor?" Tarian asked Gualtiero.

"Our Chancellor," she responded.

The small, old sedan wasn't the vehicle Tarian would've chosen for the deep snow and expansive plain. Soon, however, the engine grumbled to life and the sedan maneuvered perfectly within the tight streets of the city.

THREE

HEADQUARTERS

Peering out of the backseat window, Tarian tracked the landscape noting landmarks, as the car drove through the Quebec District.

"Where are you taking me?"

"To our village where you'll be safe," Gualtiero said.

"Are the Prevallers attacking other places?"

"Not at this moment, but we don't take chances."

"You promised to tell me the truth about my father. And now, I want to know who's after *me*!"

"I know. I will. You'll get your answers soon. I promise."

He wondered if he had the patience to wait any longer then within the millisecond of his eye blink, he'd left the city and entered a village. Tarian had no idea how it had happened.

The long, cobbled street curved around old masonry homes and stores ranging in size from fat to skinny and short to tall. The car pulled up to a wooden garage door with steel bands located in the heart of the village. The building surrounding the garage appeared centuries old and covered in stone and aged wood. Tarian admired the historic architecture.

Once inside the garage, things changed. It was modern with flat walls and glass staircases. As he looked, he saw a fleet of twenty dark green vehicles of various sizes and models. A shiny sports car with a nine hundred horsepower hover engine drew his attention for a second. How had he ended up inside a gigantic car showroom after pulling into a single car garage?

"Cadet Sergeant Gualtiero—"

"It's Audrey, here," she interrupted.

"What?"

"Just call me Audrey."

"Oh, okay." He paused, finding it difficult to disengage from the strict military academy protocol he had followed for a year and a half.

"What?" she asked, resuming the conversation.

"I'm not losing it, right? We did just go from the city, to here, instantly; and we did just enter a small garage, but now we're in a very large garage? Right?" These questions sounded crazy, but Audrey remained composed.

"You're not crazy. Have patience."

Patience, he thought. Tension covered his skin in prickly waves, and patience seemed impossible, but he had no other choice.

Moving out of the garage and into the belly of the building, Tarian noticed the four-story home filled with men and women of various ages. Each person nodded at him in recognition. Some patted him on the back, and one man even gave him a fist bump.

They were all dressed in neatly pressed uniforms, the same evergreen as the vehicles. He had been taken to some sort of headquarters, as everyone walked swiftly, purposefully holding tablets, mobiles, and/or briefcases. And like the garage, it was much more spacious than it appeared.

The foursome walked into a meeting room where two men and two women stood to welcome everyone. They were expected. Tarian sat rigidly in a comfortable leather chair that was offered to him. He hoped for the answers he so anxiously anticipated.

"Hello Tarian," a middle-aged woman said. She wore a broad smile of perfect teeth that spread her sagging jowls, creating an unpleasant bulldog-like appearance that clashed with her high-pitched tone of voice. "I am Margaret Davenport, and this is Edward Corbet, Blaise Garneau, and Nicolas Giles," she said as she walked from person to person. They were all intently staring and smiling at him. She did not introduce a man in the corner who seemed to appear out of thin air.

The man wore deep purple instead of dark green. He looked rumpled even though his uniform was obediently pressed like everyone else's. He appeared to be meditating. His eyes remained closed, and he never acknowledged anybody else in the room and no one acknowledged him. His presence, as well as the strangeness of the entire building, made Tarian uneasy.

Am I the only one who can see him? Tarian thought.

"The attacks have begun for the mortals, and we have been commissioned to help, but our priority is to find the person assassinating immortals." She paused considering Tarian's confused expression and looked at Audrey. "He knows nothing?"

"No Margaret," she said. "I was under the impression that I was supposed to bring him here first."

"Oh, well," she said, clearly under a different impression. "No, no my dear. This is not the place for him. We are handling Guardian profiles to find the traitor. Horrible, truly horrible work to pry into your colleagues' personal lives. But unfortunately, it must be done." She turned to Tarian. "I know you are ignorant about what I'm saying right now. That is why you will follow Audrey to the library where she will explain everything to you."

Audrey stood quickly, but Tarian hadn't budged. *What's going on? Assassin? Immortals? Traitors?*

"Go to the kitchen first. He needs a good meal," Margaret ordered.

"Come on, Tarian," Audrey said.

He remained seated, still in a daze, more questions piling on top of the previous ones inside his head. He thought of his family, especially his older brother Charlie. *Were they safe?*

"Let's go." Audrey tugged him to his feet.

They left the others behind in the meeting room. Audrey zigzagged through the second level hallway then up a glass staircase. Tarian jogged to keep up with her. Finally, they walked through carved wooden doors into a rustic tavern-style eatery. It was the only room Tarian had seen, so far, that matched the historic style of the exterior.

"Sit here and don't move," Audrey ordered.

He had no plans to leave without his guide since he couldn't possibly navigate this perplexing building without her. He was mindlessly following her and wouldn't be able to locate this place on his own if he had to.

"Where are you going?" he asked.

"To get you food."

"But we can order here." He pointed to the ordering screen.

"That thing's ridiculous." She shook her head and rolled her eyes.

She walked away before he could reply. The tablet for ordering lay on the table. Curious, he swiped the screen to view the numerous meal options. Before now, he hadn't even thought of food, but flipping through the images of delicious choices made his stomach growl and ache.

The mouthwatering aroma of herb-roasted turkey and stuffing wafted through the air. Scents of pecan and apple pie also tantalized his nose and teased his palate. He glanced around to view guests eating good old-fashioned, human prepared food. It'd been a long time since he'd eaten a meal that wasn't instantly generated. EMA meals were scientifically created drinks and bars, specifically tailored to each soldier's individual nutritional needs, adequate in calories, vitamins, fats, carbohydrates, and proteins. Boring.

The chef paraded around the tables, stopping to accept the many compliments showered upon him. He appeared to be a man of importance. He looked jolly with his plump belly. In fact, he was the first overweight person Tarian had seen in this building. Like the rumpled man in the corner, the chef wore purple. His suit tailored for his profession but just as impeccable as everyone else's attire.

"I got you a bowl of chicken soup and a turkey sandwich," Audrey said.

"Thank you," Tarian said, but it looked disappointing after reviewing the other plates of heaping piles of rare roast beef, honey ham, fluffy mashed potatoes, savory stuffing, corn on the cob and sugary pies.

"And a cup of coffee." She slid the steaming mug across the table.

She looked very pleased with herself, and he didn't have the heart to complain.

"Where are we?" He took a sip of the black coffee. It was amazingly creamy and sweet. One bite into the sandwich and an explosion of Thanksgiving flavors infused his mouth. Tarian had never tasted anything like it. He peeled away the layer of bread to reveal a simple thick slice of turkey. He wondered how one slice could generate the many flavors of his mother's entire Thanksgiving dinner. He devoured every magical morsel.

"We're in the Quebec District," she said, staring at a remnant of sandwich left on his lips.

He awkwardly wiped his face with his napkin. "No, we're not."

"Technically we are. However, you will not find this particular village on any map. It isn't a part of the Entente of Nations. We are independent."

With furrowed brow and pursed lips, he said, "I need to call my mom and brother. They'll be worried."

"Your family was informed that you are okay. Of course

they want to hear from you in person, so we'll arrange a contact soon."

"Are they safe?"

"Yes, we have them under surveillance. EMA was a warning. The Prevallers chose the academy because you were there."

"Why do you keep saying that? Why would the Prevallers care so much about me? I'm only a cadet." He swallowed a mouthful of soup.

"Tarian, you are very important to us. We're the Guardians of Dare. We're a dangerous threat to the Prevallers. Luckily, our Intelligence uncovered their plan before they had time to execute it fully. During the commotion of the attack, Ian planned to capture you after he killed me," she said, glancing around the tavern.

"Why?" He turned his head to view what caught her attention. He saw more curious stares directed at him. The chef strolled toward him.

"Are you done eating? I'd rather speak in private." She assessed his empty plate and bowl.

He ate enough to feel comfortable, but the aroma left him wanting more.

"Yes," he said, embarrassed to look piggish.

"Welcome," a booming voice announced, as a friendly hand patted his back.

"Hello," Tarian said.

"Hello, Chef Richard," Audrey said. "Richard this is Tarian Prescott."

"Tis a pleasure to finally meet you. Ah, your plate is empty.

Audrey, get him more food." It was an order but given in a gentle way. Nonetheless, it was still an order, and Tarian noticed Audrey didn't appreciate being told to fetch food.

"Actually Richard, we were just leaving."

"But he hasn't had pie!"

"I'll bring him back. Real soon."

The chef twitched his head and scowled at her, but then regained his amiable composure and smiled at Tarian.

"You must come to afternoon tea," the big man invited.

"Thank you. I will. It was delicious." Tarian smiled.

"Okay, let's go," Audrey said. "Bye Richard."

FOUR

PIPER

Audrey once again pulled Tarian along, but he was glad to leave. The stares of the guests inside the tavern made him uncomfortable. He felt like the seeker in a game of hide-and-seek that he wasn't aware he was playing. They ascended more stairs then entered a chilly, quiet room. Their loud, quick steps announced their approach, but the library's sparse visitors kept to themselves, immersed in their reading.

Audrey and Tarian retreated to a comfortable seating area in the back, hidden behind several tall bookstacks. A welcoming fire burned warm and constant in a giant stone fireplace. She wasn't kidding when she said she wanted privacy. *What horrible information is she about to tell me?*

Several uneasy seconds passed between the two, finally Tarian asked, "Why does everyone know who I am?"

She gave him a contemplative look, as if she didn't know where to begin. Today had been an avalanche of new information, and now he had more questions on top of the already daunting secret about his father's death. Only now, sitting across from her, the truth seemed frighteningly unwanted.

"You are inside Guardian Headquarters—"

"Did you tell him yet?" A girl popped into their intimate sitting area.

Tarian startled.

"Not yet," Audrey said through gritted teeth obviously annoyed at the girl's interruption.

"You're the first immortal to be born in five hundred and thirty-three years. We thought Eleanor was the last, but we know that to be false now." The girl spat the words out with uncontrolled excitement then paused and stared dreamily at him.

"What are you talking about?" Tarian looked from the girl to Audrey and back.

The jumpy girl heightened Tarian's anxiety and Audrey's irritation.

"Shhhh! Settle down, Piper," Audrey said as she guided Piper into a chair. Audrey kept one hand on Piper in an attempt to keep her still. It failed.

"Oh, what a story it is!" Piper rocked back and forth.

Tarian feared she would pounce on him at any moment.

Audrey turned toward Tarian and tried to regain her composure. She took a deep breath and continued, "Tarian, I'm six hundred and twelve years old. I'm an immortal. I was born Audrey Ballard in 1499. My parents were Loriners, ordinary people who made bridles for horses. Your dad's father owned a spice shop, and his mother was a powerful witch. We were neighbors. We grew up together during the time of Tudor London."

"What?" He spat loudly as he jerked forward in his seat to inspect her. She appeared to be twenty years old, at the most.

Audrey smirked and tilted her head, apparently, expecting this reaction.

"I'm five hundred and ninety-eight," Piper added with a wide toothy smile.

"As strange as it seems, it's very much true," Audrey said.

"But you're twenty and my dad was in his forties, and she is … I don't know … she looks sixteen." He glanced at Piper.

"I know. That's our physical age, not the actual number of years we have lived. We've studied our phenomenon for centuries, and we still don't know why some of us age farther than others."

"That's what differentiates us from vampires," Piper said.

"What?" Tarian asked.

"Oh, yeah, and they drink blood." Piper bobbed a shoulder like they were having a perfectly normal conversation.

"I don't believe you. You're kidding right?" Tarian tried to laugh at the absurdity of Audrey's and Piper's words. His faint laughter turned to panic. His head began to ache. He sat back on the cushiony chair and closed his eyes in an attempt to stop the throbbing.

"Piper stop talking!" Audrey scolded, then softened her tone, "I know it's a lot of strange information. We're unique. We're immortal. We're unsure exactly how we became immortal since our births happened long ago during a time of little scientific data. During the fifteenth and sixteenth centuries most people explained away strange phenomena as divine intervention or witchcraft." Audrey spoke kindly and let the meaning hang in the air.

"Yes, yes. And now, we can see our DNA. We have an abundance of methylation markers and as a result the mechanism is showing curative for any human disease in us, although we can't pinpoint how. We have regenerative stem cells. All sorts of unique traits that mortals don't have," Piper said.

As Piper's words flew from her mouth again, Audrey closed her eyes and looked as if she was defusing a bomb set to detonate inside her head.

The information spun inside Tarian's mind. "If I'm to believe this story, then how could my father die?"

"Death Serum!" Piper yelped, then covered her mouth with her hand. She looked as if she had just said the most insulting curse word.

"Piper, let me explain," Audrey snapped, and Piper cowered into the chair. "Out of all of the other creatures inside our borders, we alone could not be killed. We had no weaknesses until recently. A Death Serum has been developed, we assume, by the Prevallers." She paused as if hearing this information for the first time, or maybe she didn't believe it. "It's an extremely advanced bioweapon. Our most skilled scientists here at Headquarters have failed to make an antidote for it."

Tarian shot to his feet and began to pace. "Then we're all in danger. The Prevallers are eliminating the immortals before they begin a war."

"Exactly. We have hundreds of years worth of strength,

wealth, and knowledge. We have made this nation great since the Revolutionary War. Plus, we're the most reliable and organized of all the creatures. Destroying us is brilliant strategy."

"And my dad was killed by this Death Serum?"

"Yes and thirteen others."

"So how can you say I'm safe or my family is safe? None of us are safe!"

"The village has a magic shield." Piper jumped back into the conversation. She nodded her head and widened her lavender eyes.

"No one has been murdered within the protection of the village," Audrey said.

"And why is my birth any different than yours just because it happened hundreds of years later? I don't get it!" He continued to pace, wearing a path in the rug.

"It's a long story," Audrey said.

"I don't care. I'm sure Piper can tell me." Tarian glanced at the twitchy girl.

"Yes, yes." She sat upright, leveled her gaze but didn't get the chance to speak.

"No, I'll tell it. Sit down," Audrey ordered. "Have you ever heard of the lost Colony of Roanoke?"

"No." Tarian sat in the chair running his fingers through his stubbly buzz cut hair.

Piper resumed rocking, eyes wide with excitement, but she bit her lips closed.

"Well, those of us within the walls of London began to gather together. We traveled to the New World as the Colony of

Roanoke in 1587. Our assumed mission was to become a settlement for Queen Elizabeth and Sir Walter Raleigh. At the time, they were competing with Spain to conquer the New World. That part is in the history books, but our real mission, our immortal secret mission was strictly to protect Eleanor White Dare and her unborn child, hence the name, Guardians of Dare. In the history books, we vanished and many theories have been made explaining our demise, but in truth, we disappeared on purpose." Audrey took a breath.

Piper stared at Audrey, lips quivering. Audrey rewarded her with a nod of permission.

"Eleanor's baby was foretold to be the last-born immortal, but Virginia died of illness as a teenager. Eleanor is our Chancellor. She was the last immortal to be born back in 1568. She never had any more children." Piper finished the story.

"All of our children have died, all except you," Audrey added.

"But I'm only nineteen. How do you know I'll survive?"

"You've already survived," Audrey said.

"The bus accident." Realization ghosted through his body.

He always knew he should have died when the Salem Academy school bus skidded on black ice and sank into the icy pond. Everyone perished except for him—all of his friends. He had no recollection of the events. He'd blacked out. All he remembered was waking up inside a hospital. Several doctors called his recovery a miracle.

"Yes. You should've died when you were nine. Since that day, your father knew. He gathered a few of us together, and we've been studying your miraculous existence ever since."

"If I'm the only birth, I mean … new … immortal …" *Oh my God, this sounds even crazier out loud.* Tarian's nerves knotted. He couldn't swallow. He forced a deep inhalation then exhaled the anxiety away. Calmly he asked, "How many of us are there?"

"Right now? Three hundred and fifty. We are continually searching the world for immortals, but it has been over two hundred years since our last discovery. However, even those immortals were all born in fifteenth or sixteenth century Europe. So you see why you are so important. You were born recently and with the Death Serum—"

"The Prophecy is coming true," Piper interrupted, her excitement gone.

"Piper!" Audrey growled.

"What? Tell him about the Prophecy." Piper crossed her arms.

"What's she talking about?" Tarian quieted his movements and listened, fearing this news would be overwhelming. Keeping his thoughts in order became a difficult task.

"I told you your father's mother was a witch."

"Yes." He nodded.

"Well, her coven foretold of a new and final birth followed by the horrific destruction of our kind. During Queen Elizabeth's reign anyone suspected of witchcraft – and of course, cheating death would fall under that category – was scrutinized, tortured, and put to death. We assumed the prophecy meant we were soon to be discovered and hunted and killed. So that's why we fled England with Eleanor Dare. She was the only immortal pregnant at the time. We thought Virginia Dare was the foreseen final birth, but she wasn't. And no one has fit that description until you."

"You're it Tarian. You are the only hope for the survival of the Guardians of Dare," Piper said in a surprisingly mature voice.

"What?"

"Well, the prophecy has changed. I mean it has evolved. I guess that's the best way to explain it. The coven has said that our extinction can be stopped."

"How?"

"Well, that's just it. Prophecies are vague. Something about a tomb and other creatures."

"No, it goes like this. The savior lies in a tomb where grown men die. A young child of many is the key soon born of mortal witch and man of unending years. Do not fear other creatures from the south for their help will bring life," Piper chanted.

"Do you see what I mean? Jibber-jabber. Why can't they just tell us in English?" Audrey threw up her arms.

"It makes perfect sense. Tarian is one of four children: 'one of many,'" Piper said.

"Yes, but he's not lying in a tomb with grown men."

"Not yet," Piper added.

"Great! Something I can look forward to. What about the kid thing? None of you were able to have children? My dad was the only one?" He questioned.

"Not immortal children. We've had children and families throughout the centuries but they're mortal," Audrey explained.

"Have you ever had kids?" he asked Audrey.

"Yes," she said. "A girl, Isabella. She was beautiful. She died many, many years ago."

She didn't elaborate and Piper remained silent too. Audrey's eyes moistened, and she swallowed her lump of grief. He knew that rock-hard lump of pain. He, too, had experienced the inability to form words through the thick grief that clogged the throat.

Time had not healed her pain. Everyone at his father's funeral had promised him that time would heal his heart, and his memories would bring joy, but her pain was alive after all these years.

"I see," he said.

Then an even worse nightmare consumed him. He'd outlive his family and his girlfriend, Delia. He'd watch them grow old and die, and everyone else that he loved would die too. He would have to endure heartbreaking losses over and over forever. He could've shared immortality with his dad, but someone had taken that away from him.

"Tarian, are you okay?" Audrey asked.

"I want to find the person who took my dad's life, and I want to kill him. I could've had decades of memories. You did. Centuries! I barely got seventeen!" he said, with enormous breaths and flared nostrils. "What good is this gift of life if everyone you love dies?"

His bitter chocolate eyes glared at her, and for the first time, she looked away. He turned to Piper, but she was gone. Vanished. For a second Tarian regretted scaring her away, but he couldn't calm his rage.

"This is a damn curse!" he yelled but still Audrey had no words. "It could've been a very special gift, but someone took that from me. Who?" He pounded his fists into the chair. His lunch gurgled in his stomach. Savory Thanksgiving flavors turning sour.

"I don't know!" She yelled back at him then inhaled deeply to recompose herself.

The fire in the hearth began to feel hot instead of warm. Glances from a couple of green-suited library patrons turned into haunting stares. Now he knew why they all looked at him as if he was an infamous celebrity. He'd been twice cursed, first with immortality and second with the link to their survival or death.

"How can you not know who is killing your … our kind? This looks like quite an elaborate organization. Someone knows the truth."

Audrey flinched.

He stepped toward her. "It's one of us, isn't it? You mentioned a traitor earlier."

"That's the fear."

Tarian's eyes moistened with tears, his hands clenched into fists. The blood in his veins raced, filling his muscles with the need to move.

"I know how you feel," she said, trying to calm him down, but those were the wrong words.

Strike one!

"No, you don't." He directed his irritation toward her.

"Yes, I do," she said adamantly. "Lower your voice."

Strike two!

"Well, what do we do now?" he asked in the same voice. "I want justice. I'm an Entente soldier. I'm trained to fight. Take me to the person in charge of us, the Guardians."

"You do nothing but stay here where you're safe."

Strike three!

"Hell no! I will not." His voice boomed another decibel louder.

"Shhhh! You must. You're a protégé. We don't know your state. We need to study you and protect you."

"I'm not a lab rat."

"No, you're not. You're the first Guardian of Dare born in centuries. Do you realize how important you are? Your father died protecting you, protecting our kind. If you die, then he died for nothing."

"How dare you use my father against me!"

She held her hands up in retreat. "I'm sorry. That's not what I meant. Your father was my best friend. He loved you." The ice in her eyes thawed. "Forget the Prevallers. Forget the prophecy. Your dad thought you brought hope to us all. He thought if you could be born then maybe others could too. Maybe we all could give birth to immortal children and stop suffering the unbearable pain of their deaths."

"If you knew my dad, you'd know he wouldn't want me to hide behind your magic curtain. He sent me to EMA! The orders were in his Will."

"Zachary's back!" Piper popped back into view, rocking in her chair as if she'd never left.

"Senator Eastwood?" Tarian asked.

"Yes," Piper said.

"That fits … Right … He's immortal too, isn't he?"

"Yes," Audrey stated.

Tarian's heart dropped. He didn't actually expect her to say yes. "That's why you were talking to him … about my dad … I get it now … you and Senator Eastwood sent me to EMA … not Dad. You said the Guardians are soldiers. Not an attorney, never a lawyer like I thought, like my dad. Like I wanted. I was supposed to work in Dad's law firm. Everything changed after Dad died, and now I know why." He talked without thinking, words spilled from his mouth, words of comprehension.

"I think it's time for you to go to your room and get some rest," she said.

"What about Delia?" he inquired about the Senator's daughter.

"She's mortal, Tarian," Audrey said.

"Of course, because I'm the only one." Tarian nodded. He focused on a distant intangible image.

"Come on, let me take you to your room." Audrey placed her hand on his forearm.

He snatched his arm away from her. "It's one o'clock in the afternoon!"

He looked at Audrey then Piper. He paused then he whipped around and stormed out of the library.

Audrey's strides caught his heels immediately. He erratically paced the maze of hallways and the other floors, looking for an office that felt important. There were a lot more than four floors.

Frustrated, he turned to Audrey. "This place is gigantic. Where are they?"

"Follow me."

They went to the fourth floor and walked straight back to the last door on the left. They entered a lobby area with a set of monstrous, solid, oak doors. A mahogany desk sat empty of its receptionist. Steel framed windows with old stone on the outside, and thick, probably bulletproof, panes of glass broke up the walls. It smelled like his dad's law office: wood, leather and a smokiness that had rooted inside these materials a long time ago.

Audrey knocked on the door.

FIVE

ELEANOR

"Come in," a female voice said.

Audrey escorted Tarian into a palatial room. Richly embroidered tapestries hung from tall walls. Old tables made of spectacular petrified wood stood proudly alongside new technological advancements superior to any Government Intelligence Agency Tarian had ever seen or read about. This space couldn't possibly fit in the area provided by the quaint village street venue. It had to be an illusion. Ten-foot-tall screens lined the back wall that extended at least one hundred twenty yards. Even the Entente Military Academy with all its modern technologies had nothing to compare to this room. Misty images of charts and maps levitated in the air.

"Tarian, this is Eleanor Dare." Audrey's words pulled him out of his awed state and back into his rage. She turned to face the gentleman in the room and introduced him. "And you know Zachary. I mean, Senator Eastwood."

Tarian surveyed the two of them. Eleanor was one of what

he now thought of as the purple people. She wore a blackberry business suit, and the Senator wore his usual well-tailored, steel gray business attire. A few other people in dark green, the green people, studied charts and gathered information in the far back of the room.

"I'm not staying here to be a lab rat," he finally said to Eleanor. "No matter how elaborate your chemistry set is." He turned his attention to the Senator. The urge to punch him in the face grew. The Senator was his father's best friend, yet he'd kept so many secrets. This man was Delia's father. Resentment stung Tarian's esophagus like bile, but he swallowed it and maturely, but sternly, directed his conversation to the Senator. "You should have told me."

"As you can see," Audrey said, "Tarian is very upset with all the secrets. His new world is confusing and—"

Tarian cut her off. "I can speak for myself. I'm a fighter remember. I'm EMA, the pride of the Entente. If I die, then I die. Take my DNA. Take my blood, my … whatever you need. Keep it. Study it. I don't care. But you can't keep me. I'm going to find Dad's murderer."

"You will serve Joe best by staying inside this village," Senator Eastwood said.

"Bullshit!" Fury erupted in Tarian as his father's name slipped from the Senator's lips.

"Listen, young man, I did not bring you into my home for you to throw everything away," the Senator spoke with finality.

Tarian remained stubbornly silent.

"Zachary, I agree with Tarian. He's not Virginia. I promise you. He is going to survive," Eleanor said.

Tarian felt Eleanor's confidence and strength. She had a steady stance that emitted unabashed truth. She scanned Tarian with pride and concern. She sat down behind her desk and gestured for everyone to sit. Senator Eastwood stood, visibly upset that she'd rebuffed his position, but it was obvious, no one questioned this woman's authority. Tarian wondered where the Senator and Audrey fell in the line of command.

"What is our position?" Eleanor directed the question to Senator Eastwood.

"I'm not going to marginalize the situation. The attack on the Entente Military Academy was an enormous breach in security. The President is reeling. The press is having a field day questioning the safety of the Entente's closed borders."

As the Senator spoke of EMA, the image of the Academy lifted off of the large screen in the distance and appeared next to Eleanor like a levitating photograph. Tarian assumed Eleanor had a unique light device to create holograms, but she held nothing. She simply waved her hands, and things happened. With another flick of her wrist, the two people dressed in green disappeared from their posts in the back of the room and materialized standing next to Tarian.

"Incredible." Tarian gasped. He touched the man's arm to find he was flesh and bone, not a holographic light field.

The moving picture that floated in the air displayed some of Tarian's professors examining the rubble looking for students. Next Tarian viewed a similar image of the Government District.

"As you can see the Government District in Boston is

secure, and our resources have not been targeted," the Senator explained.

One by one the holographic light fields of these places materialized for review. Silently, they examined each important resource facility of the Entente. The uranium pits weren't damaged. The diamond mines swirled into the earth's crust, and the massive cavern system still cut across the southwest. The electricity-producing fusion power plant remained operational. And so on. And so forth. As far as Tarian could tell, the Entente nation remained intact and unharmed.

With one flick of the wrist, Eleanor threw the three-dimensional images back onto their flat surfaces one hundred feet away. The two green people also inexplicably returned at their stations in the distance.

"EMA was a deliberate attack. The reasons are known to the President and us, but obviously, we cannot tell the public," the Senator said.

"Why?" Tarian asked.

"Many Guardians hold positions at EMA, and you were there. That was the target. The Prevallers' mission was to capture and kill as many immortals as possible. Luckily, we had Recon Intelligence and were able to get all of the Guardians out in time, but there were far too many mortal casualties."

"Maria, Gabe," Tarian said almost to himself.

Everyone looked at him with sympathetic eyes, but no one assured him of their safety. He hoped his closest friends were alive, and someday, they'd be together again.

"We were lucky. We cannot risk Tarian's safety again." The Senator turned his back on Tarian to speak to Eleanor.

"He's perfect for reconnaissance," Eleanor said.

The Senator scoffed. "You are using him as a decoy."

Tarian cleared his throat to draw Eleanor's attention. "I want to know more about the assassin."

She politely redirected her explanations toward him. "Yes, yes. You, as well as the rest of the public, are aware of the threat to our way of life by the outside alliance known as the Prevallers. It is no secret that when we closed our borders and ended trade amongst other nations, we created many enemies. While we've thrived, the outside world has not."

"It was only a matter of time before the other nations destroyed each other. We had the insight to prevent such ruination from crossing the seas and affecting our nation. We fought hard to erect our borders, build lethal drones and weapons to secure our lands," the Senator stated.

"Correct, Zachary." Eleanor acknowledged his interruption. "Without the strength of the Guardians, the Entente would not exist. We helped build the peaceful society we live in today. We have battled in secret for the security of this land and our freedoms since the Revolutionary War. Our existence and contributions have always been a secret until now. Someone has not only leaked the existence of an immortal race to the Prevallers but has created a Death Serum to kill us. And that informant is feared to be one of us."

"Why?" Tarian asked.

"We don't know." Eleanor clenched her jaw.

"And that is who killed my father? One of our own?" Tarian asked.

"We believe so." Eleanor's eyes fell. Tarian saw that she mourned the loss of her beloved immortals. With one subtle sigh, she looked a lot less powerful.

Tarian wanted to fight for this woman. "I'm ready." These were his people, his dad's family, and now his. A need to protect them and punish such an evil betrayer surged his blood.

"I don't like it. We have other alternatives." The Senator's brow furrowed as his eyes narrowed.

"Zachary this is my final decision," Eleanor stated.

Tarian noted the look of resentment the Senator aimed at Eleanor. He'd never seen the Senator receive orders from anyone.

Eleanor turned all of her attention to Tarian. "You need more training. We need to test your special abilities. See how far you've developed. However, I need you in the lab first."

"How long do you need him?" Audrey asked.

Tarian felt like a pawn in a very real chess match.

"In twenty-four hours, you can take him to the Realm."

"Agreed," Audrey said.

"Tarian, I will escort you to the lab." Eleanor stood.

Once in the hall, Audrey and Senator Eastwood headed in the opposite direction.

"Senator." Tarian stopped him before he walked away. "How's Delia?"

"She's fine," the Senator said.

"When can I see her?"

"I'm not sure. It's too dangerous."

"I understand. Please tell her I'm sorry."

"I will. She knows nothing of this. If and when you see her, it must all remain a secret," the Senator said.

The Senator gave Tarian one of his sanctimonious downward glances that Tarian had received several times during his yearlong stay at his estate. Only now, Tarian surpassed him in height, and his tone didn't have quite the same effect. However, Tarian still felt like a boy that owed him a great deal. He had taken Charlie and Tarian into his home, had helped their mother financially, had prepared Tarian for EMA and Charlie for Harvard. *Will I feel obligated to him forever?*

SIX

THE LAB

Eleanor led Tarian up two flights of stairs to the lab. Everyone who noticed her made sure to say hello, and a couple of people stopped to ask for her signature.

"We are not all Guardians. We do have mortals here too. I trust the mortals in this building. They know our kind. Most of their families have been working for us for generations. It's a shame with Joe's and the others' deaths that we have all become very suspicious of one another. I honestly cannot imagine anyone in our organization as a traitor," she said.

"You must have your suspicions." Tarian watched her closely.

"Clever boy." Her emerald eyes twinkled, but she didn't expound. "Your father was curious too. You know Joe, Audrey, and Zachary were inseparable for many, many years. Then Audrey met Marco. Oh, how she went through the wringer with those two! Your dad and Zachary were ruthless on poor Marco. No one less than perfect would suffice for their best friend. Your dad was a shape shifter, did you know?"

"No." Another sucker punch landed hard deforming the image he had of his dad. *Did I even know him at all?*

"You've probably noticed the dress code around here."

The question echoed in Tarian's distracted mind before he answered, "Of course."

"Purple identifies those among us who have uncommon abilities. We have discovered these special talents are due to witches' blood. Some of the people you see dressed in purple are not immortal. They are in fact witches."

"Really?"

"Well, I generalize, but in some way or another these witches defy natural law. Call it magic, clairvoyance, paranormal, and so on. Personally, I do not like labels. We all have some unique gift."

"If my dad had unnatural abilities, do I?"

"Not sure yet, all of us were conceived by two mortals. You were not. These tests will give me more answers."

She opened the door to the laboratory and concluded the conversation with a smile. Everything about Eleanor from the gait of her walk to the expression in her smile radiated confidence. She seemed too important to be escorting him around, but he guessed he was an interesting new development in her several, long-lived lifetimes.

The laboratory air wafted ten degrees cooler and hummed a guitar solo. The style reminded Tarian of music his dad used to listen to. Fresh, clean smells of lemon and lavender filled his nostrils. Four long chairs that resembled dentist chairs, but looked much more inviting, waited in each corner. The chairs were designed to be comfortable, and Tarian assumed he would be sitting in one for a long time. When he saw the needles a chill slid down his spine, but he convinced himself he could handle a few pricks and pokes.

"Tarian, this is Henry. He is the best. Hasn't lost a patient yet," she said as an attempt at comic relief, but she wasn't a funny person, and the joke staled fast.

Henry just rolled his eyes and gave Tarian a look of sympathy.

"I'll check back in later." She left as regally as she had entered.

"Your job is to sit back and relax. The tests take thirteen, maybe fifteen hours but you can go to sleep," Henry said.

"That's okay. I'll stay awake." The idea of sleep tempted him, but he had far too many questions he hoped to ask Henry during the testing.

"The tests don't require anything on your part except to be in proximity to the equipment because of the wires and tubes. I've been doing this a long time and found the newer versions, the wireless versions, are not always better. In fact, their results have been erroneous. I like to stick to the old-fashioned, wired impulses and injections," Henry explained.

While Henry spoke, Tarian dozed off. Attempting to lift his eyelids, he saw Henry slip on a mask. A sleeping inhalant now controlled Tarian's consciousness. His anger, bravery, and confusion faded away into the numbness of drug-induced sleep.

He awoke several hours later with stiff muscles and a

cramped neck. The fog of sleep inside his brain slowly thinned, and he became aware of his surroundings. Henry still sat at his computer nodding his head and tapping his pencil to the beat of the guitar solo. Tarian opened his mouth to speak, but an embarrassing dribble of drool leaked onto his chin. He quickly wiped it away.

Henry gave Tarian a thumbs-up. "Well, my friend, you were a delightful patient. Snoozed like a baby. I got what I needed, and you can be on your way."

"Great," Tarian said. He almost complained about being tricked into unconsciousness but decided sleep had been beneficial. He hadn't realized the toll the stress had taken on his body. Whatever concoction of sleeping gas he had been given, it was the perfect combination for satisfying, restful slumber.

"And here is your lovely guide," Henry said.

"Hi Henry." Audrey grinned, obviously used to Henry's bantering style. "How did he do?"

"Very well, very well," Henry said. "I captured plenty of cell division for Eleanor to look at. Did some carrier, predictive and presymptomatic testing. Amazing cell development." The complex words seemed misplaced inside Henry's lazy drawl.

"Really, that's fascinating," Audrey said but with her back turned to Henry, she looked at Tarian with wide silvery blue eyes and raised eyebrows. "Okay Tarian, let's go. It's time to leave the poppy field." She held out a hand to assist him from the comfort of the cushiony, leather chair.

In the hall, she looked over at his drowsy face. "Enjoy yourself?"

"Yes," he said, a bit ashamed of his need for sleep. Fatigue didn't seem very soldier-like.

"Hey, don't feel bad. He does that to everyone. Henry has a way about him that makes people calm. We call him Dr. Doze," she said. "For many reasons."

"Well, I feel better than ever. I'm ready for training."

"There has been a change while you were sleeping."

"What happened?" His gut twisted. *Good change or bad change?*

"It's okay. We'll train in the Realm in four days. We captured one of their men. He's not here in the village, but Eleanor is in constant contact with Central Intelligence."

"Has he confessed anything about the Death Serum?"

"No, he's not talking but we have gathered an abundance of information from his devices."

"That's good but what about the killer," Tarian asked.

"We believe he's in Boston. We also believe he went after your family."

"What!" Tarian halted, squared his shoulders in Audrey's direction and began yelling, "You said they would—"

"They're safe. Everyone's okay."

"How?"

"Your house was broken into while your mother was home."

"Did he hurt her?"

"No. She didn't even hear or see anything. She was taking a shower while the person rummaged through the house. When she came out of the bathroom, the house was ransacked, and the person was gone."

"And Chloe, Teresa, and Joe Jr.?"

"They're fine. Thankfully, they weren't home at the time."

"So, where's my family now?" he asked.

"They're on their way here," she said.

"Good! I want to see them."

"I know you do. It's an important time for you to be with your family, and we need them to remain here where it's safe. We postponed training so you could spend Christmas together and convince them to stay here. But I need to explain a few things first," she said.

"Okay, explain." His patience waned.

"We have an Inn for people like your family. They can't know about the Guardians."

"What do I tell them?"

"As far as they know, this is a safe house for the Entente Military and Congressmen. Your mother, Teresa, and Charlie think the burglary has to do with Zachary since he's a senator. It's not a stretch for them to think government officials and their families would be targeted by the Prevallers," she said then added, "Chloe and Joe Jr. think they're on a fun vacation."

"Okay. That's fine. I'll make sure I don't tell them anything they're not supposed to know."

"Good."

An almost visible uneasiness floated around her.

"What are you not telling me?" he asked.

"Nothing, I don't like waiting."

"You don't trust this new information?" he said.

"Having a traitor among us is a new phenomenon. I'm not sure who I can trust."

"Do you trust Eleanor and Senator Eastwood?"

"Yes." She answered without hesitation, but trouble remained frozen in her icy blues.

"Tarian!" Senator Eastwood rounded the corner, determined to gain their attention. "Thank you, Audrey, I will take it from here."

She gave Tarian a diluted smile and handed him over to the Senator. If Tarian hadn't known better, he would've thought she was disappointed to leave him.

SEVEN

AN UNLIKELY PICNIC

Delia's lips met Tarian's before he had a chance to say hello. The passionate kiss extended past the point of etiquette, and Tarian knew why. Delia's favorite sport was making her father uncomfortable.

Tarian desired her and would've kissed her for hours if she chose, but she released him. Awkwardly forced to look at Senator Eastwood, he tried in vain to blink away the haze of lust lingering in his eyes. He knew better than to speak and forced the smile to leave his face. The three of them stood in triangular formation in the center of the Inn's lobby for what felt like an eternity.

"Tarian, your family is not expected to arrive for another couple hours. You may take Delia into town if you like, but do not leave the village and remember what we discussed. You too, Delia. We have limited time and even though it is safe here, we must use all precautions," the Senator explained.

"Yes, Father, I know."

Delia locked her hand in Tarian's and rushed out of the Inn. She guided him through Rue de la Magie and drew him inside a door beneath a sign that read *The Perfect Picnic.* The store was empty of customers but filled with woven picnic baskets and checkered blankets. Most normal people didn't picnic with snow on the ground, but he knew Delia well and guessed that she planned on keeping him quite warm despite the chill in the air.

Several minutes and a few zigzagged maneuvers through alleyways later, Tarian unfurled two heavy blankets in front of a secluded bonfire.

"How'd you know this was here?" Tarian asked.

"I've been here before." Delia laid out a variety of cheeses and a baguette to snack on.

"Should I be concerned?"

"Yes." She sat cross-legged on the blanket, ripped off a piece of bread and ate it.

Guilt frayed his joy and tried to destroy the moment. Tarian closed his eyes casting out the invasive thoughts about his father's killer. Tonight, he wanted to banish his duties and focus on Delia's happiness.

She leaned in and caressed his face. Her eyes rounded with concern. She kissed him briefly then ripped off another piece of bread and handed it to him.

He took the bread and watched a smile spread across her face. The sight of her smile lessened the distractions inside his head.

"Why aren't you eating?" she asked.

He grinned in response. He hungered not for food. In one bold move, he pulled her on top of him. Tarian didn't usually initiate aggressive, romantic advancements, out of respect for her position as the Senator's daughter.

She giggled with delight and stretched the length of her body on top of his. His hands found the small of her back, then wound around her narrow waist to grasp the sharp edges of her hips. She didn't pull away; instead, she pressed her body harder into his. He hungrily kissed her neck, and she moaned into his ear. Entwined in ecstasy, they explored one another with mouths and hands. Somewhat to his relief, since he knew he couldn't refuse her if she wanted more, she peeled her body off his.

She rolled onto her back still holding his hand, looking at the dark cloudless sky. "You know this fire never burns out. Isn't that weird?"

His labored breathing prevented words. Eventually, his animalistic desire faded into a manageable ache, and he could answer, "Yes that's weird. Are you sure?"

"Yes, every time I've come here, day or night, it still burns. And I've never seen any person around tending to it."

"Strange." He now recognized it as the work of a purple person, but he kept the secret.

She propped herself up on one elbow and ran the soft tip of her slender finger along his cheek. "What have they asked you to do?"

"It's classified. If I tell you, I have to kill you." He dragged her towards him again.

"No seriously." She pushed away.

"How many times have you been here?"

"We've hidden here a few times, thanks to Dad's work. And

now he's gotten your family in danger too."

"No, he hasn't."

"Yes, he has!"

He wanted to tell her about the many circumstances that brought him to this village, but how could he explain it and not reveal the truth? He'd have to lie or evade her questions. He'd have to act just as her father did, and he knew she resented her father for his secrecy.

"I'm going to be fine," he said. "And what about you?"

"I'm fine."

"You're still very thin."

"I know." She turned away.

"But you're healthy?" He treaded lightly. Her illness was a sensitive topic.

"Yes, I've already told you I'm fine." Turning back around to face him she asked, "When do you leave?"

"What do you mean?"

"Tarian don't do this to me. You know me." She looked into his eyes with strength and wisdom.

"Christmas day, our training begins in four days." He braced for her furious onslaught.

"We'll spend every minute together." She tucked her head into the crook of his shoulder and snuggled up to his robust body.

He was shocked she didn't complain about government brutality or unnecessary military actions. Normally these conversations would end in a long debate over many of the Entente's policies. Today, however, it ended much more pleasantly.

EIGHT

UNWELCOME TOURIST

The aged cobblestone road of Rue de la Magie stretched long with crooked wooden signs swinging from creaky metal chains. Bells rang crisply when vendor's doors swung open and shut. The magic and music of Christmas filled every nook and crevice of the unique village as the shoppers gathered last minute presents. The smell of baked cinnamon bread, pumpkin pie, and brewed apple cider with hints of mulling spice made shoppers stop to purchase one last item for dinner. It was Christmas Eve, and even the venom from the Prevallers' attack couldn't poison the spirit of the village.

From the stationery shop across the street, Delia watched Tarian laugh and dine on baked brie and chestnuts with a woman. The clerk shot annoyed glances at Delia, but she had no intentions of leaving her watch post. To appease the wicked clerk, she snatched a Christmas card off the shelf and paid for it. The clerk looked at her quizzically as she placed the card inside a paper bag. The card read: *To my wonderful wife: Meet me under the mistletoe.*

Delia plucked her purchase out of the clerk's hand and

resumed her post. She wasn't about to leave the store, not while her boyfriend ate lunch with a beautiful woman. The clerk cleared her throat, but Delia rolled her eyes and continued spying.

"I bought a fricking card!" she mumbled.

Tarian and Audrey sat in front of Café de la Nouvelle Natuche, a popular gathering place for the villagers and Guardians. They were lucky to get a seat, even an uncomfortable scrolled iron chair outside. The heat from the outdoor fire pit kept them surprisingly warm as tiny snowflakes cascaded to the ground.

"The weather is far more enjoyable than I thought it'd be." Tarian glanced at the snow piled high on the peaks of the rooftops.

"It is," she said with a wry smile.

Tarian caught the nudge of a lie. "What?"

"I can't have any secrets," she huffed. "That's my gift."

"Oh my God, you're a purple person!" Instantly, he regretted his words.

"A what?" She smiled.

"You know. The gifted ones wear purple." His chest caved. He sounded ridiculous.

Her smile grew. "Then yes, I'm a purple person."

He hung his head as the humiliation settled in his belly.

"Don't feel bad. It makes sense. I get it."

"So what's your gift?"

"It's small and not very helpful really. Nothing like your

dad's shape shifting. You would've been amazed."

Audrey's many memories of Dad slipped out during their conversations. At first it had bothered him. He'd been jealous and hurt over his lost memories, but soon the pain turned to fascination. Seeing Dad through someone else's eyes began to feel like a present being opened.

"What do you do?"

"I can change the weather but only in my immediate vicinity. I can't cause a tornado or anything like that. But it helps on a cold day like today."

He smiled to himself reminiscing about how Delia had been able to keep him warm in a very different way.

"What?" she asked.

"Nothing." His cheeks flushed with heat.

"Oh, you can have secrets. Whatever." She crossed her arms and smirked like a teenager.

This wasn't the Audrey Tarian had known at the Entente Military Academy. This Audrey was funny and interesting and soft. As her subordinate, he'd suffered her constant barrage of orders throughout his first year and a half, but the woman that sat across from him now demanded only camaraderie. She'd guided him into his new life, with patience, in less than four days.

"Why won't you come to Christmas Eve dinner tonight?" he asked.

"I told you, I always spend it with Eleanor and the Guardians."

"Come over afterward."

"No Tarian, you enjoy this time alone with your family. We begin training the day after Christmas, and by the New Year, if we're lucky, we'll have our assignment. It won't be peaceful for long."

"I know. At least come over a little while before we have to leave. I want to introduce you to everyone."

"I'll try." She slid an envelope across the table. "This is why I asked you to meet here."

"What is it?"

"Open it. It's your witch's blood test results. Let's see if you're a purple person too." She laughed.

He ripped it open with one swipe then paused. His heart pounded, but did it matter to him? Maybe since he'd just discovered she could control the weather, he now felt competition.

"I don't really understand most of these markings, but I'm a purple person." He cocked an eyebrow. Relief rushed through him, and again he wondered why he cared so much.

"Congratulations. Cheers!" She lifted her mug full of cider.

He lifted his. "Cheers!"

They clinked and sipped then an awkward silence snuck in between them. They hadn't been intimate friends and now they were, just like that.

"So what can I do?" He broke the quiet.

"Let me see the report." Her eyes scanned the papers. "Your ability is to be determined but look here." She pointed to a percentage notation. "This means you have more than 60% witch's blood. I bet your mother is a descendant from a witch. She probably doesn't even know it."

"Cool, but when will I know what my special abilities are?" Anxiety crept under his skin, and he put down the mug. Every day he learned a new, unbelievable fact about himself or his father. He began to wish for a normal, boring day.

"Don't worry. Once you begin the training your gifts will develop quickly. In a person without gifts, the Realm is simply an arena to hone skills, but in a gifted person, it also accelerates the special abilities hiding inside. It speeds up the natural process. If we waited for your gifts to come in on their own, it could take days or years, and we don't have that kind of time."

"Is there anything I can do to help?"

"Just concentrate on any strange phenomenon you feel. In other words, don't doubt yourself or shy away from weird things happening inside your body. Does that make sense?"

"Sort of, I get what you're trying to say."

The sharp ringing of bells startled Delia, and she nearly knocked over a glass angel for sale on the display table in the stationery shop. Once again, the clerk furrowed her bushy brow and squinted her dark eyes at Delia. Delia realized she'd better get out of the store before she was thrown out.

She needed to know what was in that envelope. It must have been good news since they toasted their cups with a smile. Jealousy filled her lungs as she breathed. That woman was one of the horrid village people, and she was luring her boyfriend into this strange world.

Her eyes burned from the constant squinting, and her shoulders ached from the tension of holding still for too many minutes. A fist-sized knot bunched in the crook of her neck. It swelled with every pretty smile from the desirable woman sitting next to her boyfriend. She knew Tarian had other things to attend to while here in the village. She'd hoped the agenda items weren't so attractive.

"Delia!"

Her father's sharp voice surprised her.

"What are you doing? I told you not to leave the Inn alone. It's too dangerous, and you are too weak."

"But it's Christmas. And I'm not weak."

"Honey." He lowered his voice. "Your illness and the Prevallers do not care about such things. Let's go."

Delia wanted to catch Tarian's eye as she left the store, but he remained focused on the other woman. To her dismay, the only eye she caught was the disapproving gaze of her father.

"What?" she asked her father. *Did he know I was spying?*

"You should have stayed at the Inn."

"Why can't I interact in the village?"

"I've told you."

"No, you haven't. You just say 'because I say so.' I thought this was a safe place for us?"

"It is."

"Then I should be able to walk around freely. I'm eighteen."

"We are not discussing this. Do not leave the Inn

unattended!"

"Whatever," she sighed.

As always he gave orders, not explanations. Her father loved her, but it was a strange love, distant and controlling. He was a secretive and powerful man.

She'd been to this village several times before but still felt like an unwelcome tourist. As they walked in bitter silence, she recalled her first visit. They'd come during a summer month. At eight years old, and much healthier then, she and her mother had enjoyed visiting the fanciful shops. When she was young, the peculiar patrons dressed in purple and green had made her joyful. Today they made her inquisitive and suspicious.

An uneasy memory came to her. She remembered strolling this same path, looking up at her father as he gazed straight ahead as if he belonged to this place. As a young girl, she couldn't explain the impression the town made upon her. Now it seemed clearer but still indefinable. Everything about the unique village filled her stomach with tingling anticipation.

NINE

CHRISTMAS EVE

The door swung open wildly, and Tarian knew it was his little sister excited to see both of her brothers at the door with presents. He'd met up with his older brother Charlie after lunch to purchase gifts for the family. Neither of them ever bought Christmas presents before Christmas Eve. At least this year, their sudden rush into hiding was a valid excuse.

Chloe hit Charlie like a miniature bull sending all of the boxes tumbling to the floor. Her youthful pink skin and beautiful blonde curls bounced as she ran. Joe Junior, the youngest Prescott, barreled into the entrance to greet them, followed by Teresa.

"What's it like?" Teresa asked with big doe eyes. She was sixteen and quite put out that she had to leave all her friends during holiday break. "Mom promised to take me shopping but she's been too busy turning this place into a Christmas wonderland."

"It's nice. It has an ice rink."

"Wow." Teresa rolled her teenage eyes and sighed.

Tarian's mom had decorated for hours. Somehow, she'd

managed to make the Inn's suite look like home. The balsam fir Christmas tree stood in the corner of the living area. Evergreen filled Tarian's nose and twinkling colorful lights caught his eye. Shiny presents were placed neatly under the branches wrapped in silver and gold ribbons. Seeing this stunning display and knowing how hard his mom had worked to make an inconvenient Christmas seem spectacular made Tarian realize just how much the traitor had stolen from his dad.

All through the night as they ate dinner and played board games, Tarian's mind dipped in and out of the past. They laughed and cried over silly details that had been forgotten. When Charlie rolled snake eyes, everyone went silent remembering that was Dad's famous roll. He could turn out two dice with a one on them whenever he needed to.

Tarian enjoyed this precious time with his family. He made every minute count, right up to bedtime. Mere seconds had infinite value, now that he knew what he was.

"And they lived happily ever after." Tarian closed the bedtime story book.

"I love happily ever after," Chloe said in a sleepy voice, eyes closed.

"I thought you were asleep."

"Nope." She smiled her sweet smile.

Tarian's heart melted. "Goodnight, Chloe." He slipped one leg off the bed and tried to sneak away.

Chloe pulled him back. "Cuddle! Just a little longer."

"Of course." He kissed her forehead and sank onto the

pillow.

"Love you," she whispered. Her body squirmed its way under his arm and her head nestled on his shoulder.

Thirty minutes later he untangled her blond curls from his neck, removed her sleeping body from his, and tiptoed out of the bedroom. Downstairs his mother cleaned up and prepared for gift opening in the morning.

"Thank you, Sweetie," his mom said, her hands soapy from cleaning dishes. "Chloe misses you. She has put all of her dolls away and only plays with army toy soldiers now. She makes her own mini EMA in her room, and all the boys in the neighborhood play at our house now."

"She's a character." Tarian smiled, but inside he worried that his little sister may never return home to play with her neighborhood friends.

"I know. The attack scared her to death. I'm so grateful for this place. Thank goodness Zachary took us all here."

"It's a nice village, so old and different from the districts."

"It's a ..." she paused, mouth pursed, eyes searching, "wondrous place, but it's not home. At least it's very Christmassy, for now." She smiled.

"Yes, almost elf-like, isn't it?"

"Yes, that's it. I wouldn't be surprised to find Santa Claus living here," she said.

He understood how she felt. He wished she knew the real magic of this place. "Has Senator Eastwood told you how long you have to stay here?"

"No. I wasn't going to worry about that just yet. At least the kids are off of school. But I do realize I have to stay here to keep my children safe. Charlie is the only one who wants to leave. He insists he's going back to Harvard after the New Year."

"I figured. He told me the same when we were shopping."

"Where are you going tomorrow?" she asked.

Tarian knew it was a loaded question. He saw the curiosity in her caramel eyes. "I'm going to be trained for a special mission. One that could put a stop to all of this."

She looked at him with knowing eyes.

Her awareness heightened his guilt. He almost told her everything, but his eyes fell to the floor instead.

"Your father had secrets too," she confessed. "I've been here before, you know. Joe took me here twenty-seven years ago. It hasn't changed at all."

"I didn't know that."

They silently continued to clean up the dinner mess. Tarian felt his mother's stare upon him, and he couldn't face her.

"Be safe," she said softly.

"Mom, it's going to be all right. I promise." He hugged her. "Go to sleep, you look tired." He pushed her out of the kitchen.

"I have to set the coffee," she protested.

"Go! I'll do the rest. You've done enough already. Love you Mom."

"Love you more." Her mouth smiled, but her eyes remained doleful.

TEN

CHRISTMAS MORNING

Christmas paper and fir needles scattered under Chloe and Joe Jr.'s feet as they scampered around the tree delivering presents to their intended recipients. Delia finally plopped down next to Tarian and sunk into the plushy couch. All morning she'd been recruited by Chloe to be one of Santa's helpers and hadn't had a minute of peace.

Delia clung to Tarian and refused to let Chloe steal her away again. His arms wrapped around her. His shoulder made the perfect pillow. All presents had been opened. Breakfast sat comfortably in her belly. She only wanted to embrace him for the remaining couple of hours they had left.

Chloe sat on her knees on the floor arranging her new army figures and the new combat tank. She organized and reorganized the figurines. Joe Jr. whizzed by riding *her* new hoverboard and knocked down all she had built.

"Joe! That's mine! Get off!" Chloe yelled.

"No! Catch me."

He sped away but didn't get far. He crashed and began to cry. Soon Teresa had set him up with some of *his* Christmas toys to play with, and both youngsters were happy. The gifts would help the children forget Tarian's absence.

Delia didn't have the luxury of such distractions. Her space would be empty. Her heart would be broken. Her time with him robbed because of what? Who exactly was taking Tarian away from her? Tarian wouldn't tell. Her father wouldn't tell. This confirmed her decision to take that job offer in the Government District. Once Tarian left on his secret mission, she'd leave on hers.

At this moment, there'd be no discussion of training or job offers. She ran her teasing fingers over Tarian's arm catching his attention. She kissed him lovingly until the objections from Joe Jr. and Chloe forced her to stop.

"Ewe, gross, kissy face," sneered Joe Jr. and Chloe.

Seconds later, Audrey walked through the door escorted by Senator Eastwood. A smile spread across Tarian's face. Delia stiffened and held tight to Tarian's arm. Turning her boyfriend over to this beautiful woman felt like feeding him to the wolves.

Together they rose from the couch. Tarian introduced Audrey to Delia and then to his entire family. They all gathered around the kitchen counter for coffee and more pastries. Delia and Tarian stood as one, arm in arm. She wanted her connection to him prominent in both her father's and Audrey's minds.

Her father gave her a look of sovereignty. Tarian was his jurisdiction now, but she wouldn't surrender him without a fight.

Her father was removing her boyfriend from her arms and delivering him into the arms of another. She cast contemptuous glances at him, and he countered with domineering glares. She'd never receive empathy from him. In her eighteen years, she'd never seen compassion in his eyes and questioned his love constantly.

As a child he'd hugged her, he'd read her bedtime stories, he'd taught her valuable lessons but all with distant emotions. That distance spread with every year, but it had made her strong. A hardened sense of duty had come from her father. Work always trumped family, especially secretive, never discussed jobs. He left in the middle of the night, locked his office door and refused to answer any of her questions concerning the state of affairs of the Entente or this mysterious village he called a safe house. She loved him but couldn't honor him because what constituted honor for her was honesty and trust, something she'd never received from him.

Now her beloved Tarian kept secrets from her too. The strange intuition that always permeated into her bones when she visited told her she was losing him. He was joining her father's mysterious village.

"So, when will we all be safe again, Daddy?" Delia asked.

Her snide tone caused Tarian to snap his head around and look at her with drawn brows and tight eyes.

"Oh Sweetie, you give me too much credit. I wish I had the control to determine the movements of the Prevallers. I do not," her father said.

"What about you, Audrey? What's your level of control

around here?" Delia turned her plastic smile on Audrey. Delia's grasp of Tarian's arm became a vice grip.

"I'm just a soldier like Tarian. Going to do whatever is asked of me," Audrey volleyed.

Delia took it all in. She glared at all of them including Tarian and his mom. She loved Tarian but at this point her simmering rage threatened to explode. She was too smart to start a sparring match with her father in front of everyone, so she rushed from the room.

"Where are you going?" Tarian chased after her. "I have another hour or so."

"I don't," she said bluntly.

"Please don't leave like this."

"Like what?"

"Angry."

"I can't be happy to see you off to God only knows where!"

"Don't worry." He placed his hands on her hips.

"Don't patronize me!" Her deep blue eyes glared at him.

"I will tell you everything when I get back," he whispered.

This sparked her attention. Would he be completely honest with her?

"I love you," she whispered, and her eyes softened.

"I love you too." He pulled her into his arms and pressed his lips upon hers.

She kissed him back with passion. She wanted her kiss to weaken his knees, to be a kiss that would live in his dreams forever. She slipped out the door as a tear cut a path down her face.

The whisper of "Goodbye," achingly forced out of her breath.

ELEVEN

DAY ONE

With one step over the threshold, Tarian, Audrey, and the Senator walked from the charming, cobbled street of the village and onto the slick, rigid tiles of the training facility. The building had Entente identifiable markings everywhere, straight lines and precise people in gray. A few familiar Guardians dressed in green and purple suits dotted the otherwise colorless environment.

"Tarian this is a joint training facility for both the Guardians and the elite Entente military. You will be safe here. The protection from the village extends into this building as well," Senator Eastwood explained.

Confused, he studied the gray walls. They emitted a dull coldness, and yet, at the same time, they cloaked and protected him.

The welcoming tour included all the usual venues but also numerous virtual simulation rooms. Suddenly, Tarian realized he would never leave the building. The fresh air he'd smelled outside was gone and substituted with imitation air designed by human beings to enhance the senses. But it smelled too perfect. He missed the harsh odors of EMA from the stench of ground-in sweat to the bittersweet smell of the fresh cut lawn.

"Here we are, your room for the next few weeks." Senator Eastwood stopped in front of a door labeled 3344. "Audrey you are right here, across the hall."

"Weeks?" Audrey asked.

"Yes, I've brought in a team. I want Tarian to train with them and a few days is not sufficient. He has a lot to learn, and we have a lot to test."

"Exactly what am I being tested for?" Tarian asked.

"Your immortal senses and strengths. I need to know how far you've developed before I'll send you on a mission."

"We don't have much time," Audrey said.

"I'll be the judge of that. Get some rest, both of you." The Senator turned on his heels and left.

The fury on Audrey's face made Tarian nervous. He reached for the doorknob to escape into his room. Wanting to comfort her, he turned around to invite her inside but saw only her door slam shut.

The luxury of his room surpassed any he'd ever seen. The room and the entire building didn't seem real. Some sort of magic hovered around and inside these walls. Like the Guardian Headquarters, the size of this building deceived and fascinated his senses, but more than that, it felt as if he'd stepped out of the village and into the Entente Military District five hundred miles away. He couldn't recall any Entente military personnel walking the village streets, and yet they lined the halls here.

Early the next morning he changed into a training uniform hanging in the closet, a camouflaged snug bodysuit made from an extremely pliable yet indestructible material. The label read 'bulletproof' but offered no other information. What would he encounter today that would require a bulletproof bodysuit?

The boots were high and came up almost to his knees. Even though he was covered from neck to toe, he felt barefoot and naked. Everything fit him snugly. The flexible material stretched over his muscles and melted into the creases of his skin. All sizes were accurate, even the high arch of his shoes.

All items of clothing inside the closet were individually wrapped. The first container labeled *The Game* hung next to those marked day five through day twenty-one. Uniforms two through four weren't missing. The Guardians' obsessive-compulsive organization wouldn't make such an error. Days two through four didn't exist because he wouldn't be changing out of this bodysuit for four days.

Audrey and Tarian collided exiting their rooms. She wore an identical bodysuit, but she had a backpack.

"Where's your backpack?" she asked.

He quickly ran back to his closet to find an identical backpack hanging on a hook. It weighed a hefty forty pounds at least.

"Have you played this game before?" he asked her when he returned to the hallway.

"Yes."

He waited for her to elaborate, but she offered nothing. They walked several seconds in silence.

"Care to explain?" he finally asked.

"It's basically a complex and challenging Capture the Flag set inside the Realm."

"The Realm? I thought we were in the Realm."

"No, we're not. This is the training facility. It houses many rooms."

"The Realm is a room?" he asked.

"You could say that."

"Err, uh," he murmured. "How many of us are playing this game?"

"Two or possibly three teams of twenty-five soldiers," she answered. "The main subject of this game is you."

"Me?"

"Yes, your immortal abilities will be assessed. You'll be put through strange tests to assist in the development of your extra strength or extreme vision."

"Cool. Maybe I can even fly." Tarian laughed.

"Maybe." Audrey's tone was serious.

"What? Seriously? Can I fly?"

"We don't know what you can do yet, hence the test."

She might as well have ended her sentence with 'idiot' because that was how she made him feel.

"Did I hurt your feelings?" She mocked then pushed him

so hard he fell into the wall with a loud thud. "You need to toughen up."

"I'm tough." With a bruised ego, he remained silent.

"Not all eyes are on you, so don't worry."

Still repairing his ego, he didn't answer.

"The Realm also trains the Elite Forces. This facility houses one percent of those who graduate from all the EMAs across the Entente. Those with the right credentials train here to become the Elite Forces. They are some of the few mortals that know about us."

"Okay. Why is this place full of military personnel, and yet, I never saw anyone wearing a military uniform inside the village? Do they never leave the building?"

"Something like that," she said.

"We're no longer in the village, are we?"

"Something like that."

"We're in both places at one time."

"Something like that." She smiled but offered no explanation.

Maybe there was no explanation, he thought. Maybe it was just plain magic. Before he could ask her more questions, they reached the door of their destination.

Approximately sixty trainees gathered into a circular all white room, no windows, no furniture. Tube-like compartments big enough for one maybe two people lined the curved wall. Each trainee stood in front of a cylinder. Tarian fell into an open spot in the circle, as did Audrey. Directly across the room stood an athletically built, brown-eyed girl with severe bruising covering the left half of her face. Next to her stood a tan, square-shaped man with a blood red suture split across his cheekbone.

Maria? Gabe?

Her hair was shorter and dyed blue, and he had a terrifying scar, but they were definitely his friends. So much had happened since he last saw them. What had they gone through? By the looks of their faces, quite a bit of pain.

Guilt crushed the carefully constructed fence of bravado Tarian had built to endure the craziness of the last few days. He bowed his head. He couldn't look into the eyes of true soldiers. He'd been rescued and whisked off to safety in a fancy tiltrotor. The Guardians had coddled him while his friends battled the Prevallers to stay alive. If he hadn't abandoned his friends, maybe their faces would be undamaged, but then again, maybe it would have been worse for them to be with the so-called 'First Born.'

Maria caught Tarian's attention with animated facial expressions. She looked excited to see him but how would she feel after he told her his story. He wanted to run across the room and embrace them both. Ripples of uncertainty swelled into giant waves of apprehension the more he waited. He needed to get the truth off of his chest, face his sentence. However, the massive Commander General that stood in the center of the room made it impossible for him to act on his eagerness.

The Commander was a huge man, as tall as he was thick. His sharply, defined muscles bulged under his shirt. These were not decorative muscles of body builders; these were functional muscles of a disciplined war hero.

Do they make superheroes here?

"Move!" The Commander shouted in Tarian's face. He'd just drunk a cup of coffee by the smell of it.

Tarian realized he hadn't heard one word of instructions. The giant man had been talking, but Tarian had been drowning in his culpability. Now he was holding a weapon that he couldn't remember accepting nor did he know how to operate it. With a reluctant step inside the tube, the door snapped shut, and he could no longer see his friends. The narrow metal tube he was encased in began to shake violently. The powerful elevator sucked him toward the sky with tremendous speed, although he had no visual reference point to confirm his sensory input.

The ascent stopped abruptly but without a jolt. Quite easily, Maria, Gabe and Tarian emerged from their tubes. The others were gone, and so were the tubes. A forested, mountainous jungle surrounded them. And it was warm, very warm. The three stood still and silent for a moment as the dizzying effect of the transport subsided.

"So, this is the Realm." Tarian looked around the vast environment. He thought about what Audrey had said. She had called the Realm a room, but this was no room. *Was it?*

"Have we been tractor beamed to like … outside the borders?" Gabe asked.

"Impossible," Maria said. "It's just a sophisticated

simulation center."

"I no longer know what is real and what is simulated anymore, but I do know they call this place the Realm," Tarian answered.

Stress laughter unexpectedly burst from all three of them. They were trapped in a child's fairytale where all their wildest dreams and nightmares were possible. They'd all experienced a surreal week that seemed to climax here in a magical forest. Tarian's guilt vanished. It seemed no time had passed between them, and they exchanged explanations of their survival. His friends didn't consider his rescue to be abandonment. Instead, they encouraged him to embrace his amazing future. They'd already been informed about the Guardians and most of Tarian's story, so they were prepared for his wild tales. He knew nothing of their past week and listened as they told him frightening accounts of the attack. Tarian couldn't believe they were lucky enough to make it out alive.

"You should see the lawn, it's awful. The beautiful grass burned to ash," Maria explained to Tarian.

"And our barracks: Eisenhower, Pershing, Bradley and Washington Hall. It's a pile of stones. It's like the Prevallers were aiming their weapons at that spot," Gabe said.

"They were," Tarian said. Accountability washed over him once more. Those buildings were destroyed because of him.

"Oh yeah," Gabe said.

Dark emotions trounced their joyous reunion.

"Stacey and Tommy didn't make it Tarian," Maria said the

familiar names through clenched teeth, and Tarian bowed his head. "Professor Novak and Major Steinhart are gone too." She opened her mouth to list more names when Gabe nudged her arm.

"It's all right. I need to know. They're who we're fighting for."

"For the Black and Gray and Gold!" Gabe shouted.

"For the Black and Gray and Gold!" They all three shouted in unison paying tribute to the nation's colors.

Saddened by the details of death and destruction, and yet exuberant to be with each other, they began their new journey into the Realm. Filled with patriotic pride Tarian marched onward holding his weapon. Embarrassment hit him when he realized he had no idea how this particular weapon worked.

"I feel really dumb right now, but did the Commander explain how to use this?" He held up the gun.

"You are too much. It's a stunner." Maria rolled her eyes and explained the mechanics.

"The effects are severe. One hit will send a two-hundred-pound man to the ground instantly. The convulsions last two minutes and from what I've heard, hurt like a mother," Gabe warned.

"That's when you get away from the enemy, or you take your victim as a prisoner," Maria said.

"Don't shoot the guys in green like us. Only shoot the guys in black camouflage," Gabe said.

"Got it." Tarian nodded.

Tarian was thankful to be with Maria and Gabe but wished for Audrey's experience. He guessed they'd been separated on purpose. Someone controlled the game. Every move was strategic, a test of survival.

Within an hour, they met up with an enemy game player. Squatting and hiding like wolves ready to pounce, they watched. The opponent girl moved stealthily through the woods. She hadn't seen them. They each turned to one another and nodded. Jumping from the foliage, armed and ready, they had her surrounded. Without hesitation, she shot her stunner but missed. Gabe grabbed her weapon while Tarian wrestled her to the ground, trapping her under his weight. Without warning an enormous man appeared. She wasn't alone after all. Suddenly he fell to the ground with a loud thwack and Tarian thought he felt the ground shake. All two hundred, thirty pounds, six-feet-five-inches of him crashed to the dirt. Legs thrashing, arms flailing and eyes rolling.

"Mike!" The girl cried out.

Gabe stood motionless. His stunner still pointed at the position where the giant man had been standing before he fell.

"Let's go," Tarian ordered Gabe and Maria.

He had the girl's stunner, and Maria grabbed the giant man's stunner. Before lifting his weight from the girl, Tarian pinched a pressure point in her neck, paralyzing her long enough for them to get away.

As they ran through the thick bushes and tall trees, Tarian sensed someone watching. He cast his glance upward to find the trees filled with red-eyed, scorpion-tailed animals. These animals hung upside down; tails curled around branches while they observed. Tarian pondered if they were possums or monkeys, but as long as they didn't attack, he didn't care. A few of them threw clumps of dirt and rocks, but other than that, the animals remained tame.

Night arrived after a grueling day of running, fighting and hiking. Maria, Gabe and Tarian made camp under the cover of the trees. Tarian guessed the time by the stars and moon in this sky.

"I can't believe it's so light out. According to the stars, it should be nine o'clock," Tarian said.

"What are you talking about? It's pitch dark," Maria said.

"Really?" Tarian asked.

Maria and Gabe looked at him inquisitively. Tarian glanced around. Through his eyes, he saw an eerie haze of light. Bright moonlight shimmered off of droplets of misting rain. It must just be a difference of opinion.

"I'm freezing," Maria said.

The damp cold also besieged Tarian's bones. They unpacked the backpacks searching for something warm. His friends stumbled in the darkness. They really couldn't see anything. Tarian found his sleeping bag first then a snaplight. He shook the stick until it glowed.

"Is that better?" Tarian asked.

"Much, thanks," Gabe said.

"I guess you can see in the dark," Maria said.

"Yeah, I guess." Tarian shivered but not from the cold.

Having his immortal senses develop in the presence of mortals rattled his nerves. He didn't want his friends to look at him differently, or worse, fear him. He missed Audrey.

The threesome formed a triangle on the hard, uneven ground. The thin sleeping bags helped with the cold but did nothing to make the ground more forgiving and comfortable. They talked about what they'd seen inside this enigmatic jungle. It'd been hard enough to plod through the thick underbelly of bushes but having strange animals and shadows crossing their path was frightening.

"This place is like nothing I've ever seen before. But it feels real, doesn't it? The humidity, the smells," Maria asked.

"Yes." Gabe stared up at the stars, heavy breaths leaving his lungs.

"I hope I can make it," Maria said.

"You will. Just keep your mind straight. Remember it may seem real but it's not," Tarian said.

"That's just it. It's scary as hell, and it's not even real. I've been through real, and this is almost as bad. Soon it'll be up to us to find and defeat the Prevallers. These people can kill immortals. What chance do I have?" Maria asked.

"We have to remain optimistic," Tarian said.

The forest's spookiness disturbed him too, but what he'd seen didn't exist in reality: phantom shadows, mechanical scorpion-tailed monkeys, burning water. It was a game. He told himself, a psychological and physical test of will. But the strange and magical sensation of this place obscured reality.

"Yeah, well, I'm trying. Watching friends die, getting the shit kicked out of me. You weren't there. You don't know," she jabbed.

Gabe nudged her with his hand, but Tarian didn't want them to change or filter their words. He didn't need his friends to tip toe around any topics just because his life was now a bizarre circus. He needed them to remain constant even if it meant getting his feelings hurt. His skin had thickened since his father's death. He'd survived EMA's tough regimen. He'd kept his calm today under a canopy of strange creatures. He could handle the truth.

"No, you're right. I was enjoying a nice Christmas." He admitted breaking the tension.

"I still don't understand why Maria and I were picked for this. We haven't even graduated. This facility is for Elite Forces and Immortals. We're neither," Gabe said.

Tarian hadn't thought of that. He hadn't had time to think. He'd been too busy running and fighting, but Gabe was right. Why were his friends here? He remembered the Senator said he'd picked a team. He must have chosen his friends for a reason.

"Did you see Delia during Christmas?" Maria asked.

"Yes."

"That's good," Maria said, followed by a long uncomfortable silence.

Maria and Delia were from two different worlds. Maria grew up in a poor mining town while Delia was a wealthy Senator's daughter. When Delia visited EMA, and they all went out together, their easy conversation became forced and awkward. Delia and

Maria were both confrontational. Their different upbringings made for extreme opposites of opinion, so disputes were constant. Both women stubbornly voiced their views, which never concluded in any agreement. There were no hard feelings between the two women. In fact, Tarian suspected they both enjoyed the verbal sparring.

"What were those things that threw rocks at my head?" Maria asked of the strange monkeys they'd encountered earlier.

"Machines," Tarian answered.

"Did you see their eyes?" Gabe asked.

"Yes, blood red." Tarian shivered. "They were lenses, not eyes. Cameras. They're tracking us. I'll bet whoever is running this game uses them to judge our progress."

"Did you see its tail?" Maria asked again clearly disturbed by the monkey creature.

"Well, they are vile creatures," Gabe said.

"How incredibly messed up is this jungle?" Maria asked.

"I can't tell if it's a jungle, a forest, or a mountain range," Gabe added.

"You should see Guardian Headquarters. It's amazing but in a good way, not like this," he said then stopped, unsure of what to keep secret.

"Well, I still can't call Cadet Sergeant Major Gualtiero by her first name. A … Au … Audrey. See it doesn't want to get off my tongue. That's just too weird for me. Remember what a bitch she was at EMA?" Maria said.

"She's still hot though."

"Shut up, Gabe!" Maria jabbed him hard with her foot.

"Yeah." Tarian joined Gabe in a series of manly catcalls.

"Yeah?" Maria scoffed. "What about Delia?" Her words were meant to finish the manly grunts. She knew how to drop a bomb on the guys' chauvinistic playfulness.

"She's hot too," Gabe responded just to annoy her.

"I wasn't talking to you," she said.

"I think she is fine," Tarian said.

"Oh, she is fine." Gabe continued to tease.

"No, stupid, he means she is doing fine," Maria tut-tutted.

"You think?" Gabe questioned jumping to conclusions. "Did she dump you?"

"No, I mean I saw her, and it was great. She's just very thin."

"She was thin before. She kept getting sick," Gabe said.

"I know, and she's never explained what made her sick. She just seemed different. I can't explain it."

Maria burst into laughter.

"What's so funny?" Tarian asked.

"Everything's different. How is a girl supposed to act? Her boyfriend's immortal—"

"She doesn't know I'm immortal," he interrupted. "Her father won't let me tell her or anyone, for that matter."

"It's going to work out, don't worry. Let's just take one messed-up crazy task at a time, okay?" Gabe joked.

"Sure," Tarian and Maria agreed in unison.

"Do you hear it?" Tarian asked, and they fell silent.

"I don't hear anything?" Maria said.

She looked at him, and he knew what she thought, another freaky immortal sense. Minutes passed as the music's volume gradually increased, but still only Tarian could hear it.

"Taps," Maria and Gabe finally said in unison.

The historic horn melody played every night before bed at EMA. A tradition that still held strong even after the Entente War.

"It must be ten o'clock," Gabe said.

"Why are they playing it here?" Maria questioned.

Tarian wondered the same thing. Was it simply a reference of time or did the Realm know *Taps* kindled deep internal feelings for him? It conjured up images of Delia. The long C Major notes played on the bugle inspired inner reflection. *What is going to happen when this is a real game? I survived one attack, could I survive another? Could I survive without Audrey's help? What if I never see Delia again?*

Tarian's thoughts drifted to his dad. As a child, Tarian shadowed him. He admired and loved his dad more than anyone else. He was an unusual child in that he would sit contentedly for hours at his father's office as if he were thirty-year-old. The staff and partners nicknamed him Master Tarian A.I.T., Attorney in Training. He even had his own letterhead printed with that title scrolled across the header in fancy gold lettering. The hopes of a father and son law firm died after the funeral, once the Senator thrust him into the military. He let out a sigh, lost in the thoughts of what was supposed to be.

He closed his eyes. The image of a Prescott and Sons, Esq.

sign drifted into his dreamlike state, waving in midair like a proud flag, and then blackness enveloped him. He slipped into a fitful sleep.

TWELVE

DAY TWO

Day two of the strenuous game began at first light. By noon, they'd traveled miles in the stiflingly, humid heat and still hadn't found their allies or their enemies.

"I have an idea. See that cliff." He pointed to a shelf-like ledge protruding from a large mountain.

"Yes," Gabe and Maria said.

"We need to get there."

"I see. Get to high ground," Maria said.

"Yes. Then maybe we can find out where the enemy base is," Tarian explained.

"Or find Green's base. It would be helpful to have more than the three of us," Gabe said.

"Maybe we can even see the flags," Maria said.

Whichever group captured the enemy flag first, won the game. Tarian wanted to win. He wanted that flag. He didn't know which end was which, like a lost pawn on a giant chessboard. Getting to higher ground would help him collect his bearings.

"Eeeekk!" A high-pitched voice screamed from behind a rambler bush.

A young woman dressed in green camouflage jumped out of the tangled vines. Tarian had thrown a rock at her, barely missing her head. Gabe and Maria jumped, spread their legs into ready position and aimed their stunners.

"Don't shoot!" She yelled, arms up.

"Sorry," Tarian said. "I saw you hiding but couldn't tell which team you were on. You're lucky I didn't stun you."

"Thanks," she hissed. Her eyes bored into him.

"I'm Tarian."

"I know who you are, First Born." Her face puckered as if the nickname left a sour taste in her mouth.

"Who the hell are you?" Maria spat.

Tarian grinned at Maria for coming to his defense.

"Jen." No smile.

Tarian wished he'd hit her with the rock.

"Well, Jen, I'm Maria, and this is Gabe. And unfortunately, it looks like we're on the same team."

"Looks like it." Jen cocked an eyebrow.

"Are you alone?" Maria asked.

"As of about four hours ago. My partner got shot and captured."

"Do you know where our base is?" Tarian asked.

"No, I was hoping you did. Scott and I searched miles and found nothing," she confessed.

"Same here. We're going up there now to get a better look at this crazy place," Gabe explained. "Do you want to come with us?"

She didn't answer.

"Fine, we'll go without you." Maria walked away.

"Look, I don't like leaving you behind, alone," Tarian stated.

"I don't need your help," she spat.

"What do you have against Tarian?" Gabe asked.

"He's the reason we're in this mess. The Guardians are supposed to protect us, not the other way around."

"You signed on to this when you chose to enroll in the military. Protect and serve," Gabe said.

"I didn't know immortals existed when I enlisted."

"If it's any consolation to you, I didn't know about the Guardians and immortals either, and I sure never wanted to be the 'First Born.' But I do want to train hard and stop anyone else from losing their life."

She gave Tarian a long, hard look. No smile. Begrudgingly and without a word, she took the lead and began to climb the mountain.

They encountered tricky man-made creatures they had to outsmart, and they couldn't find a clear path to follow. Thick branches of overgrown weeds and plants buried the trail and covered the mountainside. Vines wrapped around their ankles as they dug hard into the ground with their boots. They climbed quickly, using the deep traction on their soles to propel themselves upward. An occasional slip in the wet, dark patches brought their focus back and put a heavy scare into them. They jammed stakes into the slope of the cliff, pulling the weight of their bodies up through the slimy mud and jagged rocks.

A bright fuchsia colored insect landed on Jen's hand. The brilliant color mesmerized her, and she didn't shoo it away. Prisms of color danced on her skin as the insect fluttered its tiny, translucent wings.

Catching up to her Tarian stopped and saw the insect. "What's that?" He looked closer. It had stripes and a needlepoint nose.

"I don't know," she replied then the insect stung her. "Ouch! The little a-hole bit me!"

Tarian watched a smile fan across her face. Her head swayed side to side. Then her fingers lifted one by one from the stake driven into the mountainside keeping her from falling to her death. She let go. Tarian leaped to grab her but missed then Gabe managed to catch a loop on her backpack, but she slipped out of it and fell.

They all screamed. "Help! Help!"

She fell belly up, still smiling. Tarian winced at the thought of her spine shattering into fragmented pieces when she hit the ground. Maybe this was a test to see if he could fly. He could save her. He positioned his feet to push his legs off the side of the mountain for more speed, then jumped.

"Tarian!" Maria screamed.

Tarian dropped fast. He couldn't fly. Fear burned throughout his veins, but he managed to douse the panic with reason. *I can't fly but I won't die, so maybe I can land on the ground before her. I can catch her.*

"Look out," Gabe yelled.

Swoosh! A winged creature the size of a horse whirled by them. The creature dove gracefully placing its mouth around Jen's falling body and hooking Tarian with its clawed hoof. The bird-like creature flew over the ledge and discarded Tarian then it flew away with Jen locked inside its beak shaped mouth.

More fuchsia-colored insects flew around Gabe's and Maria's exposed hands and heads as they continued to climb.

"Move!" Maria screamed at Gabe.

They began to jab their stakes into the mountainside without care. Driving the metal sticks in a ladder pattern. Their feet following up and up and up. As they climbed, they shook their heads and swatted anything that came close to their exposed bare skin. Finally, the two of them threw their torsos over the top edge of the ledge. Tarian grabbed their hands and pulled. Rolling onto their backs their chests heaving with oxygen gulps, finally safe.

"Do you see any more of those bugs?" asked Gabe still lying on the ground.

"No," Tarian said.

"Where do you think that flying … horse … hawk … thing … took Jen?" Maria asked.

"Probably out of the game and back to the training facility. That's my guess," Tarian answered.

"I thought she was so dead. I thought we'd be picking up body pieces at the base of this mountain." Maria spoke slowly, her eyes to the sky, spine flattened against the ground, head swaying back and forth rhythmically. "And you! Did you think you could fly?"

"No," Tarian lied, then stuttered out an explanation. "I … I … just … thought … knew if I fell, I wouldn't die … so maybe I could soften her landing."

"Whatever," Maria scoffed.

The three of them fit nicely onto the spacious ledge without fear of falling. Looking down the side of a mountain, two hundred feet in the air, instantly brought a better perspective to the game. Tarian could see the layout of the playing field as if drawn on a map. The size was daunting. From his vantage point, the enemy camp perched north of the mountain. They'd built their headquarters in a circle with prisoners held in the center. Very clever. It made for a difficult recovery.

"Look over there," Tarian pointed south of the mountain. "Is that our base?"

"Maybe, I can barely make out some tents." Gabe strained and squinted his eyes.

"Yes, it is. The others must've banded together to create it. It looks well organized, but I like the circular idea of the enemy's better. Our prisoners are too exposed," Tarian said.

"What prisoners?" Maria asked. "I can maybe see tents but

not people."

"I believe the tent to the left of that large pine tree is housing three prisoners. It's hard to see them from this far away."

"No, it's impossible. It must be another *immortal* sense. Some sort of super sight," Maria said.

"Maybe. Well, we need to get some food and rest."

Tarian didn't like discovering his new strengths in the presence of his normal friends. He kept to himself and got busy setting up camp for the night. His body might be immortal, but his muscles were still subject to weariness and ached.

The ledge created a breezeway. The cold air made Maria shiver and it reminded him of Delia. The Eastwood Estate remained a constant sixty-five degrees year-round, and Delia hated it. She wandered around shivering dressed in sweatpants, sweatshirt, and slippers during the evenings before bed. He missed her. A smile crossed his lips as a mental image of her paraded around his closed eyelids. He raised his arms and put his hands behind his head, keeping his eyes closed until her image had vanished.

The rushing wind moaned. He heard the rustling of leaves in the trees as they settled back into place after the air had passed through them, only to be moved again and again as the wind kept blowing. Animal sounds grabbed his attention, grunts and groans, hard to pinpoint the location. He didn't hear *Taps* tonight.

"I really think we've been transported," Gabe said.

"Still impossible." Maria's voice was drunk with sleep and her tone annoyed. He'd awoken her. She rolled over in her sleeping bag.

"After everything I've seen in the past week, nothing's impossible. These people can bend space. I'm not sure how they do it, but it can be done. I've seen it. We're inside it right now," Tarian said.

"Am I the only one who feels like I'm in over my head?" Gabe asked.

"No," Maria answered—the shortest answer she'd ever given. She always responded at length sarcastically and critically. For her to think inwardly meant things were serious.

Tarian hoped her brevity was just due to exhaustion.

"I guess that's why we're here training so hard. It seems unnecessary or repetitive, but they have a reason. I'm sure of it." Tarian tried to restore their equilibrium. They had their roles—Tarian the optimist, Maria the smart-ass critic, and Gabe the suspicious theorist. Any conversation that dipped out of this pattern was trouble.

THIRTEEN

DAY THREE

Six hours later, beams of bright sunshine shone on their faces. The sun rose on the east side of the mountain and stole their comfortable shade. By the time the haze of sleep lifted, and Tarian became fully aware, he had already overheated inside his sealed sleeping bag. He peeled it off his sticky skin and tried to cool his extremities with wiggling movements, but it was no use. A sweaty, frustrated, miserable day lay ahead.

The climb down the mountain proved to be just as difficult as the ascent. They had to rely more on feel and less on sight, causing them to lose their footing several times, falling a few feet. Gabe twisted his ankle dodging one of those fuchsia insects and worried he wouldn't be able to walk fast enough to keep up with the others. He had warned Maria and Tarian that he would slow them down, and they must leave him behind to fend for himself. They'd protested. Maria called him a burro. Tarian laughed.

One, two, three, thud, thud, thud—six feet landed safely at

the base of the mountain. The ground gave but not enough to protect Gabe's ankle, and he buckled to the grass in pain. Tarian wrapped the ankle with the supplies in his backpack, but Gabe still moved too slowly and clumsily.

Gabe's left side sunk with every step as if he were walking on lopsided quicksand. It agitated Tarian. At this rate, it'd take hours to reach the Green camp. Then the inevitable happened. Gabe collapsed to the ground. Maria and Tarian turned back to him, and in a split second, realized he didn't fall because of his ankle. Without a word, they both pivoted and ran at full speed. Gabe was out of the game, and their only hope was to escape. They never looked back. They'd been trained not to since it'd slow them down. But also, they refused to witness their friend convulse in pain.

Once they were safe, they stopped to catch their breath.

"Did you see them?" Tarian asked.

"No! Not at all. I feel like scum. Thankfully this is a simulation. That is scary as shit!" She gasped between each sentence.

"Yeah, scary as *shit*." He grinned.

"Let's get moving. I feel like I'm being watched." Maria's shifty eyes darted around her tense face.

Tarian understood. He couldn't shake the ghostly feeling of shadows lingering around him. Then he wondered if they were spared stunning on purpose. Maybe that was the game plan all along. *Follow the leader.*

"Maybe we are," he whispered, "Let's not head directly back to base until we know for sure we aren't being followed."

She nodded.

He led Maria into an overgrown forest of thick trees, sharp holly bushes, and low spreading junipers. He stopped once engulfed by foliage and they both sat in silence, hunched low, eyes keen but seeing only various shades of green. Tarian held his breath to listen. Nothing. No one. His legs began to tighten, but he refused to kneel.

The faint rustle of human footsteps stalked closer. Snap. Snap. Branches broke under the feet of their pursuer in an uneven pattern. The enemy didn't know Tarian's location.

He stayed motionless and pondered whether to act or lie in wait. Maria wouldn't make a move unless he did. He measured the choice since he'd only heard one person in the brush. He sprang.

Tarian overpowered the man and wrestled him to the ground, but the man had more height and weight. Tarian lost his leverage. Knees hit ribs, fists cracked jaws, heads butted. The man managed to pin Tarian's shoulders to the ground until Maria's thick, muscular leg kicked him hard to the gut. Tarian jumped to his feet.

The man's melon sized fist charged into Maria's right side. Her ribs crunched, and she stumbled. Rage whirled inside Tarian's blood giving him a strength and courage he'd never had before. The man didn't stand a chance against Tarian's immortal strength. Hog tied and gagged, the man finally stopped fighting.

"Why didn't you just stun him?" Maria held her side and bent slightly in pain, her breath wheezed.

Tarian's jaw throbbed as the blood rushed to it.

"I need to know if there are more of them and where they

are." Tarian stared down his opponent. "Are there more of you?"

"Of course, there are," the man spat.

"Where are they?" Tarian received a defiant stare. He pulled the stunner out of its designated pocket and repeated the question.

"You think that's gonna make me talk, First Born?"

"I don't know. Let's see!" Tarian stunned the man without delay.

The man's look of surprise contorted to one of pain. Tarian surprised himself too. He hadn't hesitated to use such a pain-inducing weapon. As the man convulsed noisily on the ground for two minutes, no other opponents came.

"Well then, I guess you were lying. There is no one else with you." Tarian turned to walk away.

Maria's eyes widened with amazement. "What about him? Are you just going to leave him here in the dirt?"

"Oh yeah." He shoved the gag in his mouth.

"No, that's not what I meant. We aren't going to take him with us?"

"No. He'll only try to slow us down. That tracking monkey," he pointed to brown fur and crimson eyes peeking from behind a tree," will report a man down. Come on. We have to hurry."

Maria followed him as the man squirmed and attempted to yell through the gag.

Tarian marched confidently on. The fight felt good. The pain made him feel alive with power. He'd impressed himself with his quick decision-making under pressure.

"Stop," Tarian whispered after they'd been walking for a while. Maria knew they were close but didn't know why he advised the halt. He put his finger to his lips and with his other hand, pointed two feet in front of them. A very fine, black wire zigzagged from tree to tree for about ten feet.

"Do you see any wiring over there?" He pointed to the right of the pine tree.

"No," she said. "Let's go."

They cautiously approached the clearing. He felt every minor movement inside the fibers of his muscles and carefully controlled each advance. His vision cleared and brightened. His mind keen, working as a computer to calculate escape routes if needed. He located every obstacle to overcome. His acute hearing heard the flutter of a bird's wing, the crunch of pine needles under his feet and the unwanted click of a stunner. In an instant, Maria fell to the ground. Next, he heard a second click but felt nothing.

"What the hell!" barked a voice from an enemy opponent in the bush. "You're the First Born!"

He stood up and proceeded to tackle Tarian. In that split second, Tarian roundhouse kicked the man in the head. Tarian knocked him out cold. Tarian swung the convulsing Maria over his shoulder and started to run full speed the remaining fifteen hundred yards to the camp.

Her convulsing stopped halfway, but he refused to put her down. She pounded his back with her fists and cursed at him viciously. He ran faster. She gave up. Once past the secure border, he flung her to the ground and doubled over breathing heavily.

"Smooth landing. If you're going to sweep me off my feet, at least have the courtesy to put me down gently." She wiped the dirt from her hands. "I'm not a small girl. Are you all right? That was a long haul."

"Yes, fine," he said between breaths. "Yeah! That felt awesome." He grinned from ear to ear. He loved the thrill of the hunt. With every brutal exhalation, the warrior inside him grew stronger.

"You know that stunner hit you?"

"Yeah, how did it feel?" he asked.

"No, I meant weird that you didn't react. But it felt like shit," she said.

"Really? What does shit feel like? Honestly, Maria, you need to find better descriptors."

"Okay. It felt really, really, really horrible. Is that better? Did it look like it felt good? What kind of stupid question is that?"

"Are you two finished bickering?" A blonde-haired man said in an annoyed voice. "How'd you find us?"

"Where's Audrey?" Tarian asked.

"In the captain's quarters." He pointed to a very large tent.

"Audrey?" he politely asked, standing outside of the tent. He was unsure of the correct procedure before entering someone's tent. The three-knock rule couldn't be used on a door made of fabric.

"Come in, Tarian," she said recognizing his voice.

Tarian held the flap open for Maria. Audrey leaned over a

table studying charts. He could tell she was working her atmospheric magic as the interior felt dry and cool.

She sized the two of them up with one quick glance. "We have set up a makeshift bathing area by the stream. I would suggest you two go for a swim and tend to your wounds."

"Yes ma'am," said Maria, still in EMA mode but Audrey didn't correct her.

"They captured Gabe, and we know where their camp is," Tarian said.

"Yes, I, too, know where the camp is," Audrey stated.

"What else do you know?" Tarian wondered if she'd been observing him through those monkeys.

"That you need a shower."

He stared at her trying to read her unreadable face.

"What is it, Tarian?" Audrey asked.

"Nothing," he said. Her Cadet Sergeant persona offended him.

"You've all done well, now tend to your wounds. You both can sleep in tent seven tonight," Audrey said courteously but abruptly.

At the stream, Maria stripped down to her underwear without inhibition. She was tall and built solid like an athlete. She jumped into the water. Tarian undressed then cannonballed. She splashed him back, pretending to be annoyed. She challenged him to a race, but Tarian won.

They swam in the refreshing water and let the liquid clean

their dirty, sweat-covered bodies. Tarian burst through the water into the air and let the clear droplets fall away from his face. Eyes closed. Relaxed. It felt good. He didn't want to leave but it was time to return to camp.

"That's a nasty cut you've got there on your shin," Maria commented on his gash while he stood soaking wet in only his underwear.

He felt uncomfortable, but Maria was like a sister to him. "Yeah, I know. I hit a rock when I jumped in. Watch this."

Slowly and ever so slightly, the droplets of blood surrounding his sliced skin returned into his body. The tiny fibers of tissue wove back together. Even the purple tinge of the bruising steadily faded to match his natural color tone.

"Wow! That's amazing!" she blurted mouth agape.

"I know. I'm getting better at it. Of course, I didn't know what I was doing at first. The more I concentrate on healing, the faster it happens."

"I wish I had that ability."

"How's your side where he punched you?"

"I've had worse. I have brothers. Just a scratch." She fumbled to secure the tape around her elbow with one hand.

"Here, let me help you." He offered to wrap up the dressing. The slice and lump came from a nasty fall she took after Gabe went down from the stunner.

"Thanks." A look of defeat blackened her brown eyes.

"He's fine you know. It's just an exercise. You couldn't have done anything differently," he said.

"I guess so, but I feel so stupid. I should've had his back."

"You did. It was an accident. He got injured, and that was the problem."

His words made him think about Maria's delicate mortality. The responsibility lay within Tarian. He was the immortal. Like Jen had said, "The Guardians are supposed to protect us, not the other way around." He began to understand the power of his new position and what his eternal role as a Guardian meant. He'd been born to protect the weak.

Tarian finished her dressing, and they proceeded to find tent seven. It was smaller than Audrey's tent with no special climate control and two pitiful cots, but it was a thousand times better than sleeping on the hard ground of the mountainside cliff.

At two o'clock in the morning, Tarian awoke abruptly. His dream had been vividly disturbing. Touching his lips with the ends of his fingertips, he sensed the phantom presence of a girl's mouth, but which girl? The sensation of pleasure lingered inside him as the feeling of deceit pumped through his heart. In his dream, he'd been enjoying an intimate encounter with Delia. As his lips kissed hers, she morphed into Audrey and his hunger increased. He wanted more. Then someone slapped his face. Blackness engulfed him, and he woke up. The sudden leap out of dream world left him disoriented. It took seconds to regain his bearings. Embarrassment crept into his conscience, and he turned to look at Maria. Relieved to see her rapid deep sleep eye movement.

He cast off the sheets hoping to hurl away the pleasurable heat that swept through his body. Humid air clung to his skin and pulsating pain beat into his head. There'd be no more sleep. The throbbing increased. Soon violent pounding consumed his head. He needed water. He realized he hadn't eaten or drank much in the last forty-eight hours.

Carefully he snuck from his cot so as to not wake up Maria. Her eyelids twitched, and her mouth dripped saliva. She looked as if she was running from something wicked. If not for the pain, he'd have laughed. But if he woke her, she'd punch him hard.

He took his backpack outside to try to find a painkiller and water. He located the medicine and wondered if it'd be strong enough for immortal pain. Maybe he just needed water. His mouth felt like sandpaper. He rummaged some more, but no water. *The stream.* He could drink form the stream.

Halfway down the path he heard Audrey's voice. He froze. *Where was she? North, she was north.*

Audrey walked through the moonlit woods with someone. He bent low and found a thick Mountain Laurel bush to hide behind. The guilt of his romantic dream rushed back to him, and he prayed for invisibility. The other voice was high-pitched and familiar. He lifted his eyes above the Laurel bush. Two figures walked in the distance. Shadows from the full moon laced their faces, but he could see the other person was a Guardian. The woman wore a green Guardian suit. He recognized the face, but the name wouldn't come to him.

They argued, but he only caught general words at the end of their discussion. Audrey pressed her mouth into a thin line while she furrowed her brow. The lady dressed in green showed Audrey photos and paperwork that made Audrey scowl. Then the lady kissed Audrey on the forehead and walked away. Tarian felt an urge to approach, but Audrey quickly turned on her heels and marched back to camp.

"Margaret," he mumbled. "That's her name."

The vexing fog of forgetfulness lifted. He'd met her right after the attack, the lady who profiled Guardians. Soon his suspicions got the best of him, and many possible scenarios flaunted themselves in his brain. Trust was a tricky thing and easily doubted.

Within seconds and distracting him once more, his headache screamed for attention. The vicious thirst returned to his throat and cast away all his suspicious thoughts. He continued to the stream and knelt down to retrieve a cupful of clean spring water. He not only drank it, but he also violently threw it against his skin, wishing it would sting or hurt. He needed to rinse away his mixed emotions of lust and infuriating distrust. He poured one last douse of chilly water over the top of his short, dark hair, pinning it to the surface of his skin like a tight ski cap.

It had been a dream, *hadn't it?* He desperately wanted to trust Audrey. He tried to grasp the meaning of the dream. For some reason, the dream had driven him into the woods where he found her.

Why? What did it mean? The water turned frigid once the breeze hit his skin eliciting energy from his flesh. He'd hoped for clarity not wakefulness. He ran back to his tent.

FOURTEEN

THE FLAG

Before Tarian had reached the tent, Maria snapped, "Where've you been? I've been searching for you!" She looked at him sideways. "Why are you soaking wet?"

"I had a headache and needed water. What happened?"

"They've ordered us to line up."

"Whose orders?"

"I don't know who they are. We just met them two days ago. Someone woke me up and got me out of bed," she spat.

They ran to their tent to retrieve their gear then fell into line. Audrey, Sophie, and John handed everyone a small device. Tarian turned the flat, lightweight, oval object over in the palm of his hand.

"This is the egg, as we call it," John said then he touched it.

At once, all the eggs lit up. It resembled a mobile phone only much lighter in weight with no visible controls. John slid open the thin top layer, splitting it into two parts and revealing a secret compartment where a miniature egg-shaped piece hid. He stuck the tiny egg behind his ear.

"This smaller piece," he said, "controls the egg. Once placed behind your ear, the conductor responds to your thoughts. These tiny devices have many functions, but we will use them mainly to communicate to one another as we attack the enemy camp and get our prisoners back. It's also a trap finder and a tracker to help us find the base as well as each other. Audrey's team will be in charge of capturing the flag. The sooner you find it, the sooner we can get out of this muddy hellhole."

The tiny egg showed no visible signs of adhesive, but when Tarian placed it behind his ear, it stuck like a magnet. He held the larger egg in the palm of his hand. A map appeared on the egg's face.

Audrey informed, "The egg will guide us to the enemy flag. It's 9.6 miles away, which means three hours of hiking. The enemy camp is only three miles away. Do the math."

How could this all be an illusion? Tarian desperately wanted to know how they made this Realm possible. The sheer size boggled his mind. Was it magic or advanced science far beyond his comprehension? Maybe Gabe's theory of teleportation was correct.

"Let's go," Audrey ordered, and they began trekking through the woods.

Tarian placed the egg inside his pocket, but it zipped out into the air where it hovered in proximity. It remained a constant companion as he marched on with his troop. He could hold on to it if he chose, or he could let it float.

After an hour of treacherous plodding, a thick curtain of

heavy rain swiftly blew in, and forced them to take cover under a canopy of trees. Rain-soaked leaves dripped water onto their heads, prolonging the agonizing journey. Maria and Tarian huddled close together to stay as warm and dry as possible.

"This thing is helpful," Tarian examined the egg.

Audrey smiled at him.

"Can it get wet?"

"Yes," Audrey said.

"Did you help develop it?" he asked.

"It's a Guardian advancement, but we've run into some problems with it."

Tarian tossed it up and down. "It barely has any weight to it."

"It's made from digitally fabricated carbon fiber filaments," Audrey said.

"It's also cold," he said.

Audrey smiled again. "Very observant, Tarian."

"Boron arsenide as an electrical insulator." Maria murmured as she fondled her egg.

Audrey grinned. "I forgot your dad's a miner."

"My brothers are too. I'd been on that path, but Mom didn't want me going down in those caverns. She insisted I go to college."

"It's a tough life," Audrey said.

The Audrey Tarian trusted was back, and then she wasn't.

She stood up abruptly. "The rain has stopped. Move out."

Audrey waited for everyone to exit and took a place behind

Tarian. She whispered, "Your best friend is smart."

He grinned as her breath brushed the back of his neck.

After another hour of hiking, their V-formation scattered. Audrey held the position in the front with Tarian on her left. Without warning, everyone to the right of Audrey fell into a deep cavity. Audrey and Tarian were the only two people left standing above ground.

"Dammit!" Audrey hissed and shook the egg as if it hadn't worked properly.

"Maria," Tarian called out.

"I'm okay. It's a long drop, but the ground is level." She moaned in aggravation. "Those jerks put out a trap."

"Is anyone hurt?" Audrey called down into the pit.

Several 'no ma'am's' voiced from below.

"Keith, survey the damages for our men. Lori, walk the perimeter. Let me know if there's an exit."

Immediately both went to complete the tasks and within minutes reported back. They were all in good health, no sprained ankles or broken bones. The pit was roughly ten feet in diameter with an opening of five feet. No visual signs of an exit.

"I'll alert John and Sophie of our setback. Sit tight, help will come for you soon. Tarian and I will continue. We have to capture their flag before they capture ours. Winning means eating steak instead of canned rations," she said to the disappointed grumblings of those stuck in the hole.

Tarian felt miserable for Maria.

"Move!" Audrey ordered when he hesitated.

In the forty-five minutes it took to hike, walk, and swim to their destination, neither of them said a word. His dream and what it meant, moreover how it made him feel, continued to preoccupy him no matter how much he tried to focus on the task. He sensed she wanted to talk to him as well. Questions swirled as he recalled what he'd witnessed between her and Margaret during his trek to the stream. Audrey and her Guardian friends had centuries of memories and secrets. He didn't like being odd man out. Wasn't he part of the Guardian world now?

"What's going on, Audrey?" he finally blurted out.

She continued marching through the root and rock-filled, uneven ground. "We have to capture the flag."

"I saw you with Margaret in the woods," he said.

"I don't know what you think you saw."

"You were arguing with her." He'd gotten the conversation rolling, and the momentum pulled him forward.

"This is complicated. I cannot share all my information with you." She kept her head faced forward as they walked side by side.

"Why not? Back at Headquarters I seemed pretty important to everyone," he said, still walking.

"After the game," she said, finally bringing her eyes to his.

"I want to know everything. I'm an integral piece in this puzzle. People hate me because of it."

"What?"

"Never mind."

The conversation halted at the site of the enormous river they had to swim across. They'd exited the forested mountaintop and emerged next to an embankment. On the opposite shore was a vast meadow where the Black team's flag stood waiting.

Tarian's tense body relaxed under the buoyancy of the fresh spring water, and the frigid temperature healed his inflamed muscles. The water prompted an unsolicited race between them. She won.

They moved on. She still didn't speak, but he assumed she surveyed for more booby traps. The beautiful meadow of yellow wildflowers and green grass seemed too good to be true. It simply couldn't be as easy as walking through a flower-filled meadow to capture the flag.

As soon as Tarian had stepped one foot into the calf deep grass, his throat swelled shut. Panic filled his senses. His eyes bulged from his head. He fell onto Audrey like a zombie clawing at her for life.

She pushed him to the ground, placed both hands on his chest and pumped twice. "It's okay. Don't panic." She looked down at his face while straddling his torso.

He looked up at her choking.

"Shhhh. You're not dying. It's a trick." She gently stroked his chest and arms.

He wanted to believe her but being unable to draw breath terrified him. He gathered every ounce of will he had and managed to calm his chaotic nerves. Little by little, second by second, oxygen crept into his lungs.

"Don't gasp!" she ordered. "Breathe steady."

He tried, fighting his instincts to gulp in the air. His eyes never left hers, and he appreciated her patience. He mirrored her slow breathing pattern and soon regained normal oxygen levels. He fought the tears.

"What was that?" he asked still a little breathless.

She crawled off of him. "It's an oxygen dump. It's an immortal weakness. We already have a much higher blood oxygen level than mortals."

"But I felt like I had no oxygen."

"I know. It's a strange phenomenon and would have the opposite effect on a mortal. I'm surprised your reaction was that bad since your body was cold from the water."

"Why didn't it affect you?"

"I'm trained to recognize this trap. You're not."

He staggered to his feet still weak. Together, they moved a few steps in the direction of the flag.

"Stop!" Audrey said. "There's an electric barrier."

Tarian stopped as ordered but didn't see the barrier.

"Right there." She pointed low to his right. "Can you see that disturbance in the grass?"

"Yes." It was barely visible, but the grass vibrated. Once he noticed it, he could see the faint line encircling the flag.

"You think the stunners are bad, this would've thrown us twenty feet," she said, a voice of experience.

"The stunner didn't affect me."

"It didn't?" she asked.

"No. Is that unusual?"

"Well, it's rare," she replied, and her eyes narrowed.

Was she impressed or envious? "Why didn't the egg detect this?" The egg had been extremely valuable for navigation and communication, but it missed both booby traps.

"Like I said, it's still in the developmental stage. It should've warned us," she said. "I've seen a lot in my life, and human intelligence and instinct are still the best weapons."

"How do we disarm the barrier?"

"We don't. We must find the hole. I'm sure the disarming device is in the hands of the enemy. Whether the enemy is close by or not is something we'll find out soon enough."

She walked the perimeter of the barrier shaking the egg device violently. She spat a slew of expletives at it. Twice they walked it, and Tarian felt as useless as the egg.

Finally, she saw the gap. "The opening is less than two feet," she warned. "Enter sideways, turn your shoulders and suck in your gut."

Her pixie-sized body walked straight through.

"We're in, and I didn't have to suck in my gut." He sneered at her.

"That's not what I meant. Geez. Touchy. Now watch out. If it were me, I would've installed ejection pedals all the way to the target. We'll see," she said.

With her gift she froze the grass into tiny icicles, he assumed to stop any pedal ejection devices, then she ran full speed for the flag. He followed her lead. Without interference, she snatched the flag and sat down.

"Now what?" He said in huffing breaths.

As she relaxed, he stood braced for action.

She smiled and motioned for him to sit down. "We wait. We've got the flag, and that's the end of the game."

"Oh, okay."

It all seemed very anti-climactic to Tarian. He didn't know what to do with himself. After four days of intense field simulation, he was supposed to sit still and relax? His arms hung cumbersome and awkward until finally he shoved them in his pockets. Audrey looked at ease, which unnerved him even more.

"Well, I can't fly." Tarian sat down and tried to relax.

She laughed for several seconds. "If you had, you'd be the first."

"So no immortal can fly?"

"Nope. What else did you discover about yourself?"

"I can see in the dark and very far into the distance compared to Gabe and Maria. My hearing is also much more acute than theirs."

"You're displaying soldier traits."

"Compared to what?"

"The immortals that work in the labs at Headquarters don't usually display soldier skills."

"What are their strengths?"

"Things like being able to look inside a cell without a microscope, and photographic memory. Our skills predispose us to be either soldiers or scientists. This organization of abilities leads me to believe that God did intentionally make us the way we are. We're not some mutant race. We serve a purpose."

"We sound like some overgrown ant colony."

Audrey laughed, and Tarian joined in.

"I did feel a surge of super strength during a fight. Maybe it was adrenalin," Tarian said.

"Did this come after one of your friends was threatened or hurt?"

"Yes, how'd you know?"

"It's common in us. We have an aggressive protection extinct. Sort of like the vamps but different."

"Vamps? Like vampires?"

"There are all sorts of creatures in this world Tarian."

"Are there red-eyed, scorpion-tailed monkeys?"

She laughed, "Possibly in the Wastelands. Let's just say they're the result of an animal weapons experiment from fifty or so years ago that went awry. Maybe they've all died out now. I haven't had a mission outside the borders in a long time."

Tarian had spent his entire life inside the Entente. No one went outside the borders anymore. There was no need. Plenty of wonderful cities spread across this nation to fill up a lifetime of vacations. Now it seemed ridiculous and narrow-minded. He realized just how incredibly sheltered his perfect little life had been.

A single tubular pod appeared out of thin air. They both squeezed inside. Cramped and entwined together, Tarian once again desperately tried to banish all thoughts of his dream.

They were uncomfortably but successfully delivered back to the familiar room where the game had begun. When the door opened, their twisted bodies tumbled into a room filled with cheering soldiers. Maria and Gabe hurried over to congratulate them. Their team had won the challenge. That evening Chef Richard prepared a scrumptious buffet but taking a hot shower and sleeping in his downy bed was Tarian's best reward.

FIFTEEN

FENG AND JUSTICE

Delia's heart dropped when she stepped into the law offices of Feng and Justice. The last time she'd been in the building Mr. Prescott was alive. She remembered traipsing through the halls and hiding in secret rooms at age ten with eleven-year-old Tarian while their fathers discussed important business matters. A typical occurrence during her adolescence but as she grew older, she lost interest in playing with Tarian. Their silly childhood games turned into thorny pre-teen anxiety. Looking back, she wondered why things changed so vastly. When and why do children become self-conscious?

Today, two days after Christmas, she walked into this office as a striking woman ready to begin the New Year and her new life. She vowed to be independent and never be smashed under her father's thumb again. Mr. Feng had promised her an internship where she could gain on-the-job training while continuing her Harvard education virtually. She deserved this job. But no matter what she told herself, the guilt still crawled under her skin. She'd deliberately kept this opportunity a secret from Tarian. She told herself she was sparing his feelings, letting his dad rest in peace. In truth, if she was honest with herself, she wanted a secret of her own. He'd left her. He'd gone away with a beautiful Entente agent doing who knows what for the government. None of it made sense. It helped her sanity to have her own undisclosed affair.

In preparation for her interview, Delia did a background check on Mr. Feng. She found very little information about him as a young adult due to his secretive Xia heritage. Rarely did a Xia marry, educate, or work outside the community. She did learn they are required at least two years of college-level medical school before deciding on another major. Most Xia adults worked in the medical field and lived close to home on the west side of the Entente. Mr. Feng did neither. In fact, Mr. Feng had become an attorney. He'd sued the world-renowned Xia Technologies Inc., received millions for his victory, and lived on the complete opposite side of the continent from his family.

Joe Prescott had promoted him to partner at the young age of twenty-eight and by thirty, when Mr. Prescott died, he'd made senior partner. But what intrigued her the most, he'd refused to work with her father. The Entente Government District surrounded his law office, and he worked closely with many other Senators. Mr. Prescott had handled all of her father's business affairs when he was alive, but now, Mr. Feng wouldn't take her father's calls. She had her reasons for alienating herself from her father, but what were Feng's reasons?

"Follow me, Miss Eastwood."

The young, well-dressed male receptionist led her down a lengthy plush hallway she didn't recognize, and into Mr. Feng's office. Everything was new. Ms. Lucy, Mr. Prescott's old receptionist, no longer greeted clients and the dark wainscoting she used to run her fingers across had been replaced with modern, textured designs. She reached out, allowing her fingers to skim the new walls. Sadness overtook her, but she only allowed a moment of nostalgia. She erected her posture and squared her shoulders. The past was the past.

But the past wouldn't rest. As she passed Mr. Prescott's old office, her mind drifted back to Ms. Lucy. She had been the one to find him lying dead on his office floor. Tarian's mom had called her at three a.m. after her husband hadn't come home that evening. It was normal for him to work late, but one a.m. was always the latest. When Carolyn couldn't contact him, she called Ms. Lucy. Ms. Lucy insisted Carolyn stay home with the little children while she went and checked the office.

"Miss Eastwood," the young man said again.

"Pardon me." She snapped out of her reminiscence.

He held the door open for her. "Come in, please. Mr. Feng has left you instructions on the desk."

He shut the door leaving her in solitude. She swiped the tablet and read the note. It instructed her to write an essay about herself and then turn on the wall display. She did as she was told, finding it all extremely strange.

Roman Feng watched the lanky young woman in his office from behind a hidden two-way mirrored wall. He'd already researched her and knew her qualifications surpassed the low-level internship position, but like everyone else, she'd have to start at the bottom and work her way up. They'd met at Joe's funeral where she never left Tarian's side—a day that changed Roman's life for the worse.

"Delia Eastwood," Roman whispered to himself. He studied her as he kept her in his office far past the conclusion of his required instructions. He wanted to see how she reacted to his absence. She fidgeted in the chair and then rose to walk around the room. He admired her choice of classic style dress. She carried herself with a grace far older than her eighteen years. She leaned over to view the photos on his table. In no way did she seem inhibited or nervous. He continued to ponder her true motives.

"Do I hire you? This will change everything." He'd read her anonymous blogs. He'd followed her short but impressive Harvard career, but had she left her home? He wondered if it was an act, a trick. She may be a spy for her father.

Roman didn't want her because of her intelligence nor because she was Zachary Eastwood's daughter. He wanted her because of the disease. Her overly thin frame confirmed his suspicion. He needed to work on her. He needed to delve into her fascinating medical history, but would she let him?

"Hello, Miss Eastwood," Roman introduced himself.

"Hello." She spun around to find him standing behind her.

He seemed to have appeared out of thin air. She feared he'd been in the room, possibly sitting in a chair in the dark corner all along, and she hadn't noticed him.

"It's a pleasure to see you again, Mr. Feng." Delia didn't spook easily and regained her composure without a hint of a derailment.

"Welcome to the law firm of Feng and Justice." He held a firm warm grip on her cold, rigid hand long after the handshake had ended.

His yellow eyes frightened her, but she managed to keep poised. She remembered how his eyes had entranced her at the funeral. All the research books she'd read claimed tiger-eyes were a common Xia trait.

"It's an honor to be a part of this firm."

"Do you have a place to live?" he asked.

"Yes, I'm staying with a friend," she replied.

"Very well. Let's get started. We have much to accomplish."

SIXTEEN

EBONY6

The last seven days consisted of one thing: extreme physical exertion. Up at 0500 hours, eat, run, weight train, eat, simulation room, cardio train, eat, sleep, and repeat. Inside the simulations, Tarian fine-tuned his immortal abilities and overcame his immortal weaknesses. To say the least, he was exhausted. So, today, when he received the note under his door that read, *Meet in the library at 0800 hours*, he almost jumped with joy.

Ten minutes early and proud of himself, Tarian strutted into the library grinning. He wanted to get a head start on the assignment before anyone else showed up.

"Always the bridesmaid." Audrey mocked his arrogant gait.

"Hello, Audrey." He narrowed his eyes at her and gave her a smug smile.

Of course, he was second. He hadn't beaten her at anything yet. Her perfection was getting old. Plus, the constant help she gave him teetered on fanatical. Worst of all, she thought of him as a boy.

He secretly hoped he'd age to thirty, ideally, maybe even thirty-five. He'd still be young but old enough to be respected by mortals without question and, best of all, physically older than Audrey.

"You look happy," she said.

"Oh, do I? Well I feel great. Been kickin' ass around here." In reality, he was as exhausted as a med student pulling an all-nighter in the ER. Top that off with cramping muscles and a headache.

"Coffee?" Piper asked.

She appeared out of nowhere, earning a startled yelp from Tarian. He cut off the sound, hopefully, before he looked too foolish.

Audrey snickered.

"Thank you, Piper." He took the cup of steaming black liquid. "I knew it. We're in both Headquarters and the training facility. Aren't we?"

"Something like that." Piper zestfully raised her shoulders.

"You see—" Audrey began to explain.

"Never mind, I don't want to know." Tarian interrupted sighing and shaking his head.

"You sit there." Piper pointed to a seat with the name First Born attached to it.

Eight oversized, pliable leather reclining chairs waited for readers. Each chair had an accompanying table with a stack of books. Labels pinned to the chairs listed the eight nicknames given by the Commander over the past week. Since the end of the game, he'd only been training with seven other people.

Tarian sat in his designated chair. A surge of rebellion struck his core, and he decided he would rather sit next to Audrey in Sparkplug's chair. He had a few questions he wanted to ask her, but the obedient student in him dragged his feet back to the chair labeled First Born.

"Chicken." Audrey watched him play musical chairs.

"Yeah, well, have you seen the size of the Commander?"

She laughed. "Oh, I thought you were more scared of Sparkplug a.k.a. Maria."

Tarian sneered at her then sunk into the comfort of the chair and let its soft hide embrace his sore backside. It felt like sinking into a cloud. He closed his eyes and exhaled ecstatically.

"You know this doesn't mean the end of physical training," Audrey said.

"Shhhh! Don't ruin my heavenly moment," he said without opening his eyes.

"Haven't you been to the therapy room yet?" Piper asked.

"No." He opened his brown eyes wide at this new and appealing information.

"I'll take you later," Audrey offered. "First, I'll put you in the cryotherapy chamber. Second, I'll squeeze you into the compression suit." Her mouth curled wickedly.

The weight of her playfully sinister gaze rested on him. He wasn't sure he liked the idea of her enclosing him inside of something or squeezing him into anything, but his stinging calf muscles and burning shoulders insisted he allow it. For now, he tilted his head back onto the cozy leather again and stole a few minutes of relaxation before the remaining trainees filled the room.

The smell of antique leather against the pungent aroma of printed ink on paper brought back memories of high school nights spent studying with Delia in the Eastwood Estate's vast library. They'd escape their homework and the harsh monitor light to treasure hunt through the delicate vellum of centuries-old books stacked on rows of shelves. Scavenging to find the oldest book or personal journal became a competition that led to a game of imagination. They loved history, and these books brought them back in time to foreign and fascinating places. Hours would pass, and their homework would remain undone. Thinking back, Tarian wondered how he ever passed any of his subjects while he lived in the house with Delia.

The old and new books sitting next to him on the table would be studied in conjunction with virtual learning. The next phase of training dealt with the government, culture, geography, language and history of the Guardians, the Entente, the Wastelands, and the Prevallers. Not an easy task.

After everyone had arrived, Piper appeared holding folders. She handed one to each of them. "Here are your agendas from the Commander. He'll not be in today but will return for your training tomorrow. He asked me to remind everyone that you are on a deadline, and he expects all of you to have completed all the tasks listed on page one and two by 0800 hours tomorrow." She smiled brightly, did a small bounce that Tarian thought might be a curtsy then disappeared.

A note slipped into Tarian's *Phosphorus Phacts* textbook read: *At eleven o'clock, meet me in classroom 12-C. Audrey.* He turned to her in acknowledgment of her note, but she didn't look up from her reading. An hour later she was called out of the library leaving him stewing for two more hours. He tried to concentrate on his studies, but his mind raced with ideas about their secret meeting.

With some difficulty, he found room 12-C—an old and forgotten classroom packed full of wooden desks and one antique chalkboard. A thick layer of dust gathered on the furniture, and most of the light bulbs didn't work.

Audrey sat in the back corner of the dimly lit room with a thin, portable laptop. She appeared ghostly as the blue light hit her face.

"What are you doing?" he asked.

"I've found something interesting," she answered. "I wasn't honest with you about Margaret's and my conversation during the game."

"I knew it," he spat. "And you should also admit you weren't very friendly to me either."

She raised an eyebrow at him and didn't smile.

He sat next to her.

"I wasn't sure who the blogger was back then, but I had my suspicions. I'm not positive what it means or if it's connected to the murders. And I'm not telling anyone. Got it!"

"Doesn't Margaret know?" he asked.

"No, she handed the investigation over to me over a week ago when it was still ambiguous."

"What did you find?" Tarian asked.

"Your girlfriend's anonymous blog page."

"What?"

She nodded.

"Is it current?" he asked.

"I have about six years' worth. They change servers twice a year, April and October. She also deletes entries, so it's difficult but not impossible to find them. The past three months are still missing," she said. "The first four years are very basic, kids' stuff. Most of her blogs are school related or generic, but in the past few months, her voice has changed."

"How?"

"It's almost like a depression fell upon her or—"

"How did you find out?" He interrupted. "You said she wrote them anonymously. I know Delia. She's thorough. She wouldn't have blogged lightly. Not now, maybe when she was fourteen, but definitely not now. And what could she have possibly written?"

"Her blog was flagged because she writes about the Prevallers."

"Why?" he said but he knew the answer. She was a conspiracy nut. He could only imagine what she wrote under the guise of anonymity.

"She's one of millions of bloggers around the world

carelessly dropping flagged words, but I happened to notice some other statements. My instinct triggered and linked onto her site. The more I researched, the more I believed blogger Ebony6 was actually Delia Eastwood."

He didn't like the suspicious tone in her voice nor the dark look clouding her eyes. Delia was on trial, and he would defend her to the death.

"Exactly what are you accusing her of?"

"Nothing," she said. "I brought you here to have you read them for yourself. You know her. You can help me figure out some of the most encrypted blogs. Here's one from a year and a half ago after Beast Barracks at EMA and just before you began your first year."

August 15
Today I get to see T for the first time in 7 weeks. I'm nervous. We will only have a couple of hours so I cannot discuss serious topics. I will have to force myself to keep the conversation light. I do not want to burden him with my suspicions. I want to kiss him. I want to hold him close to me. I miss him more than I ever thought possible. It's like having a hole in my chest. Yes, that's it. I'm not whole when I'm not with him. I'm broken, incomplete. But I am torn. Does he have a right to know? But there is nothing he can do while he is at TGL. And it really doesn't prove anything. What is it really? I don't have all of the facts yet. I will wait. Once I know more, I'll tell him. I'll get my car in the next couple months and drive up to tell him. I cannot believe I waited so long to get a driving permit. What was I thinking? I guess I took driving for granted, always having a driver and my brother around. Why do you need a permit anyway, the car basically drives itself. Permits are simply a way for the government to keep track of us and charge us fees. But the vial of her blood in that package to Father! It has to mean something … but what? Why did he need a vial of T's mother's blood? Oh, have

to go. It's time to leave for TGL. Until tomorrow.

Fortis est veritas

Ebony6

Comment: XOXO25

You have to tell him. You love him. He's a good guy. It's his mom.

Ebony6

Love you XOXO25, you're always rooting for him. I'll see.

Comment: Zigler88

Come on! Dad is obvs connected!

Ebony6

Shut up Zigler88! We've discussed this already.

"I'm T, I guess," he said.

"I'm assuming so," she responded. "And TGL is The Gray Line, an old reference to the army academy."

"She never mentioned a vial of Mom's blood. Maybe there's a logical explanation that she found out later. Knowing her, it has to do with her illness that she won't discuss with me. Everyone says she's fine, but I'm worried about it. Maybe she needed Mom's blood …" he rambled then drifted off in thought. The information inside the blog terrified and unnerved him. "You said that was almost two years ago."

"A year and a half."

"Okay. After that blog I spent all Christmas and summer with her, and she never mentioned it and seemed fine. Her health had significantly improved," he said. She wasn't truly well though.

He often thought her cocoa complexion dipped into a gray zone and her slender frame too thin. He worried about eating disorders, but she dismissed his questions. She once ate an entire banana split in front of him just to prove she wasn't anorexic.

"I know it's not definite. Here's one from this September, on her eighteenth birthday. I checked Harvard's records. She did miss two weeks of classes."

September 30th
I woke up in a pile of my own vomit again. What a way to begin my eighteenth year! I felt miserable all day. Happy Birthday to me! I've been through three prescriptions of medicine and nothing is working. This is the weakest I've felt in a long time. I don't understand why the doctor can't figure out what is wrong with me. Mother is beside herself with anxiety, but I can't hide my symptoms. I've tried to vomit quietly without her knowing, but she doesn't leave my side. I'm so thankful for her care, but it's breaking my heart to see her suffer. We're both at our wits end with frustration. Mother is worried they are going to quarantine me soon and forbid me to go back to College. It's obviously not contagious or I would have already gotten someone else in my home sick, and no one is showing symptoms but me. I'm going to begin my own research today. I need to get myself healthy before holiday break. I cannot let T see me like this.
On a more interesting note, Biggie went west again. If I were the Prevallers I'd hit the West first. I think Biggie is in charge of border security. Also, his weird North Pole friend visited the house again. I was too sick to eavesdrop this time.

Fortis est veritas
Ebony6

Comment: SkyEartHater
Attacking from the West is beneficial. It's the Energy District. They'll attack big! The Prevallers' objective is to terrorize.

Ebony6

They are after something. You said yourself there is a reason SkyEarth is investing heavily from Flagstaff to Dallas.

Comment: Jugular8
Boron you morons!! Oh and feel better Ebony6

Ebony6
Thanks Jugular8

Comment: Jugular8
Got rid of T yet? Let's do dinner.

Ebony6
Goodnight!

"Who is Jugular8?" Tarian asked with no attempt to disguise his jealousy.

"That's not important," she stated.

"Who is Biggie?" Tarian asked, anger still present in his tone.

"I don't know yet." Her look suggested she had an opinion but refused to divulge her suspicion until she had all the facts, or maybe she was waiting for his input.

"What's out West?" His voice now even.

"Our Fusion Power Plant, our Wind-Solar Tower, and like Jugular8 says, the cavern system produced by the meteor storm, but he shouldn't know that. The craters are confidential and very well guarded."

"Maria knew."

"Her family lives and works there."

"Why are the Prevallers after the craters? Is her family in danger?" His heart thundered at the thought of another person he cared about getting hurt because of him.

"The craters are an abundant source of pure chemical element Boron. But not just that, scientists are discovering things inside the connecting cavern system that don't exist here on Earth, not only is it valuable, but it's dangerous. There's energy down there that will control the world: volatile lithium, unstable nuclear activity, and much, much more. And we haven't even reached the bottom yet."

"What? I didn't know they were that deep?"

"It's classified, but the meteors' impact created mines as well as caverns. It's an explorer's dream. I think Ebony6 and her blogging buddies are all well-connected teenagers."

"What do you mean?"

"I mean the sons and daughters of senators and generals. Suspicious kids who snoop in their parents' offices."

"Is Biggie on our side?"

"It's not clear," she responded.

"I can ask her. She tells me everything."

"Does she?" Her ice-cold eyes and doubtful mouth crushed his confidence. If Delia was Ebony6, she was obviously not confiding in him.

"This is teenage social networking. It means nothing," he protested, mostly to himself.

"Agreed. Listen, I'll give you this laptop. Read them. There are hundreds. She posts at least three times a week, sometimes every day, and yes, most of them are totally meaningless. Weed through them yourself. We'll talk later."

SEVENTEEN

BIT BY THE FAMILY DOG

Tarian didn't know what to expect on day twenty-one. He put on the last article of clothing inside his closet. Today's minimal itinerary included eat, run, library, eat, and conference room. Everyone assumed they'd be given their mission in the conference room.

An elongated, shiny metal table covered with blueprints of buildings centered the room. Holographic images of weapons and persons of interest hovered over the table. Tarian's team flipped through the papers and studied the images. No one looked pleased. It was real now, the commencement of their official assignment.

The company assembled for this mission had been training with Tarian for the past eighteen days and included three-centuries-old Guardian warriors, Audrey, John, and Warren, and two Central Intelligence Agents, Sophie, and Keegan. Together they possessed exceptional knowledge and because of this fact were given rare, unlimited authority. As for Gabe and Maria, they had simply been in the right place at the right time. If they hadn't sat next to Tarian in the mess hall the first day of Beast Barracks, they'd probably be home right now, uneventfully waiting for the restart of their second year at EMA.

"I see all of these papers and images but no plan of action Commander," John stated.

The Commander grunted and continued to shuffle around the data like Tarot Cards but found no mystic answers.

"Commander?" Audrey probed. Her jaw set with disapproval.

"We don't have our target." The Commander had no other option but to tell his soldiers the truth. Failure didn't flatter him.

"For three weeks we've prepared. We've helped you to educate and train Tarian, Gabe, and Maria under the impression that we were creating an elite reconnaissance team to find the traitor. Now you're telling me, not only do you not know who he is but you don't know where he is?" Sophie slammed her hands onto the tabletop of data.

Perturbation bubbled over as the group of veterans began to complain and argue amongst themselves. Losing wasn't an option for them. Their loved ones had died. They wanted progress. The room burst with turbulent hand gestures and angry overlapping voices.

As if on cue, Eleanor walked into the conference room. In seconds, her presence silenced the stormy chaos. She pulled Commander General Smith aside for discussion, showing him something on her slender notepad. The ever-present tablet never left her side. Tarian imagined it held centuries of world secrets that others would kill to get their hands on.

"Hello everyone. We have our assassin," she said with a look of delightful satisfaction.

One flick of Eleanor's wrist produced a light field image of a three-dimensional man's face. Tarian recognized him. A stab of pain wrenched through his heart as if the family dog had just turned on him. He stood face to face with his dad's law partner and friend, Roman Feng.

"Roman Feng is the man who killed Joseph Prescott, our friend and a Guardian of Dare. He is the Prevallers' hitman and guilty of at least six of the thirteen murders. We have reason to suspect he is also the developer of the serum. He is a Xia," she said matter-of-factly.

What was so special about the Xias? Tarian knew them only as a highly intelligent and extremely secretive community of people that lived mainly in the Technology District.

"Our sources are working diligently to collect as much information as possible on this man," Eleanor concluded.

Tarian's body urged to sprint out of the room. Run far and fast. He'd spent nineteen years in an isolated dome of privilege and naiveté only to have it crash down upon him. He laughed out loud considering his so-called superior private school education with its fancy professors. *What had it taught him? Lies!* In twenty-five days inside a magical village and strange training facility he'd found truthful learning. All of the Entente's secrets had been dumped upon him. All of his family secrets had been dumped upon him. He shrunk under the weight.

"It can't be Roman," Tarian said.

"I'm sorry Tarian. I know it is difficult to ingest all of this in the short period of time you have, but the success of this mission will depend on the eight of you being able to do just that. You are the lucky, or maybe unlucky, few that are privileged, or shall I say, cursed with this classified information. The eight of you have been purposefully trained these past three weeks in our most lethal simulators to find this man and to defend the Entente. You must find Roman Feng and bring him to us alive. He *must* be alive," she said and looked directly at Tarian.

His irritation grew with this news. This loathsome man befriended his father and now Tarian couldn't kill him.

Commander General Smith brought up holographic renderings of the blueprints of Entente Government buildings. They studied the Capitol where they'd soon work, and the office building that housed Feng's law offices, Tarian's father's old firm. As a team they thoroughly examined the inner workings of the buildings.

"Tarian, Audrey, Maria, and Gabe are here to lure Feng out of hiding. It would be perfectly normal for the four of you to remain together after the attack on EMA. You have been allotted an internship under EMA alumni until you can return to your schooling. This shouldn't raise suspicion. Our goal is to appear organic. The four of you can interact in public without a problem. The rest of you must only acknowledge each other in private.

Outside you are no more than work related acquaintances. Roman Feng has been untraceable and out of his office for weeks, but we have reason to believe he is returning to the Government District quite soon. Our agents believe that his orders are to kidnap Tarian," Eleanor explained.

"Not kill?" Audrey asked.

No. Study. We have evidence that the Prevallers attempted to exhume Joe's body for study, but we were one step ahead of them. His body is not in his grave." Eleanor's sympathetic eyes landed on Tarian. "We are a mystery even to ourselves, so I understand the value of studying our kind. The Entente has performed several studies on us with our permission, but if we fall into the hands of the Prevallers, the tests may become cruel under the guise of scientific advancement."

"Tarian is the most valuable of us all," Audrey said in a whisper, contrary to her character. Louder, she continued, "Isn't he?"

Tarian's gut flinched with pleasure at her concern for his wellbeing. She meant more to him than just a compatriot. Their friendship had matured, and he knew he'd protect her with his life as she would him.

"Of course, he is the First Born," Eleanor said.

EIGHTEEN

BITTERSWEET HOMECOMING

The frigid wind kissed Tarian's face as he descended the private jet's staircase. He inhaled a lung full of the familiar city air and grinned. The smell of fuel and deep-fried food mixed with the hint of evergreen and harbor sea life flooded his senses with nostalgic memories.

On the tarmac, two four-passenger sized green hovercrafts waited for them. Tarian, Maria, Gabe, and Audrey slid into one. It flew them to the rooftop of the Towers of Longfellow. Meanwhile, John, Warren, Sophie, and Keegan took off for the Leverett Saltonstall Building, the building Tarian's father used to work in, the building where Tarian had grown up. Could he go back to that place?

"You okay." Maria placed a hand on Tarian's shoulder.

"Yeah, I'll be fine. This place just brings back a lot of memories," Tarian explained never removing his focus from the scenery outside the window. He'd never ridden in a machine like this before. He'd seen them. Top government officials traveled in them.

The apartments were true to Guardian form, eerily accurate. Unrivaled attention to detail met Tarian at every turn of a corner and open of a door. He slid the refrigerator door open to grab his favorite drink, orange soda. He knew it'd be there, just as he knew size twelve shoes would sit neatly in a row on the floor of his closet.

"Did you see the closet?" Gabe asked from his bedroom.

"I know," Tarian responded.

"Did you see it! Even my drawers are filled with socks, underwear, everything!"

"What's your favorite drink?" Tarian smirked.

"Personally, I enjoy a nice peach tea," Gabe said, head held high, proud and unashamed of his choice of beverage.

"Yep, I remember. Look in the fridge."

Gabe glanced at him suspiciously. He walked to the fridge, opened the door and gasped. Six bottles of peach tea sat next to Tarian's orange soda. "Who are these people?"

"They're very thorough."

"Let's go to the girls' apartment," Gabe said. "I want to see how perfect their fridge is. I'm going to give Maria two days before she has it out with Audrey."

"I give it five." Tarian placed his bet.

"Come on." Gabe motioned with a wave of his hand as he went for the door.

"No man, you go. I'm tired. I'll see their place tomorrow." Tarian wasn't tired. He just wanted to be alone.

Gabe nodded and walked into the hall.

Tarian collapsed onto the saddle brown leather couch, propped his feet on the glass coffee table and stared up at the vaulted ceiling and angled walls. Two ceiling fans dangled above him, and a modern fireplace stood grandly in the corner. He finished his soda and stood to recycle the bottle but walked out onto the balcony instead.

The ink black night lit by a thin crescent moon and a few scattered stars entranced him. The skyline sparkled with infinite city lights. Tarian looked down from the thirty-fifth floor and reminisced about the days when his feet walked the very pavement below with his father. Memories flooded his mind, filling him with a bittersweet homecoming. Breathing in one last whiff of crisp air chased with a lump of grief, Tarian retired to his bed and drifted into dreamless sleep.

Seven-thirty in the morning, Gabe and Tarian entered The Wicked Good Coffee Shop. Patrons jammed the little store. Visiting this place, they assumed, would be a normal morning ritual, and they wanted to appear as ordinary as possible. Tarian needed to show himself at all the local hot spots to attract Feng.

Gabe and Tarian entered the facility first and proceeded to join the winding line of twenty-to-thirty-year-old executives. Audrey and Maria came in two minutes later and landed ten spots behind them.

The sliver of a girl behind the counter, phantom-like dressed all in black, glared at him. She'd already whipped through fifteen orders at lightning speed. "Ready?"

The unfamiliar, extensive menu of morning energy drinks confused him. Coffees, teas, vitamin shots, enhancers, and concoctions to be drank traditionally or inhaled as vapors proved overwhelming. There'd been no choice at EMA. Everyone got black coffee. As the line grew longer and angrier, phantom girl's face soured. A revolution of angry coffee consuming regulars broke out. He finally chose a drink and chose it quickly.

"Black coffee," he blurted.

Phantom girl laughed in his face. "That's it. Black coffee!"

Gabe asked for The Wicked Good Special: a triple grande latte with maple-honey. He ordered with incredible ease, and phantom girl smirked approvingly as if to say, *I can't believe the two of you are friends.*

Tarian reconsidered his order. Gabe's drink sounded delicious, but he figured phantom girl would bite his head off, so he took his boring black coffee and retreated to a table.

The four of them sat at a small high-top barely large enough to contain the three coffees, one tea and four breakfast sandwiches. They felt very anonymous in the crowded back corner of the establishment, yet they didn't chance a conversation that was anything more than shallow gossip.

"I can't believe I'm going to say this, but I miss Piper," Audrey confessed.

"Yeah, she brought me my coffee every morning when we were in the library. It was always perfectly brewed." Tarian's face softened.

"Such a boy," Maria said, and Audrey agreed.

"No, she is very sweet unlike phantom girl over there." Tarian cast his eyes in the barista's direction. phantom girl caught his look and narrowed her gaze at him. He looked away quickly. "Did you see that? She hates me."

"Yeah, I think she does." Audrey laughed.

They left the busy coffee shop and joined the hundreds of common staffers marching swiftly onward until they all piled up at the entrance of the Entente Government Capitol. The front of the building sprawled an entire city block. The steel and glass monstrosity stretched its body tall reaching the blue of the sky. Security had been increased after the EMA attack. Only one set of doors out of a dozen were now permissible causing an impatient traffic jam.

Mumbles of complaints bounced around the crowd: "I've worked here for a decade." "This is crazy." "Why am I subject to such harassment?" "I have to get up an hour earlier now."

Plenty of expletives could be heard as everyone entered in a single file line then spread out to pass through intimidating security machines. Giant-sized, scowling men sat in high official's chairs peering down at those who entered, daring them to set off the alarm.

As Tarian looked into the eyes of his watcher while he passed through the terrifying machine, a bead of sweat gingerly rolled down the back of his neck, luckily hidden out of view. He hoped the machines weren't sensitive to sweat. Just then the screen in front of his onlooker glared red. Tarian forced himself to remain calm. The observer took a second glance at him, but the husky man didn't pounce.

Tarian kept a steady pace and slipped through the scanners unnoticed. Under his clothing hid weapons designed by the Guardians and guaranteed undetectable by the Entente. They'd each been instructed to carry them at all times, even inside the apartments.

Once inside the establishment and after several attempts, Tarian found his office space. The horror stories he'd heard were true. Rows upon rows of robotic people stuffed into tiny cubicles inside noisy, gray office domes. At least he had adequate desk space that faced Audrey.

The surrealness of holding a position inside the Entente Government Capitol didn't escape him. A month ago, he never would've predicted his life would end up here under such outlandish circumstances, surrounded by so many influential decision-makers. Tarian felt both pride and terror at secretly being the most important person inside the room, a person whose pure existence could spark an attack.

The Prevallers would soon ignite a Border War. Tarian knew what the past war had done to the old capital cities, and he didn't want the same fate for Boston. Decades ago the Entente War destroyed Washington District of Columbia, Mexico City, and Ottawa City. The disabled governments transitioned to Boston while the expensive and time-consuming reconstruction replicated the spectacle of these historic places. Boston became temporary housing for government officials. After reconstruction, the new government had no desire to return to the old ways and coveted a practical, more effective space for business. The old Capitols turned into historic museums for tourists, and Boston became the permanent Government District.

Tarian became bored fast with his data processing cover job. As time passed, the glamour of working inside the prestigious walls of the Government Capitol became commonplace and uninspiring. He missed the rugged running trails of the EMA and the challenging professors and classes. He missed the thrill of the game and the ever-changing trials of the simulations. He glanced around at the employees and wondered how they could be happy with such a monotonous job.

Fortunately, he had Audrey to joke around with. They played laser tag between cubicles and exchanged messages. Unfortunately, the days rolled on slowly as they waited for more instructions. Day in and day out, they marched in formation into the gray government building and sat behind their efficient computers and trudged through their daily work. No new information from the Guardians came.

He knew Eleanor worked hard plotting the capture carefully and that it had to be executed with precision, but the delay tortured him. The lack of communication with his family weighed heavy on his heart. He'd read through the one thousand three hundred and twelve blogs Delia had written over the past six years, but they didn't comfort him.

The blogs started out funny, a dip into the mind of a preteen girl. He had sisters and assumed he understood girls. He didn't. As she grew older and found a community of blog mates, the posts became intimate and uncomfortable. The more he read, the more his heart sank. These anonymous friends knew more about her than he did. He resented Audrey for giving him another secret that he had to hide from his girlfriend. It terrified him to think he might accidentally mention a detail from one of these posts. Delia would never forgive his trespassing, but could he forgive her secrecy? It felt like she'd cheated on him.

Discussing the blogs with Audrey made it worse. Laughing at his girlfriend's expense with another woman felt wrong but growing up could be a funny adventure especially in retrospect. Audrey continually pressed him to read more. She insisted that even the tiniest clues were vital.

He justified snooping by reassuring himself that searching for clues dropped by teenagers of influential parents insured national security. Her blog group gradually posted more and more political rants, conspiracy theories, and threats of violent protests. Leaning on Audrey's shoulder when the burden of his girlfriend and family's protection became overwhelming; spending hours speculating over his girlfriend's loyalties; defending his girlfriend's treasonous words to Audrey, an Entente loyalist—it all polluted his mind and didn't make sense.

One night he read October through December. Audrey had just located the blog page only to find Delia had deleted her most recent entries, so January was still missing. The last entry sent a chill down his spine.

December 27
I left today. I couldn't get away fast enough from this strange, seemingly innocent town. I wrote my mother a sincere note of apology but not him. After what I have discovered, I am ashamed. He let my brother go back to university but not me. I had to leave secretly. I cannot live in a house of lies any longer. He still has not admitted he knows anything about T. The government would not trust T with a secret mission. He's too young. Everyone is accusing me of being crazy, but I'm not crazy. Everyone around me is crazy. I followed him and I saw where the colorful people work. It's not normal. I don't think he's even human. None of this makes sense. I'm going to X.

Fortis est veritas
Ebony6

Comment: Fantastic5
The government is doing strange things right now. Maybe he is telling you the truth about T.

Ebony6
Even if he is, he is putting him in grave danger.

Comment: Fantatsic5
You should see the massive security around this place. Two more miners died and no one's telling us anything. It takes me an hour to leave the mines. I have to go through six security checks coming in and going out. I'm telling you, it's aliens.

Comment: Jugular8
You left the North Pole?

Ebony6
Yes

Comment: Jugular8
Come stay with me!

Ebony6
I might just take you up on that.

Comment: Jugular8
You know how I feel about you. You're always welcome.

Ebony6
Thanks ☺

Comment: Fantastic5
No one wants to talk about the aliens on our planet? Seriously!

Tarian's blood boiled after reading Jugular8's advances. He wondered why the Senator hadn't contacted him. *Did he know where she was now?* Desperation twisted through him accompanied by an urgency to read the most recent blogs, but Audrey hadn't recovered the deleted entries yet. *Where had she gone after Christmas?*

He cursed Audrey for finding these blogs. He could've spent his evenings reading a good book and not these torturous paragraphs. *What did it matter anyway?*

As if she'd leaped out of his mind, Audrey marched into his bedroom unannounced and plopped herself next to him on his bed.

"I'm amazing," she boasted.

"You found them?"

"I found this year's blogs and recovered the deleted entries. It took me a while, but I did it. They're clever, but I'm smarter. Anyway, read this." She shoved her laptop in his face.

"Okay, have you read this?" He shoved his at her.

She glanced at the date. "Yes."

He glared at her. Of course, she'd read ahead of him. He should've known. She'd had this evidence before he did.

January 15
I'm feeling a lot better. The office work has been educational and needed to keep my mind off of reality. X is the most amazing person I have ever met. His medical background from the West and the papers from his partner have helped him to create an antibiotic for my mysterious disease. I hate Biggie. He has used me as a pawn in his game for the last time. X and I will make him pay for what he has done to me. X has a plan. And we will find T. My work with X is the only thing keeping me sane. He's the only person in my life who is telling me the truth. I have learned more from him in these last three weeks than my six months at university.

Fortis est veritas
Ebony6

Comment: XOXO25
I can't believe T lied to you.

Ebony6
I know XO. You always liked him. I don't think he understands it all. I don't blame him.

Comment: Jugular8
Miss you. Glad you are better. You looked pretty weak.

Ebony6
Cannot repay you enough Jugular8. Thanks for your hospitality.

Comment: Jugular8
Anytime! Wish I could have been more hospitable.

Ebony6
Don't ruin this moment with your perverted thoughts.

Comment: Jugular8
Sorry, can't help it.

"What does this mean?" Tarian asked Audrey.

"I won't know until I know who X is, but I do think she is here, in the Government District," she said.

"What?"

"Yes. I know she left the North Pole which we already had figured out was the Guardian Village. She stayed with Jugular8 who is Jack Silsbury."

"Who?"

"Jugular8 is Senator Daniel Silsbury's son, Jack. Daniel is a Guardian. He was very close to both Joe and Zachary. Jack lives and works in the Government District. Jack's older than Delia, but I know he was good friends with her brother, George."

"Okay, that makes sense. Fantastic5 is definitely a government employee at the cavern system. And there is a lot of activity going on around there. Hasn't Eleanor told you anything about that?" Tarian asked.

"No. She's being extremely vague and has kept me in the dark. It's frustrating."

"She doesn't trust anyone," he said thinking out loud. "This is bad."

"I know, but it'll be fine," she said.

He heard the trepidation in her voice. He reached for her hand, and she took it. If a woman who had lived centuries was concerned, he was petrified.

"I think Biggie is her father," Tarian said.

"I agree," she said.

"Who is X?"

"I don't know. I tried again today to contact Eleanor and I'll try tomorrow."

"She still is not returning your communications?" Tarian asked.

"No."

"Have you spoken to John and Warren? Have they heard from Eleanor?"

"I talked with them yesterday. They're in the dark just as much as we are. We just have to keep waiting. It's important to keep the chain of command intact."

"Let's go to Jack Silsbury's place tomorrow." Tarian wanted to meet the man who was flirting with his girlfriend. He was over dealing with the chain of command. The chain was broken.

"That's a possibility," she hesitated. "Or maybe I'll contact his father."

Tarian turned to look at her. He watched her taut face and fierce eyes stare at the ceiling. Her chest heaved up and down to a methodic rhythm. *Was she willing to go against orders?* He knew she'd been a maverick in the past, he needed her to be one now. The waiting had taken its toll on him, and he couldn't continue to sit still doing nothing, maybe she felt the same way.

Together, they conspired for another hour then fell asleep and woke in the morning still on top of the denim blue bedspread with their laptops sprawled across their chests.

NINETEEN

WATERFALLS

Tarian wrote down places Delia may be working in the city, but only scribbles sprawled across his notepad and the phrase *needle in a haystack*. The Government District's tentacles stretched far in all directions, an overpopulated metropolis that could hide anyone.

"I didn't know you were an artist." Audrey snickered at the doodle drawings.

"Frustration and boredom at its finest." He leveled his gaze at her without a smile.

"I know, but this is part of it. Soldiers wait for orders, soldiers follow—"

"The chain of command," he concluded. He'd heard the speech a hundred times before.

"She said she'd be in touch soon."

"That was four days ago," he argued.

She sighed in response. Her shoulders sagged, and her eyes fell. Her belief in the system broke down right in front of him, and he'd use it to his advantage.

"Are you hungry?" he asked.

"Starved," she answered.

"Mel's?"

"Sure."

Lunch at Mel's was quick and cheap: burgers and fries, the kind of meal Tarian loved but made Delia cringe. He thought of her as Audrey devoured her greasy beef. A river of ketchup and mustard flowed out of the burger and onto the plate with a few remnants left at the corners of her mouth. She rubbed the evidence away with the back of her hand.

"I guess we don't have to worry about clogged coronary arteries," Tarian said.

"Nope," she laughed. "Perks of being superhuman."

A twinge of guilt caught in his thoughts. *Is Delia eating well? Is she healthy? She claimed in her blog that X had the ability to make her better. Could he?*

"Maybe X is a doctor's office or rehab center," Tarian said.

"Possibly, but I still think it's a business or law office."

"Maybe we should have Gabe and Maria read the blogs," Tarian pondered out loud. Before, he hadn't wanted his girlfriend's deepest thoughts on display, but now, he'd risk anything to find her.

"No," Audrey snapped.

She'd always agreed that no one else should know of the blog's existence. They'd excluded Gabe and Maria from all discussions about Delia and her possible link to the Prevallers.

Luckily, Sophie had them working surveillance. This week they were tucked in an alley behind a Chinese restaurant called Wok Out. According to an anonymous informant, Feng frequented the joint.

"Let's walk around a bit," he said, putting his plan in motion. "We don't really have to be at our jobs." He winked at the inside joke.

"Actually, yes, we do have to be at our jobs." She didn't wink or smile.

"Okay fine, but we can extend our lunch break a little longer since we finished eating so quickly. It's a nice day to be outside. The snow has stopped."

It was bitterly cold, but no deterrent for a gifted purple person like Audrey.

"Don't think you're fooling me, Tarian."

He flashed her a foxy grin and walked faster. She followed struggling to keep pace and swearing at her uncomfortable shoes.

"Miss your EMA combat boots?" He smirked.

"Hell yes," she said.

Luckily for her feet, they ventured only two more blocks. Tarian ducked into an alley then scurried three-quarters of a block to a hidden door.

He pulled and jerked the handle then grinned at Audrey. "It still works."

"We can't go in there. We don't have our orders yet," she complained.

"Screw the orders." His tone more suited for Maria.

"Maria's rubbing off on you," she jabbed.

It was true, but he didn't mind. A lot had changed. The naïve boy from Salem Prep didn't exist anymore.

"No, then I would've said something much worse."

The exterior door shut eclipsing the bright sunshine. Audrey wobbled until her eyes adjusted to the severe darkness. Tarian guided her down a long, cold hallway. The exposed water pipes and A/C corridors made the air damp, cold, and musty. She clutched his sleeve and pointed to a camera with a panicked look on her face.

He shook his head. "Hasn't worked since I was ten."

She let go of him and cautiously continued in his shadow taking off her heels to silence the hollow clicking noises.

He didn't remember the corridor being this long. Finally, he heard the sound of water, lots of water. As the path brightened, his skin shivered, and his lungs ballooned with excitement.

Audrey pointed to the light. "Too visible."

She grabbed him again, slowed his pace, but he jerked her forward like a stubborn dog on a leash. Then they saw it: a gigantic blanket of cascading water, blue and green and gold glistening reflections of millions of twinkling prisms.

"It's beautiful," she said loudly. Her volume muted by the noise of the water pounding into a pool below.

"I know."

The ice in her eyes thawed as she admired the mesmerizing movement, her hand still clenched in a vice grip on his forearm. She had a habit of grabbing onto him, usually due to her impatience.

Now that she could let go, she didn't.

This was no ordinary place for Tarian, and he felt blessed to be back. "I used to come here all the time. Whenever my dad took me into the office, and I disappeared, he knew exactly where I was, and I knew he'd find me. He always did." A tear formed in the corner of his eye. He forced it to stop. He wouldn't cry. "He'd have chocolate or an ice cream cone. He'd have two, one for me and one for him, and we'd stay here long enough to eat our treats. We wouldn't talk. We'd just stare at the magnificence of something as trivial as water and eat."

"That sounds like Joe. He was always the strong, silent type," she said with a lost look of remembrance.

Audrey's reminiscent gaze triggered a whip of envy that struck him at his core. His heart stopped and his muscles clenched. He didn't want to ruin the intimate moment with his petty jealousy, so he bit his tongue. It wasn't her fault she'd lived by Dad's side for many years and shared centuries of memories. He realized his agony didn't stem from lost memories with his father but from the desire to know her as deeply as his father had.

He let the thick silence and inner reflection linger before he spoke. "You can see people through the water, but they can't see you. That always intrigued me as a boy. Why was the water a one-way mirror? I think there're two reasons. One, the light is on that side of the water and two, others are moving while we are standing still."

"Yes, I guess so." She laughed softly. "You're so observant.

I love that about you."

Her expression was as unguarded as he had ever seen it. He had to look away to avoid falling victim to her raw beauty.

"I watched you intently at EMA."

She hesitated to say more, but he'd already pieced the puzzle together. It wasn't a coincidence that she'd been assigned to be his Cadet Sergeant. She'd been sent to spy on him a long time ago.

She continued, "I noticed your eyes were always twitching, but you would stay perfectly still. I realized it was your way of taking everything in, logging all details of what you saw and whom you met. You live in the moment. That's a good thing. As an immortal that's a necessary quality. For too many years, I lived in the past while trying too hard to meet the future, but to live in the moment is the key to an immortal's happiness. It took most of us hundreds of years to master that. Except for Eleanor, she's lived in the moment for as long as I've known her. Zachary is still searching, and your dad was finally at peace because of you."

A woman appeared on the other side of the waterfall and broke their tranquil moment. Tarian shot a couple of steps to the right and startled Audrey. He listened intently. He couldn't be certain that it was her that he saw through the curtain of water.

"Tarian! Stop!" Audrey yelled.

He halted but so did the woman on the other side. Audrey had yelled his name too loudly. The woman had heard them. Audrey and Tarian stood petrified as Delia walked closer. Delia reached her hand up to touch the waterfall, but the stream was so thick, her hand didn't penetrate to the other side. Audrey saw Tarian raise his hand to the spot where Delia's hand was. Audrey tugged on his shirt. Delia shook her head, then lowered her hand and strode away. Tarian's hand remained outstretched until Audrey gently pushed it down.

Tarian sprinted down the hall in the opposite direction of the exit.

Audrey yelled, "We can't. We have to go!"

He ignored her. Instinct took over, and he no longer thought about orders or the chain of command. He needed to see her. He'd go against all protocol. He'd break all the regulations ingrained over two years of intense training just to hold her. He'd found her.

Audrey ran after him.

Tarian knew the building like the back of his hand. Audrey fumbled inches behind him. He knew the alleys, short cuts, and secret hallways that didn't show up on blueprints. He reached a cut off. He opened a door and led her into an ordinary hallway with generic brown carpet and tan walls. This could've been any one of the twenty-two floors of the building, but Tarian knew exactly where he was. He spotted the plaque labeled Feng and Justice, Attorneys at Law. He had his mark!

Tarian never made it to the door. With brute force, Audrey tackled him. They rolled onto the ground arms and legs banging against the walls. The noise was sure to attract curious workers.

"Dammit, Tarian. What are you doing?" Audrey's frantic tone snapped him out of his recklessness.

Tarian had shattered the implacable façade of the one person he could count on to keep him in line.

Suddenly, voices sounded from around the corner. Audrey grabbed his elbow and dragged him away. Tarian forced her back and detoured into the men's bathroom. He pulled her into a stall, their mouths inches apart, and their bodies wedged together. They stayed motionless and silent for minutes, dreading discovery more than embarrassment at the proximity of their sweaty, adrenaline-filled bodies. The intimate position went unnoticed until the voices disappeared, and they exhaled.

Tarian regained his senses and released his grip on her. Time stood still as he stared into her crystal blue eyes. He leaned in with an urge to kiss her, but she shoved him backward. Before he knew what had happened, she had his hands pinned against the wall of the stall and her knee threatening his manhood. She had the strength of ten men, but he'd grown stronger. He pushed her back into a powerless position that she wasn't accustomed to. She squirmed and thrashed against him in the tight space. The stall door burst open, and they spilled out gasping for breath.

"Let's go now," she demanded, completely annoyed.

He would've been mortified with embarrassment, had he the time. He simply acquiesced, following her as she precisely led them back underground behind the waterfall and into the alley. Her faultless memory and sense of direction impressed him.

Once out of the building, they blended in with other pedestrians hoping no one noticed their stressed faces or wet armpits. She didn't speak, but her anger emanated a heat that scorched his body. He'd crossed a line in their job and their relationship. The split-second urge to kiss her was merely a by-product of exhilarated adrenaline. Nothing more. *Could it have been anyone? It meant nothing. I'm an idiot! Anyone would have tried it.* But he couldn't rationalize his stupidity.

He shook his head to clear his thoughts and banish his guilt. Now, away from the intensity of the experience and thinking plainly, Tarian realized his girlfriend worked for a killer. X was Feng. He tried to understand what this meant for Delia. Delia may know confidential things that could put her life in danger. He pressed his eyelids together and prayed she hadn't stepped too deeply into the hornet's nest.

They didn't return to work. Instead, they walked directly to their apartments. Tarian opened his door but turned back to look at Audrey before he entered. He caught her glance back at him as well. She flashed him a small smile. Relieved, he grinned back and shut the door.

TWENTY

THE BAR

Never had information on a mission been withheld from Audrey. Not having all the facts compromised her assignment to safeguard Tarian, and this terrified her. Her repeated unanswered calls to Eleanor were infuriating. Tonight, she vowed to find answers.

The celebration of Entente Victor's Day incited the noisy bar. The crowd of people got increasingly intoxicated by the hour. Waves of loud cheers swooped through the bar when the Boston Bruins scored a goal against the Montreal Canadiens. The historic sports rivalry always played on Entente Victor's Day. The entire city awash in alcoholic revelry made for the perfect night to seek out Zachary.

Audrey flagged him down as he forced his way through the people cheering and dancing in his path. He scowled with distaste, and Audrey wondered when he'd lost his sense of adventure. This used to be the kind of place Zachary, Joe, and she would hang out. Now they were too serious saving the mortals from their own destruction and paying a fatal price for it.

Zachary caught her waving arm in the air with his eyes and swiftly pushed his way past the drunks to seat himself. As usual he wore a designer suit and looked like a politician. He always had a well-tailored, professional style even before his personality got so uptight, but now it really fit him.

"Grant's on the rocks, and I'll have a Harp," she said aloud as she placed the order on the touchscreen display, ignoring his disapproving gaze.

"Why did you call me here?" he asked.

"Delia is here." She got right to the point. Without Joe, she didn't enjoy conversing with Zachary. Joe could bring out his dry sense of humor, making him more entertaining.

"Yes, I know," he said slowly.

She wondered if he was hesitating to give up this information or surprised she'd found out.

"What's going on? I've never been kept out of the loop this long," she said.

The server brought the two drinks and a small bowl of peanuts. She glanced at Audrey to confirm the accuracy of the order.

"Thank you," Audrey said to the young woman.

"Is this your first beer?" he asked after the server retreated, but she didn't answer.

The appearance of his antique Pierre Frédéric Ingold watch threw her back in time. As he reached for his glass, the watch peeked out from beneath his sleeve. The woman who'd given him that watch so many years ago was the love of his life. Now Audrey remembered the Zachary she used to enjoy so much, the Zachary pre-lost love. After Cecilia's death in 1856, Zachary had changed. At that point in time, he and Audrey had formed a common bond over their depression. She'd already suffered the loss of her greatest love. Together they drifted into the dark abyss of grief.

For years, Joe had to deal with two intoxicated immortals spiraling out of control leaving a path of destruction in their wake. Joe hadn't found his intense love until much later when he met Carolyn, Tarian's mother. He wouldn't have suffered as they did. He would've had Tarian to ease him out of his grieving.

During these dark days, Zachary and Audrey had found themselves in many seedy bars only to have Joe rescue them before the wrath of Eleanor came down. Zachary had crawled his way out of the pit sooner than she had, but it cost him. He created another family and then another, but he never allowed himself to venture back to the intimate place Cecilia would forever inhabit. That part of his soul was sealed shut by a thick, iron bolt. Encased with her love was the part of his personality that enjoyed living. He became less and less human as the years since Cecilia's death accumulated. He had wives to provide for and children to educate, but his compassion for their mortal struggle diminished.

"Audrey?" He snapped a finger in front of her face.

Her eyes shot up still uncomprehending his words. *He still wears that watch,* she thought.

"Something is wrong, Zach. I feel it." The words came from

her heart. She confided in her old friend. She wanted him back. No, she wanted the good ol' days back.

"There is nothing to worry about. Eleanor and I have the situation under control. It will not be long now."

"Where's Feng?" Her blunt question caught him off guard.

"We had a lead." Zachary swirled the copper liquid around in his glass.

Audrey considered his words then slowly drank her beer. *Did he mean that stupid Wok Out Restaurant that Gabe and Maria had staked out? No. No,* she pondered shaking her head ever so slightly.

"Had? What happened?" she asked. Her knuckles went white as she gripped the beer bottle, desperate for answers.

"A lot is confidential right now," he said, his face expressionless.

She realized she'd been put on a need-to-know basis. She never operated on a need-to-know. She was always the one with access to all the information.

Her stare became a dagger aimed for his head, so he continued. "You must understand. Every minor detail must be calculated, or the Guardians' existence is at stake."

"I know that." She took a long swig of her beer. Her patience worn, she concluded he wasn't going to provide her with any insight. She'd been downgraded.

"Dammit, Audrey! Don't make me feel guilty! You chose your position. And if you ask me, you are getting a little too close to Joe's son," he spat the accusation at her.

She flinched. "Joe's son? Screw you, Zachary!"

"Look out there," he said pointing to the few screens surrounding the bar without the hockey game.

Images of fire and destruction, along with captions across the bottom tallying the death toll caused by the Prevallers' attacks were being broadcast on local news stations. She knew the situation had escalated in the past few days. Innocent people were under fire while they sat in a bar drinking and watching hockey. The Entente was a vast portion of land, but soon the violence would reach them. Soon a war would break out. She knew this and resented him for pointing it out.

"Exactly! We are running out of time," she said.

"No, we are cautious. You need to remember who you are and who Tarian is."

"What's that supposed to mean?"

"You are getting too close to him. Your awareness is clouded by feelings of …" he hesitated.

Audrey instinctively denied his accusation, yet she worried he was right.

She'd been assigned to Tarian for two years now. She'd kept him safe. He'd come to the EMA as a clumsy, confused teenager, and she'd groomed him into a top-notch, fighting machine. She lurked in his shadows protecting him from his enemies. During drills and training, she pushed him beyond his limits without him ever suspecting her attention focused fully on him and only him. She slyly set up the friendship with Gabe and Maria, knowing he'd need a small but strong core. She cared for him deeply but as what? A friend? A brother? Or more? She couldn't fall in love with Joe's son.

"I want to talk with Eleanor. Tell her if I don't hear from her by noon tomorrow, I'm taking Tarian and heading back to the village. Got it?" she demanded.

"Got it." He took one last sip of his scotch and removed himself sophisticatedly from the unrefined chaos of the bar.

After he'd gone, she noticed a hundred credit on the table. Had he thought she'd been sitting in the bar drinking for hours before he got there? The nerve! Furious, she ordered another beer and a round for the four, good-looking young men gathered at a neighboring high top.

She soon regretted her reckless decision. They mistook her generosity for flirtation and huddled around her table, giving her lascivious looks. She was about to give them one last polite excuse before she kicked the leader in his balls when Tarian approached. The men begrudgingly returned to their high top, disappointed.

"How'd you find me? Guardian mobiles are untraceable."

"The tracking unit in your jacket," he sarcastically reminded her as he sat down uninvited.

I must be losing it, she thought. Of course, he could track her every move as she could his.

"Ebony6 just posted a new blog."

"Show me," Audrey reached for his tablet.

January 30
Today was my last day at the office. The virus is spreading again and X insists

I need to rest. I have to agree with him. I think I'm beginning to hallucinate. I thought I heard T's name today. I felt his presence but I know he's somewhere far away. Probably defending the useless Entente. I worry for him every day. X and I are going somewhere safe. His life is in danger. He has been careful but I fear they want him dead. Soon the war will be here and we will all have to flee. It's better we hide now. I put my trust in X. He has advanced information and only he can cure me of this poison inside my body. I know he can. I'm too tired to continue writing.

All my love to you guys. Be careful!

Fortis est veritas
Ebony6

Comment: Jugular8
I'm coming to see you. Message me where you are.

Comment: XOXO25
Love you girl!

Comment: Jugular8
My dad can help. You know he can. Let him try.

Comment: SkyEartHater
Good luck!

Comment: Fantastic5

I agree with you. Two more arrests today. Men in suits asking lots of questions.

Comment: Jugular8
Answer me! I'm giving you two days but that's all.

Comment: Zigler88
Hang tight!

"She just signed off. What if we don't find her again? What if he hurts her? I knew I should have talked to her today." His voice cracked with regret.

"No, we did the right thing."

"How can you say that? She was our only lead and she just checked out," he snapped.

"They have leads. Trust me!"

"I do trust you," he exhaled and paused, exhausted. "She didn't respond to her blog mates. She never does that."

"I know. Makes me think this is the last blog. She and Feng are up to something," Audrey said.

"What are you doing in this bar anyway?"

"I met with Zachary."

"What'd he say?" Tarian blurted before she had a chance to explain.

"He told me nothing. Said they were close, and we would hear soon."

"Did he know about Delia? She's here, possibly in danger." The urgency in his voice was palpable.

"Yes."

"Bastard!"

"You have to understand Zachary. His mind operates on the grand plane, not on the finer details."

"Oh, that's right. I forgot, just another mortal to have to die. Oh well." He shrugged.

"It's not like that," she explained, but she knew his portrayal of the Senator was accurate.

"Why would Zachary put his own daughter at risk?" he asked.

"I don't have the strength to answer that question right now."

"You don't have a choice," he barked attracting the attention of the men he'd warded off only minutes before. "I didn't ask to be invited to this party late, but now that I'm here I deserve to know what I've missed."

"I don't doubt that he loves her, but he would risk her life for the benefit of the greater good. He's a politician and a soldier. Zachary has married six times. Six times he's watched his family die while he lived on. Honestly, I find it repulsive," she paused. She didn't say anything for a long time. She did find it abhorrent, but she couldn't blame him for erecting his wall of indifference. She too had powerful walls erected for emotional protection. At some point during their drunken rehabilitation, he'd withdrawn, becoming an almost robotic version of himself while she'd sought solace in stronger social connections. Her loss had given her an insight to others' suffering, but his loss had brought a haze of inevitable doom.

"I know it's difficult but," Tarian broke the silence then paused. He opened his mouth, and then closed it.

He regarded her intently with his warm brown eyes. He looked so young, she thought, but appeared wiser with every secret she revealed to him. Now she felt she owed him one of her secrets.

"After losing my first family and discovering what I was, I did meet a man that I fell in love with," she hesitated, "He was Italian with the face of a god, absolutely impossibly good looking. We shared one beautiful daughter and a long happy life together but when they died, I died too. I disappeared, away from the Guardians and spent most of my time drinking in bars. I attempted suicide." She laughed out loud at the absurdity of an immortal's suicide. "I didn't eat. Eleanor and Joe tried everything to help me get past my grief. Then Zachary lost Cecelia and succumbed to a life of depression with me." She paused to recall a distant amusing memory. "Zachary and I actually had some funny episodes. We were quite a motley crew. Zachary's grief for Cecelia was real unlike his other losses, but he grieved with style. When he drank, he never got messy. I drank myself into a coma." The brief levity passed, and her smile faded into a hauntingly absent stare.

"I'm sorry." His lineless and sincere face soothed her.

"Life was cruel. The seasons continued. The snow fell. Then the sun shone, over and over again, but I was alive and well." Dewy moisture built in her eyes, but she was too stubborn to cry. Maybe she'd already cried all her tears a long time ago. "I came back home to my family of Guardians and devoted my life to the protection of mortal people, vowing never to fall in love with any of them again."

"I understand," he said.

She knew he was being polite. She feared he truly would understand the pain of immortality someday.

"But Zachary is different. He needs the company of

mortals. He needs a wife and children, but I don't think he's capable of true love, true compassion, anymore—not after Cecilia's death. I think he has a God complex and considers himself superior to mere mortals. He feels their death is part of a grand plan in which his continued life is a blessing from the Divine. He has always treated his wives and children with the utmost respect. In the past and present, he's been a good provider, a good father, but a lousy caregiver. If Delia is useful to the operation today, and she's going to die anyway tomorrow, of course he'd use her."

This last sentence widened Tarian's eyes.

"Okay," he said, moving the conversation out of the past and into the future. "Delia went to work at Feng's office. X is Feng. Zachary used this opportunity. He has a team spying on her, and Eleanor is waiting to see how this all plays out. Is that correct?" he asked, and she nodded. "Delia can get a hold of this elusive killer, but the Guardians can't?"

"Sounds wrong, doesn't it?"

"Yes," he said.

"Because it is," she said.

TWENTY-ONE

TAXI

The cacophony of the bar faded as Audrey and Tarian walked back to their apartment building under flickering streetlamps. In the distance, another couple stumbled to their car. The man wasn't drunk, but the woman could barely stand. He laid her down onto the backseat of his car. Just as he opened the driver's door, he turned his head to face them.

"Feng," Audrey said.

"Delia," Tarian said, as the car drove away.

They sprinted back to the bar where several taxicabs waited. Throwing open a door, Tarian told the driver to head down Cambridge Street toward Congress.

"Just enter your location," the cab driver stated.

"No, just drive!" Tarian shouted.

"Listen, that's how it works. You enter the location, and the car takes us to it," grumbled the wrinkled faced cab driver.

"I know, but not this time. I don't know where I'm going,

and you're wasting my time."

The taxi stood still. Audrey flashed a hundred credit. The cab driver grabbed the money and sped away. On Congress, they spotted the dark blue, four-door and told the driver to follow it at a safe distance.

Audrey looked at the secure mobile on her wrist. "Should I call Eleanor or Zachary?"

Tarian shook his head hesitantly.

"I agree. I'm not sure whom to trust. I don't want to tip anyone off."

The vehicle stopped at what appeared to be an abandoned fishery in the seaport district. The sedan pulled into a garage and as the taxi drove by, the garage door shut.

"Drop us off here." She handed the cab driver another hundred credit for a thirty-credit ride. "There's another hundred in it for you if you pick us up here in forty minutes. And give me your jacket."

He scoffed but finally removed his jacket after she handed him another hundred.

"Okay," the small, elderly cab driver said. He didn't smile, nor did he ask questions. He left.

Tarian and Audrey looked doubtful at each other wondering if he'd return even for another hundred credit. She slung on his jacket. The polyester blend stunk of a long hard day's work, but it was black and exactly what was needed to cover up her cream-colored sweater. She thrust her hands under Tarian's sweater, startling him, but he didn't pull away.

She lifted the fabric up. "Perfect," she said about his black, long-sleeved undershirt. She ripped the sweater from his body and grinned. Their dark clothing would camouflage them in the black of night.

Looking through the ground level windows, they saw nothing but Feng's empty car. They walked down a dark, narrow alley where a raggedy, old woman lay asleep against the wall covered by a ripped, dirt-covered blanket. Her shopping cart, filled with empty cans and bottles, stood beside her. The woman opened one eye but shut it immediately. Audrey didn't take any chances and smashed one of the bottles over the woman's head. She slouched against the wall, her blanket tucked under her legs. Audrey hesitated to see if anyone heard the noise. Silence. She tucked a hundred credit inside the woman's clenched fist.

"At this rate, I'll be broke by morning," she muttered under her breath.

Tarian stilled. This was his first in-the-field operation. In a simulation, he also would've acted quickly to silence the woman, yet in real life, he froze not thinking on his feet as Audrey had. They'd come unprepared. All the state-of-the-art devices were back at the apartment. They had to use their instincts and improvise with whatever was available. She did that well, and he took note to learn from her. He worried that he'd fail her. He was too green. He needed to pay close attention. He wouldn't screw this up and put her life or Delia's in danger.

He followed Audrey up the catwalk to a narrow ledge they could stealthily walk across. Her cat-like feet never made a sound unlike his. She gave him an irritated look, and he walked more lightly, but he couldn't silence his one hundred and eighty-five pounds on metal. She'd worn sneakers to the bar and not high heels. She'd looked frumpy and out of place then, but now she looked and sounded perfect. They passed several small windows and peered down into a warehouse-type space but saw no movement. Then they heard a door slam.

"We should've informed someone of our whereabouts," she murmured.

"The cab driver knows where we are," he reassured.

"All he can do is identify our dead bodies," she said.

He knew death was a new and unsettling reality for her.

Scurrying a little further on the ledge, they found a broken window and climbed into a room. She leaped quietly making a hint of a sound. She landed a little off balance and grabbed the edge of a desk. Dust scattered like tiny fairies. This place must have been abandoned for years.

Tarian followed but lacked her grace and stumbled. Luckily, she caught him, and he recovered. He stifled a sneeze. Dust and the unmistakable rancid odor of a rotting animal burned his sinuses.

Time had trapped the aromas of decay inside this abandoned executive office. One of these office spaces held Delia.

Audrey glanced at her watch. "Twenty minutes," she whispered. "We only have another twenty if we want to have a safe ride home."

"I'm not leaving here without Delia," he whispered.

She gave him a look of impatience. "Look Tarian, it's important you follow my lead. Right now, you have to be impartial. You have to be a soldier. Emotions have no place here and can get us killed."

She was right. He'd try to treat this as any other mission, but his heart beat irregularly. He felt nauseous.

The door was shut and opening it would be an extreme risk. He let Audrey's more delicate hands unlatch the lock. Turning the knob steadily, she paused then pulled millimeter by millimeter. Success. Still no person in sight. *Where the hell was Feng?* Then he heard the clang of sharp objects, and cold fear slithered up his spine.

They followed the sound and located Feng. The room looked like a makeshift dentist office. Delia's unconscious body slouched in a firm chair, her blouse off with electrodes strategically placed around her chest and in her hair. Screens monitored her heartbeat while a mask covered her mouth and a tank administered gas. Several syringes filled with different colored liquids lay on a table next to the chair. Feng hummed to himself and ate noodles out of a Chinese restaurant carton marked Wok Out. Tarian wondered if he was waiting for someone else. All they could do was wait and watch, hoping to catch a glimpse of his accomplice, but no one came.

Tarian felt worthless. He had no weapon. He'd unprofessionally left his apartment without it. Delia lay a few feet away from him, and he couldn't save her. The unbearable anxiety built, and he attempted to hold steady. He must have triggered a response in Audrey because she put a calming hand on his thigh. She patted him like a child. It soothed his angst. She seemed in control. He prayed she was.

Once he relaxed a bit, he thought clearer. *What were the facts? Her heartbeat was steady. She wasn't dead. Feng seemed calm. He was using her for testing, not murdering her. That meant she was valuable. He would not or may not kill her,* Tarian hoped.

A horn blared and interrupted his thoughts. The cab! The old man had come back and honked repeatedly. He wanted his hundred credit. The horn also startled Feng whose jump to his feet was loud enough to mask the noise caused by Tarian's surprise. Delia, however, didn't move. Feng pulled a pistol from a drawer then ran down the hall, cursing. Tarian silently prayed for the life of the small, elderly cabby.

Audrey used the distraction as an opportunity to enter Delia's holding room, and Tarian followed her. Tiny track marks covered Delia's arms. This must not have been the first time Feng had brought her here. The fresh prick mark and empty syringe made his heart twist.

Audrey surveyed the room for a container and found several inside the cabinet. Snatching two she put a few droplets of liquid from the syringes into them. Audrey shoved the two containers into the jacket pockets. She pushed hard and a vapor stick broke, scattering waxy liquid everywhere. Tarian gave her a nervous look. Quickly, Audrey wiped up the fluid, but the pungent aroma filled the air.

Desperate, Tarian grabbed more containers. He wanted samples of everything. He wanted to save Delia, but he didn't have time. He froze over her body. He stroked her short, espresso hair. She looked different, gaunt and ghostly, and she'd cut her beautiful locks. Audrey pulled his arm away, but his feet planted.

"We have to leave her," she said.

Feng hadn't returned but the honking went on relentlessly. So far no gunshots.

"I can't." He slipped his hand in Delia's.

"Dammit, Tarian! We're not prepared or equipped to take her. I promise we'll come back tomorrow with a plan of action. Look at her arms. He needs her. I guarantee she will be here tomorrow," she pleaded.

He knew she was right. They had no plan, inadequate weapons, and no reliable information as to what was really going on.

They left her still, helpless body in the chair and went back to the dusty room they'd entered from and peered down at the street below. They could see the bright lights of the taxi and a shadowy figure hobbling toward it. Out of the dark stumbled the old woman Audrey had hit over the head with the bottle.

Delusional, she yelled, "Oh my darling, you've come back. Take me. Take me away."

The cab driver looked at her crossly, but as she waived the one hundred credit Audrey had given her, he simply said, "Get in, Lady."

As the cab sped away, Feng looked around confused. He reentered the building, and Tarian and Audrey swiftly exited through the window, crossed the edge, and descended the catwalk. Their ride was gone, but Feng had no idea they'd been there tonight. Together Audrey and Tarian slipped undetected down another vagrant-filled alley and headed in the direction of Congress Street.

TWENTY-TWO

TEAMMATE

"Where's Audrey?" Tarian asked when Maria arrived at the Wicked Good Coffee Shop without her.

"And a good morning to you too." Maria rolled her eyes.

Last night, Tarian and Audrey had agreed to start the morning as ordinarily as possible, but it was anything but an ordinary day. "Sorry. Good morning, Maria. I was just wondering why Audrey wasn't with you."

"She's sick," Maria explained.

"Oh." Tarian attempted a smile, but debilitating suspicion took over his senses. *She's planning to leave me behind.*

As he looked around the crowded coffee shop routing his exit, he noticed many sick people. Most looked hung-over from last night's Victor's celebration, and he wondered if Audrey could be hung-over. But she'd been alert and sober at the warehouse. Contrary thoughts boomed inside his head, but Gabe and Maria seemed oblivious, engrossed in their own conversation, of which he hadn't heard a word.

The table felt wrong without Audrey. The vacant chair next to his was an empty void. Gabe and Maria huddled close to each other. Their conversation bland without Audrey. The same topics discussed: weather, basketball, hockey. They went on about the lack of orders from Headquarters, their boring jobs, EMA and how much they missed it, and so on and so forth. Even though the conversation was the same, Tarian felt disconnected. He thought of the many topics he'd rather be discussing with Audrey right now. He realized the four of them had become two teams, and he missed his teammate.

"Earth to Tarian." Maria slapped his hand.

"Oh sorry," he mumbled.

"You look a little sick too," Gabe added.

Tarian used those words to his advantage. "You know, I do feel tired and have the chills." He'd fake illness to excuse his absence from work today.

"You and Audrey sick. Hmm! Were you swapping fluids last night?" Maria said bluntly.

"No." Tarian stiffened his shoulders and tried to appear offended.

"Maria, he has a girlfriend," Gabe argued.

"Yeah right! A woman he hasn't talked to in weeks," she said.

"That's not his fault," Gabe defended.

"Thank you, Gabe," Tarian said.

"Oh, come on, Audrey's beautiful, and the two of you spend a hell of a lot of time together," she cross-examined him.

"It's our job! And I could say the same about the two of you. Suddenly, I'm feeling very sick." Tarian pushed his chair away from the table.

"Where are you going? To check on your other half," Maria joked.

"Ha, ha. I think I'll go home and rest, and yes, I will check in on Audrey," he said.

Maria's devilish smile infuriated him, but he'd let it slide, keep them on the wrong track. If they thought he was having an affair with Audrey, then so be it. That's a great cover.

Tarian opened the door to Audrey's apartment after she failed to answer his several knocks.

"It's me," Tarian said in a panic after hearing her chamber a weapon.

"Tarian!" she screamed. "I almost shot you!"

"It's okay. I'm sure I would've survived." He chuckled. She was half dressed. He turned around. "So, are you really sick or is that our reason for skipping work today?"

"So, you think us immortals can survive a gunshot yet still contract the common cold?" She secured her weapon and placed it on the end table. She walked into her closet to find a pair of pants.

"Actually, I thought you were hungover."

"It takes a lot more than three beers to get me hungover."

"So, we don't get viruses?" he asked.

"No. Our bodies feel pain and fatigue. We'll sneeze or cough due to the elements, but that's it. We're immune to all infection. That's why the Sanoxine made you sick. Your body rejects any antibody because it doesn't need it."

"What is our plan?" he asked. The yearning to return to the warehouse began to stir in his gut.

"I need to eat. Do you want anything?"

"No."

She busied herself around the kitchen making breakfast. He paced. His anxiety building until her shoulders slumped, and she set the box of cereal down on the counter. She turned around so he could see her face, and the beauty that shown through her vulnerability struck him. She'd always looked so fierce and assured. It made her face hard. The beautiful angles and features were sharp as a blade, and he'd envisioned her slicing up her lover as they kissed. Now, with her wet hair, make-up free face, bare feet and pale blue tee-shirt, her beauty seemed soft and accessible.

His anxiety shifted to fear. She was his rock in this chaos. If she let her guard down now, then things would go terribly wrong. He trusted the six hundred years of experience behind her twenty-year-old face. He didn't know how to react to this emotion. He reached to touch her, but she withdrew, and the hardness returned.

She straightened her spine and broadened her shoulders.

"Listen Tarian, I was up all night trying to put the pieces of this puzzle together and nothing makes sense," she said. "People I've trusted for years, I don't trust anymore, but yet, I know in my gut I still should. They just seem so damn suspicious."

"Who?"

"Everyone—Zach, Eleanor, plenty of others too, even Joe. I can come up with a million different scenarios, and all of them seem plausible and at the same time ludicrous."

"I know, but together we can make sense out of it," he said. "I realized something when you weren't at the coffee shop this morning."

"What?" she asked.

"That we're a team, you and I. That I was glad you were with me yesterday when I saw Delia. I was glad I showed you my secret boyhood hiding place. I also realized that this weird bond we share feels a lot like the bond I shared with my father. It's very strange as I look back on my life with him now knowing what I am, what he was. I do think we had a different connection than just son and father. I can't explain it. It's just a feeling, and I feel it when I'm with you. A trust, an unbreakable trust. The weird thing is I felt it when I first met you. When you were my Cadet Sergeant, and I had no reason to trust you," he explained as he paced the floor.

"Do you feel the same with Delia?" she asked.

"No." He stopped pacing. He trusted Delia but he never felt comfortable around her. He had a hunger for her that he didn't have with Audrey—a romantic connection. He hesitated to share those thoughts with Audrey.

"Do you think she is immortal?" Audrey asked.

"What?" he said.

"Has she ever been in any accident where she healed quickly?" she asked.

"Oh my God, could she be?" he questioned with audible happiness.

"Well, Feng was running tests on her last night."

"But Senator Eastwood would've kept her close to him. Eleanor would know. Zachary wouldn't just let her wander around."

"There's a lot you don't know about Zachary. And actually, he's the one I'm concerned with. If it were just his allowing Delia to be in the line of danger, I'd get it. He's not the most compassionate person. He's very logical, and he's seen a lot of his loved ones pass on and he accepts it. But the fact that he claims not to know where Feng is, and he's right here in Boston, that's not adding up," she said.

"But she's been sick a lot," he said. "You just told me immortals don't get sick."

"What do you know about this illness?"

"Not much except what I've read in her blog. She kept it from me," Tarian admitted.

"If the 'Biggie' in her blog is Zachary and Delia doesn't trust him. She doesn't trust her own father." She worked all the information over in her mind.

"So, she doesn't trust a lot of people. My dad trusted him

with everything, with his family. There's no way," Tarian said. The thought of the Senator being involved in his dad's murder was too much for Tarian to comprehend. It didn't fit, but then again, what did?

"Me too. He's been an officer for the Guardians from the beginning. I'm sure there's a logical explanation."

"Delia never fully believed anything her dad told her," he said, giving Audrey a wondering glance.

"Well, he was lying about a great deal in his life. I'm sure she picked up on that."

"That's true. What should we do now? I want to get Delia out of there as soon as possible. Who knows what chemicals he's pumping into her body?"

"I'm still not comfortable acting without Eleanor's approval," Audrey said.

"I'm going to the warehouse, with or without you. You made me leave her there with a murderer." Tarian whipped the accusation at her.

Audrey threw up her hands. "We didn't have a choice. We couldn't risk detection. Delia is of some value to him." She closed her eyes, swallowed hard then added, "She's not dead."

"Yet! She's not dead yet. Isn't that what you meant to say? Where is your compassion? I guess you've gotten numb to death too." He moved closer to her.

"Don't assume that because you've known me for a few months that you know my life and my beliefs. You don't know me at all," she said, her body still and her eyes never leaving his.

He couldn't look away but refused to apologize. He felt terrible about what had transpired, but he hurt too much, and his pain fixed him stubbornly. Silent tension lingered in the air for several minutes.

Tarian ran a hand through his thick hair. "Let's go. If she's still there, she may be in danger. We need to watch them, gather evidence. We need to do something!"

"Okay, we'll go there first," she said, but he could see her mind still turning.

TWENTY-THREE

BETRAYED

Clothed in dark field pants, sneakers and a charcoal, long-sleeve shirt with a tight fitting, but stretchable black jacket, Tarian and Audrey began their mission. The Guardian-issued clothes hid a multitude of tiny but lethal weapons and a tracking device. Audrey purposefully removed the trackers from their jackets.

"What are you doing?" Tarian looked at her with suspicion.

"We don't need anyone finding us as easily as you found me in the bar last night," Audrey said.

"Let's hope we don't need finding." He raised an eyebrow.

They had difficulty recognizing the building in daylight. All the buildings looked dilapidated and abandoned. She asked the driver to maneuver slowly past each alley as they looked for the vagrant woman's shopping cart, but there were many carts. They strained their eyes trying to recognize the fire escape they'd climbed, but a fresh layer of snow hid recognizable details.

"That's it." She pointed to her left. "Stop right here." She told the driver.

Once more, Tarian followed Audrey up the fire escape and in through the broken window they'd entered the night before. The filthy window smeared with dead insects showed a hint of blood along one edge of the shredded glass. He didn't remember snagging on it, but he'd erase the DNA just in case. He showed the light over the blood and watched it disappear.

With the cloak of darkness removed and daylight shining in, the room's grotesqueness glared. Thick, avocado green dust covered everything except Audrey's slender handprint indented in the grime on top of the desk where she'd placed it to gain her balance last night. She wiped it clean.

"We were sloppy last night." Audrey rubbed the entire desk clean.

She proceeded to clean all of the office equipment. He wondered if all this cleaning was smart, but she moved determinedly. To his relief, the creature responsible for the foul odor remained at large. Tarian figured it had died confined inside the walls.

The open door exposed them to the hallway. Another sloppy move. He prayed their trespassing was still unknown, and Feng hadn't suspected the cab last night had been intended for them.

He heard soft voices. Whom they belonged to or how many voices were impossible to tell. No fear or anger, just normal conversation.

Audrey and Tarian crept down the hall, hugging it and staying far away from the railing that looked down into the warehouse. Last night Tarian had glanced into its depths to a black hole. Today, filtered light shone through windows opaque from dirt. He could make out cement flooring several feet below along with old, forgotten machinery but no people. For a split second, the diffused sunshine tricked him, and he thought the building had electricity. However, he had misjudged it. Only the small dentist-like room held power via some generator. Feng was using this building illegally. There'd be no trail of electric invoices to prove his existence.

They reached the room where Delia had been unconsciously experimented upon, but she was no longer there. Panic froze Tarian, and then a wash of relief brought warmth back to his limbs. Nothing had been removed from the empty room, suggesting it'd be used again. He wondered if Feng had even noticed the stolen containers. Tarian removed an entire syringe and shoved it into his jacket. His desperation to know what they contained overtook him. There were several more, Feng wouldn't notice. He grabbed another one.

The vacant room showed no sign of a struggle. *He hadn't killed her.* The rush of desperation consumed him. Then his heart sank as the realization of an empty room meant uncertainty. *What was better, finding her dead or unconscious in a torture chair, or not finding her at all? Answer: None of the above!*

The voices floated on the air and into the room. The empty room became instantly irrelevant. He needed to find the people behind the voices. He motioned to Audrey to go. She took the lead.

Faint whispers lured them deeper down the hallway but still

they found no one. Tricky echoes bounced from upstairs to downstairs, from left to right. The sounds skipped around an unending carnival maze of metal warehouse walls and tinny staircases. Tarian closed his eyes to stop the maddening disorientation of the sounds. He concentrated on a female voice muffled inside a distant room, and with his eyes closed he could more clearly identify its location.

Walking with eyes shut, the voices guided him toward an office that sat halfway between the warehouse floor and the upper story. The room hung in the air with a staircase connecting it to the downstairs, but no visible stairway led upward to where he and Audrey stood. Now having pinpointed the voices he opened his eyes and inched closer, carefully hugging the wall, following Audrey. Tarian bumped into her. He glared at her, but she returned his stare with unblinking, wide, worried eyes, and a heavy swallow stuck in her throat. He snapped his head around to gaze inside the office. What he saw froze every muscle in his body to rigid stone.

Delia's laughed. She tossed her head back, her long neck exposed until she whipped it into place with another laugh. Her face filled with joy, and her ocean eyes twinkled as she looked into the yellow eyes of Feng. Then she kissed him, and his hands left his side to find the small of her back and the crook in her neck. Their passionate embrace pierced Tarian's heart.

This scene contradicted the one from last night, and it sent waves of shock pulsating through Tarian's veins. He'd rehearsed how he would remain professional at the sight of her tortured body or even her death, but the sight of her in Feng's arms never occurred to him. He had no practiced response to cling to. He felt the floor under his feet disappear. He leaned against the wall for support.

Audrey turned and pushed Tarian's bulk backward toward the escape route, but he was an immovable brick wall. She persisted. He looked at her chocolate eyes bewildered.

She gently whispered, "The first betrayal always hurts the worst." Her many heartbreaks marked her face like bold tattoos.

He melted into her defeated, stunned, and immobile.

Audrey managed to nudge him, but he hadn't fully committed to leaving. She delicately slipped her hand in his, linked his fingers to hers and dragged him away. It worked. He retreated.

Careful to crawl back out the same window, she inspected it for traces of their blood or clothing but saw none. She guided him down the fire escape and a safe couple of blocks east of the building then she ordered another car.

The drive back felt like hours. They no longer held hands. They sat at opposite ends of the backseat, not touching or looking at each other. Even the driver could sense the thorny silence as he attempted small talk about the weather. The cold but sunny day only dampened Tarian's mood as it mocked his tortured heart.

Once at the apartment, he plodded straight to Audrey's balcony. She followed. She assisted him into a chair. She released a sigh of relief when he sat.

Did she think I was going to jump off the building? This life hadn't worn him down to that point, yet. Sure, he was overcome with sadness and confusion, but not desperation.

"I don't know what to say, Tarian," she said, a long pause followed. "We knew she admired him. She said as much in her blog."

"I know," he murmured.

The apartment door swung open. Audrey and Tarian jumped to their feet, both reaching inside their jackets for a weapon when they heard laughter. Maria and Gabe had sneaked home from work to check on them, laughing as always and carrying sandwiches.

"What the hell, you two!" Maria tossed the food onto the table. "We have all the boring work, and you don't. Spill!"

"Maria! Something happened," Gabe scolded. "You ok, Man?" He studied Tarian's distraught expression.

"Oh my God, Tarian. You look horrible!" Maria finally noticed his irritated eyes and red dotted face.

"Last night we saw Delia," Audrey explained.

"Tarian's Delia from home?" Maria asked.

"Yes." Audrey told the story from the blogs to the waterfall, to the bar, to the kiss.

"Harsh man. I'm so sorry." Gabe placed a thick hand on the back of Tarian's shoulder.

If Tarian had any feeling coursing through his body, Gabe's bear-sized hand would've consoled him, but he was numb.

"Well, what do we do now? What does this mean?" Maria punched her palm with her fist angered by Delia's betrayal. Like the rest of them, she was going stir crazy from the weeks of sitting behind the bland cubicle looking at fake pictures of fake people in their fake lives at their fake jobs. Maria's excitement for action burst from her aura even though her mouth frowned at her best friend's pain.

Tarian had remained silent for almost an hour while his friends tossed worried glances his way. They spoke in hushed voices and careful words.

Finally, Tarian snapped out of his trance. "Delia must be involved."

"I'm afraid I agree," Audrey said.

"She never trusted her father. She always spied on him and questioned him. She must've found out the truth of his immortality. Maybe she got angry. Maybe she learned I was immortal and got angry. She knew something at the village," Tarian said to Audrey.

"I don't know. It's hard to say. I felt a sense of envy as if she didn't like you going off on a mission without her," Audrey commented.

"Or *with you*," Maria stated.

Audrey jerked her head around toward Maria in objection.

"Yes, I felt it too," Tarian said ignoring Audrey's overreaction. "I knew she was uneasy. I just thought she was worried about me. It still makes no sense. I spent an entire year with her after Dad died. I know she knew nothing then. She couldn't have had anything to do with my father's death. It doesn't fit." Thoughts mixed like unsettled weather patterns. The rain stopped, the clouds parted, and clear skies formed only to be darkened again with more rain and clouds. More questions.

"I agree. I don't think her involvement happened until after Joe's death. Maybe after you went to EMA. She could've felt isolated or left behind," Audrey said.

"Like she felt now when you left with Audrey on this mission?" Gabe opened the bag of sandwiches and took a huge bite.

Tarian smiled at his friend—never one to let his emotions get in the way of a good meal.

"Or somehow Feng got to her. Who knows what lies he's told her? Let's give her the benefit of the doubt. She's a young woman. You abandoned her in a sense," Audrey said glancing back and forth from Tarian to Maria. "I mean EMA doesn't permit much communication. You had two weeks over Christmas, and then a few weeks over summer, then the attack. Now you've vanished. You're asking her to wait. That's tough."

"I know you're trying to make her look less guilty, but she's very intelligent. I've always sensed a distance between her and her father that didn't exist with her mother or brother. And as much as I love her, she has a spiteful side. Knowing others are immortal and she isn't could piss her off," he said still outwardly calm but inwardly frantic.

"Knowing *you* are immortal," Maria emphasized.

"Yeah, but her involvement came later. I'm sure of that. We were inseparable that year. I would've seen something or sensed something, but the blogs. It's all right there. What I've read, the hidden codes. I see it now," he said to Audrey who'd read them all too. The pieces of the blog puzzle that didn't make sense cleared up.

"What does it matter *when* she got involved? She's involved, and we need to tell Eleanor. Let's go." Maria bounced on her toes.

"Yes, let's go," Audrey conceded. "I have to get this evidence to Headquarters." She turned the vials over and over in her hands. "And we need surveillance on Delia and Feng."

"You can't reach Eleanor," Tarian reminded Audrey.

"It's okay. I'll be able to soon. We just need to get to the train before we get caught."

Audrey took charge of the group. "Maria, you and Gabe go straight to see John. Explain to him what's happened. Tell him we need a tail on Feng and Delia 24/7. Got it. Take shifts. If Zachary shows up, tail him also."

"Got it," Maria said.

"And these are Eleanor's orders not mine. Understand?" Audrey leveled her gaze square into Maria's hazel eyes.

"Got it." Maria smirked.

"No. We can't lie to our team," Tarian protested.

"Why not?" Maria asked.

"Tarian, we've waited long enough. Something's not right," Gabe said.

"I don't like it. I don't like any of it. I don't want to leave you guys behind," Tarian said.

"We have to get the information to Headquarters in person as fast as possible, and we need people here we can trust. Who can we trust more than Gabe and Maria?" Audrey asked.

"Go Tarian. I got your back," Gabe said.

Maria shoved Audrey and Tarian out of the door and reassured them several times that they had it all under control.

Audrey and Tarian caught the northbound train with the evidence tucked safely inside her jacket pockets. In a few hours, they'd board the tiltrotor that would bring them back to Quebec District, then the car to Guardian Headquarters. Four torturous hours sitting next to Audrey, trapped in a passenger car, scattered with worn out people. The two of them had gone over every possible explanation, yet he worried nothing had been solved.

Tarian turned his head away from Audrey and watched the buildings roll by faster and faster. His anxiety mounted the further away the train sped from his friends and Delia. His forehead leaned against the icy window sending shivers rippling through his body, but his mind burned hot and active. Memories of his dad's funeral flooded into view, and he tried to remember the entire event, to piece any clues together. He scoured his memory for even the tiniest of details to find a more reasonable solution than what he'd seen with his own eyes. Every fiber inside his body yearned to talk with his father, to know what he'd known.

Sleep stole up on him without warning. His forehead stuck to the window, pulsating clouds from his breath growing and shrinking on the glass. Audrey gently placed a pillow between his face and the window then attempted to sleep as well.

TWENTY-FOUR

DREAM TARIAN

Tarian's smudgy, faded dream body stood over an empty hole where his father would be laid to rest. Unlike the real hole that Tarian's conscious mind remembered, this dream hole dove down for miles, deep enough to stack a hundred bodies one on top of the other. It felt strange to be dreaming while being aware of dreaming.

Tarian glanced around the cemetery and spotted a true memory exaggerated by dream enhancements. The green of the leaves gleamed an unnatural margarita hue, and the branches swirled fantastically until they reached the curling pink clouds of the sapphire sky. Day was night and night was day—a place without time.

Even though the ground he stood on and the sky he looked at seemed impossible, his thoughts remained logical. He thought just as he had the day of Dad's burial, focusing on the irony of an estate attorney not having a life insurance policy. That was Dad's job: planning peoples' lives so they could keep their money for the future or their children's future. Tarian guessed that he was too busy planning other peoples' lives and falsely assumed he had more time to plan his own.

Tarian had a flashback inside a flashback, which mocked his conscious mind, yet he still didn't wake. As he teetered on the edge of the hole, he remembered his teenage years spent at the law offices. He recalled his father's first law partner, the ancient Mr. Jones, who walked with a cane. Mr. Jones materialized and hobbled over to peer down into the pit. Mr. Jones ignored Tarian. Tarian reached out to touch his elderly, translucent skin.

"Stop it, boy." Mr. Jones' spittle flew from his lips.

Tarian withdrew.

"I told you not to go behind the waterfall. I told you Zachary's girl was no good for you," Mr. Jones spat.

Tarian, too befuddled, didn't wipe the spit from his face. He tilted his head and furrowed his brow. "This didn't happen before. You never said anything like that."

"What?" Mr. Jones yelled.

Tarian said nothing. Mr. Jones wouldn't hear him. The device filling his ear had never worked. He may have been deaf but he had a thick nest of hair curled on top of his head, white as copy paper. Then his hair unraveled into paper banners.

Banners that read, "Enjoy your retirement Mr. Jones," flew like birds across the dream sky. The banners circled around Tarian's head like snakes in flight then dropped into the hole disappearing into the blackness of its depth.

Mr. Jones effervesced. In his place floated the smiling, smooth face of Roman Feng. No body just a giant, friendly face. Tarian laughed with Roman, just as he had in the past. Tarian remembered how happy he was when Roman replaced Mr. Jones.

The dream shifted again. The scenery remained the same, but the events changed from funeral to retirement party to a celebration for Roman. A man stood behind a podium and began to recount all of Roman's accomplishments.

"Roman Feng graduated from Stanford Law School at twenty-four. He landed the most high-profile, lucrative case inside the Industrial Science District, Xia Technologies Inc. vs. Marybeth Feng. His aunt netted twenty million dollars, and he became the most sought after attorney in the Entente. Somehow Joe got him to leave the Xia community and work for Prescott and Jones, PA." The man's voice boomed without a microphone.

The crowd roared with applause.

The mobile on Tarian's wrist buzzed just as it had two years and eight months ago. His brother, Charlie, messaged him to come inside the den of the funeral home. Charlie was handling the well-wishers with ease and charm, but now it was Tarian's turn. Tarian observed the reception, his back against the wall. His mom accepted the many hugs doled upon her: big bear embraces, small gentle pats, and formal cheek kisses.

All the caring people turned to stare at Tarian. They wore sympathetic looks and spoke kind words, but each word floated through the air and morphed into tiny hornets that stung him. The poison swelled into tiny bumps, but he didn't care. He studied each face. He recognized all of them, whereas before when he was seventeen, he'd not known these people. All the faces belonged to Guardians he'd recently met in person or seen in photographs. Once again, his conscience filtered into his dream, yet he remained asleep.

In an instant, Tarian stood at the edge of the gaping hole again. His father's casket lowered into the bottomless black space. Once the casket disappeared all the guests vanished.

"No!" Tarian yelled. He paced the edge of the hole. Threw his hands in the air. He turned to see only his family. He looked into his mother's eyes. "I saw him."

"Saw whom?" Carolyn asked.

"Dad's killer."

Tarian's family, along with Roman, circled the gaping pit holding hands. Without warning they all jumped, forcefully hurling Tarian in with them. Fear flashed within him. His body outside of his dream jumped, but his mind remained asleep. He fell into pure darkness and came out into the yellow light of the kitchen inside his childhood home.

Without reason or logical explanation, he sat with his family at the table. The fact that the violent leap into the hole took them to the serene chairs at the breakfast table seemed perfectly reasonable to everyone, including Tarian. Again Roman's presence brought warmth and peace.

Exactly as it had happened two years and eight months ago, Joe's will was read, and the memorandums handed out. Tarian received Dad's favorite novel *The American* by Henry James. Tarian had read the book and didn't like the ending at all. He never really understood why Dad liked it so much, but he was grateful to have it. Dad had written in the margins and dog-eared some pages. Even a chocolate stain smudged page one hundred and five. Tarian ran a finger across the brown mark.

Charlie got Dad's first law book that also had little characteristics of Dad's personality hidden throughout the pages. Teresa, the sister born after Tarian, got a very old, gold, and emerald ring that had been in Dad's family since the 1500's. The ring looked like a wedding band, but Dad never spoke of it. He just kept it securely in his bedside table drawer.

Chloe, Tarian's youngest and closest sister, who was sitting on pins and needles for her memento, received the Teddy Bear. She knew she'd get the bear and couldn't wait to hold it. Roman gently handed it to her with a wink. In her seven-year-old mind, Daddy was up in heaven with Trigger, their Labrador, and they were playing fetch like they always had.

Roman handed Joe Jr. a beautifully gilded knight's sword from Queen Elizabeth's court. The sword usually hung in Dad's office.

The ordinariness of what transpired inside Tarian's dream returned to the abstract. The kitchen table became a flying merry-go-round. They each sat atop a life-size teddy bear, whirling and bouncing. Tarian's book *The American* and Joe Jr.'s sword glowed neon yellow and levitated in the air inside the spinning ride.

The carousel jerked to a halt when Audrey appeared. She'd stabbed the heart of the machine with Dad's sword. Charlie leaped from his teddy bear to take Audrey's vacant arm, and together they strolled down a sidewalk. The family and Roman followed. Charlie and Audrey engaged in an intimate conversation, faces locked on one another and bright cherry mouths hovered mere millimeters apart, as they lead the group back into Tarian's childhood home.

Tarian stood heavy and mute while his other family members appeared carefree and floatable.

"Go to your room," ordered Charlie.

Tarian went and sat in solitude for what felt like hours. Every person and every thing inside his dream vanished. He lay on the black comforter covering his bed, alone and tired.

Tarian's mother faded in and out until she materialized in his room. She sat next to him on his bed. She spoke in her real voice and existed without dream alterations of color and substance.

"Your Dad has special plans for you and Charlie. Plans I wasn't even aware of." Her makeup smudged around her eyes as they puffed with tears.

"What kind of plans?" Tarian asked, but he knew the answer. He'd already had this conversation with his mother the night of the funeral.

"He arranged for you and Charlie to live with Senator Eastwood and his family," she said.

"No," Tarian stated.

"That was my immediate reaction too, but your father's

wishes are quite clear."

She handed Tarian two handwritten notes one addressed to Tarian, and one addressed to Charlie both signed by Dad. His intentions and reasons were plainly stated and hard to contest. Official, typed legal documents followed Dad's note. Obviously, his dad thought it best for the family. He trusted his dad more than anyone. Dad never made a move without thinking it through. In fact, Tarian refused to play chess with him after he turned twelve because he never won and knew he never would.

"I read through everything, and I feel the Eastwood's can give you a lot more than I can at this time. He's a very powerful man, and he's one of Joe's closest friends. Plus, you and Delia are very close, and Charlie practically lives over there with George anyway. Luckily, I finally got my real estate license last year, and now I can put it to good use. I have enough money saved up to work from home. Once I sell a couple of houses, it'll be fine. Without you boys, my grocery bill will be a lot less." She babbled on, trying to convince herself she was doing the right thing. The tears reappeared at the end of her last sentence.

The tears brought the abstract back into his dream. Carolyn's teardrops became a river that swept Tarian away from her.

He screamed as he floated on the swift current, "It's going to be okay. I'll go live with the Senator. It'll all be fine!"

Terror struck him as the waves crashed into his back causing his sleeping body to jump. Inside his dream, he tumbled somersaults in the water. The violent force of the flow poured Tarian onto a gigantic chessboard. He stood dry and on the board in the position of the pawn directly in front of the queen. Queen Audrey and King Charlie stood behind him. Mother and Teresa set in the bishop positions, and Chloe and Joe Jr. were rooks. Gabe and Maria sat on top of bucking black stallions. On the opposing side stood Senator Eastwood's family. Zachary and his wife occupied the king and queen squares while Delia and her brother George posed as bishops. Strangers sat upon the white horses. The end rooks, Roman and Dad, stared him down.

Tarian shot two spaces forward. He wore his EMA gray jacket with black collar, as did the pawn directly across the board from him. The game began and pieces whizzed passed him at lightning speed.

Soon his father knocked him over and screamed, "Get out of here! Don't trust the babies!"

"What?" Tarian asked, still down on the floor and completely confused.

The pawns morphed into crawling infants. Adorable big round eyes and plump bodies inched toward him, and he wondered what he had to be fearful of until blood red droplets dripped from their fanged teeth. A scarlet pool rolled toward him, covering the black and white checkered spaces on the chessboard, spilling over the sides like a wicked crimson waterfall.

"Get some rest Tarian," his mother said, no longer standing as the queen on the chessboard.

Ferociously looking around, Tarian saw that he'd returned

to his childhood bedroom, nightmare to dream just like that. No blood. No babies. All was as he'd remembered the night of the funeral.

"I plan on sleeping in and doing absolutely nothing tomorrow," his mother said with a small smile. "This is yours."

She handed him EMA paperwork, Dad's handwritten note about his future at EMA, and the nomination letter obtained from Senator Eastwood to endorse his application. All the other requirements and forms nestled in a file, neatly organized.

Tarian pulled several unfamiliar photographs from the file. A piece of white paper with his father's writing stuck to the photos. It had an equation on it. The numbers and letters wouldn't stay still. They danced across the page.

"Stop!" Tarian ordered.

The train stopped. Tarian awoke. The haze of temporary amnesia set in, filling his brain where his thoughts had just been. He scrambled to recollect the images. The faces he'd so easily recognized were now mere shadows. He'd seen some clues in his subconscious, but now they'd disappeared. Only eerie feelings of mixed emotions lingered.

"Oh, you're awake." Audrey entered the cabin. She carried two bottles of water and an assortment of nutrition bars. "It's important we hydrate, and I thought we should eat a little something."

Tarian's thoughts shot to the Guardian Headquarters' kitchen upon seeing the unsatisfying bars of food. His stomach growled.

"Damn it," he said.

"What is it Tarian?" she asked.

"It's gone, and I can't get it back. Now I'm focused on food," he grunted, discouraged, his stomach rumbling.

"What's gone?" Her brow furrowed.

"Why are we stopped?" He noticed the absence of the vibration.

"We're at a station. It's not our stop yet, though," she explained.

"How much farther?" He gulped the water.

"We're the next stop. What's gone?" she asked again.

"My dream," he sighed.

"Oh," she murmured, turning to face forward and unwrap her bar.

"No, it's not just any dream. It was like a vision. I was back at my father's funeral, and it didn't make sense. It made sense to me in the dream. It was clear who the killer was, and it wasn't Roman, but now it's vague," he rambled.

"Roman? You've never called him Roman before. In your dream was he your friend." She nitpicked details like a veteran detective.

"Yes, no, I mean he's better than Dad's old partner, Mr.

Jones. Roman's young, energetic and very intelligent."

"Smart enough to create Death Serum."

"Perhaps, but that wasn't the feeling I got. It was all so perfect while I was asleep."

"You said you knew who the killer was?" She leaned in.

"Yes and no. I just remember seeing his face at the funeral reception, and I knew he was guilty. But now I only have the feeling, not the face." He slumped back into his seat.

"You can't force it out of your subconscious. Relax. It may come back to you."

The familiar and oppressive energy that had burdened him for so long after the funeral returned to his shoulders. The revisited past slid under his skin weighing on him like an unwanted spirit. He closed his eyes, rested his head against the bench and waited for the ride to end.

TWENTY-FIVE

HISTORY

The tiltrotor descended onto the blanket of freshly fallen snow covering Battlefield's Park. Tarian tightened his grip on the handle above his head and steadied his breathing in an attempt to settle his stomach. Audrey, not holding onto anything, glanced at him and smiled. Humiliated, he let go of the handle. Seconds later, after a rather turbulent shift of the aircraft, his hand shot back to the trusty grip. Audrey's shoulders bounced. He knew she was laughing at him.

The same dark green, unmarked sedan sat empty and frigid as they entered it, and again, the engine started after a little encouragement. Thoughts of his last trip into the village washed through him. He'd discovered unbelievable facts about himself and the secret society of immortals he belonged to. What mind-blowing information would he learn today about Delia?

The familiar roads now narrower with more snow squeezing the banks closer together wound around the city just as he remembered. He recognized storefronts and predicted the winding turns before they tossed him to one side or the other. The sedan crossed the threshold into the quaint magical village and zipped inside the mouth of Guardian Headquarters' garage.

Two female Guardians dressed in green uniforms awaited as they exited. The two women hugged Audrey and shook Tarian's hand. "Welcome back, so good to see you. Come, come, Eleanor is waiting," said the blonde-haired lady.

The brunette's hand pressed on Tarian's back, gave a slight shove, and moved him forward into the elevator. She pressed button six. The elevator doors opened to find Eleanor standing stiffly in front of them. Her boney shoulders acted as precise hangers for her pristine white lab coat covering her thin frame. Her long, gloved hands took the vials of evidence Audrey and Tarian carried. Without words, she turned on her heels.

Inside the lab, purple people placed the liquid from the vials onto glass slides and peered at them. Others dribbled the clear droplets into test tubes immediately transforming them into a rainbow of colors. A human test subject sat in a sterile chair awaiting injection if necessary. Eleanor and her staff worked like buzzing bees but made no sound. Tarian looked questioningly at Audrey, but she wore a blank face. They waited and waited and waited.

Finally, Eleanor walked toward them with her tablet. She showed them the encrypted codes, which meant nothing to the unskilled eye.

Eleanor quickly explained. "None of the vials of solution are Death Serum or any sort of antidote. It's also not like our immortal DNA of any kind," she said with a straight face.

Tarian's heart leaped but his exterior remained as calm as Eleanor. He hoped this meant Delia had zero involvement with the murders.

"Then what is it?" Audrey asked.

"One seems to be some sort of painkiller but unlike any common analgesic. This particular painkiller is highly complex. It seems to repair cells, reduce inflammation, and sedate the mind all in one. In my opinion, this pharmaceutical is used after being injected with the first vial. The first vial is still evasive to our tests but when mixed with sample DNA, it rips it apart."

"Is it a virus?" Tarian asked.

"No. It's synthetic, man-made. I don't think it has been perfected either. It does not fix, repair, change the DNA, but it does add biomarkers tags to the nucleotides. Further study will be necessary. So far the test results are inconclusive," she said.

"You've only mentioned two. What about the rest?" Tarian asked. He looked at Eleanor hoping to gage some indication of her true suspicions, but her icy expression revealed nothing.

"Patrick, any change in J or K yet?" Eleanor called over her shoulder to her lab assistant.

"No," Patrick responded.

"Inconclusive." Disappointment at her failure crossed her pale face.

"What does this mean? What are Roman and Delia up to?" Tarian asked.

Before Eleanor could answer, a man walked into the lab to announce the arrival of Senator Zachary Eastwood. Audrey looked at Tarian. This was it, time to discuss their findings with him. Audrey had already lectured Tarian to treat this as any other investigation and warned him not to make it personal on any level.

After Eleanor spoke to Patrick, she removed her lab coat and with a flick of her telekinetic wrist, it obediently placed itself on its designated hook. She wore her deep violet pantsuit and stiletto heels. Her respectable attire reflected her power as Chancellor.

They met Senator Eastwood one floor below in a plainly decorated conference room. Eleanor showed him the lab reports. He was in a navy business suit making Tarian's field clothes look out-of-place. But as Tarian watched Audrey take control of the debriefing, pride replaced insecurities. The field clothes had done the dirty work while the suits sat behind desks.

"As I told you before, Audrey, I have not had contact with my daughter since she left. She is an angry teenage girl who lashed out. She probably has no idea what she's gotten herself into," Zachary explained.

Audrey glared at him. The air inside the small room grew heavy. Without releasing Zachary from her stare, she continued, "I still don't understand why the location of Feng was an issue." She turned toward Eleanor stretching herself tall but dwarfed by Eleanor's height in heels. "Eleanor, you have people in the field, and you couldn't locate Feng? Meanwhile, Delia waltzes into his office and not only gets a job but some weird relationship with him."

Audrey's strong and insinuating voice made up for her petite size.

"Audrey, our people are spread thin. The Guardian's survival is top priority, but I also have the Prevallers to contend with. Your team of eight is large. Most of the missions are limited to two and are spread from the cavern system to the fusion power plants to the Wastelands overseas." She closed her eyes and released a brief sigh. "Nothing suspicious has occurred. We know their cause, but the true leader has not surfaced yet. These are terrorists we are dealing with, cowardly phantoms. The actual leaders of the Prevallers are still just a long list of possible suspects. Our information is not reliable. The duplicity of this situation travels far."

"You know who they are," Audrey said with a strong jaw and piercing eyes.

The muscles around Eleanor's mouth tightened a fraction of a millimeter, and for only a brief second, but it was a tell. Zachary twitched, noticing it too.

Audrey's body emanated intense heat, and Tarian took two steps back. He'd never felt her release such a furnace blast before, but then again, he'd never seen her lose control. Her stance and voice displayed a confident, self-restrained Audrey, but inwardly she was breaking.

"Eleanor, if you have information, the government must be informed. We are being attacked and a full-scale war is imminent. We have to work together. We cannot repeat the past." Zachary flipped his mobile over and over in the palm of his hands.

"What?" Tarian blurted out. "Eleanor, you're withholding

information from the Senator? And Audrey couldn't contact you?"

Eleanor pivoted in the direction of the door. "Tarian, Zachary, Audrey," she addressed them in precise, punctuated breaths. "I assure you I have every intention of working with the Entente, but I have nothing to share at this time. I'm needed back at the lab. Everyone get a good night's rest. We will adjourn this meeting and resume after breakfast tomorrow." She left without even a nod.

Audrey's shoulders slumped and she looked exhausted. Zachary folded his arms around her for as long as he could stand the heat. Tarian studied this embrace. Audrey didn't welcome it. It seemed like a gesture made out of habit rather than out of genuine concern and affection.

"Audrey, I know what you are worried about, but it is different this time. What happened *then* will not happen again." Zachary stood tall over her. His condescending tone matched the look of superiority in his eyes.

"What happened before?" Tarian was sick of being uninformed. He wanted answers.

"War of course! That's all mortals do. Kill each other."

"Stop it Zachary, there's a lot more to it," Audrey said.

Zachary smirked and began to leave the room.

"Wait a minute. I have a right to know. And I also want to know why you're so flippant about your daughter being involved with Roman." Tarian's nerves trembled inside his gut, but he forced his body not to shake. He refused to be intimidated anymore.

Zachary halted mid step. He turned a stern eye on Tarian. "Year after year, century after century, I have protected this great nation. I helped build the Entente after the war. Piece by piece, the Guardians helped the people of North America unite, close the borders, and become financially independent and productively resourceful. No little girl, not even my brilliant daughter, can bring down my success. Ludicrous! I'm wasting time explaining myself to you. If you need answers go to the damn library." Zachary didn't wait for anyone to respond. The door slammed shut behind him.

Audrey sunk into a chair and covered her head with her hands.

"We've learned nothing!" Tarian blurted then noticed Audrey. "What is it? What are you thinking?"

She said nothing. He placed a supportive hand upon her shoulder, but she pushed it away. Standing next to her for several minutes, he felt helpless and angry. He silently slipped out of the room.

Tarian tromped through the crooked halls, walked down two flights of stairs. He entered the library intent on finding more answers. The familiar chill mixed with the tranquility of people silently reading comforted him. The busy laboratory combined with the whirlwind of the last few days had caught up to him. All he wanted to do was search for Piper and relax in the cozy chair by the fireplace.

He trudged the long corridor to his destination but no Piper. "Piper," he whispered. "Piper!"

"Tarian," Piper squealed, appearing from nowhere as usual. She wrapped her arms around him, hugging him with such force that he felt pain.

"Hi." He hugged her back then pried her off of him.

"You're back. I missed you. How was it? What happened? Do you want coffee?" She disappeared before he had a chance to answer any of her questions. Reappearing seconds later with a steaming cup of coffee, she shoved the cup into his hands.

"Thank you." He inhaled the sweet aroma then sat in the big, leather chair and set his cup on the table.

Piper didn't sit. She pulsed with energy above him.

"Please sit down Piper. You're making me nervous."

"Oh, sorry." She obediently sat, legs crossed, in the giant chair, rocking back and forth.

"Our mission was a success." He wasn't sure why he'd lied. Disappointing her exuberant face seemed cruel.

"Where is he? The Killer?" she asked.

"Well, we're watching him." He paused to gather his thoughts. "Piper can you please explain to me what happened during the Entente War."

Piper's perpetual movement suddenly stilled, and she focused on Tarian.

He'd never paid noticed to the lavender color of her eyes. He wondered just how powerful she was.

"I'm sorry Piper, but I need to know the truth, not what I learned in my history books at school. I need the Guardians' version of history."

"Okay," she said back to her perky self. Again, she was gone, then back with a stack of books two feet high. "Here, everything you need to know."

Tarian thumbed through a book entitled *The Mind Ring*. The stack in front of him would take him days to read.

"Piper can you please summarize for me what these books say?" Tarian utilized his best puppy dog eyes.

Piper jumped to her feet visually stressed, like an exploding firecracker shooting around the room. Then she stopped. "Oh, Tarian. It was a horrible time, horrible. Blood, lots of blood. Frankie." Piper sniffled.

"Was Frankie a friend of yours?"

"Yes. We lost so many friends."

"It's okay. I'll read the books."

"No, I can do it. I want to tell you. Well, first off we have come so far since then, so far. The United States government was bad, very, very bad. It had taken over completely. All the states of the United States no longer had rights. The federal government controlled everything, like a dictator. It pushed us away. The Guardians had always been there to help, to give advice, but the government had turned into a giant monster that listened to no one. Whatever it said was the law, no questions asked. No Congress, no free will, no checks and balances, no different branches, just one big tree!" She'd been still through her entire speech, but it seemed to be too much for her. She needed to move. She zipped up and down the corridors asking all library patrons if they needed anything.

Piper was incapable of long periods of serious conversation. That's okay. He'd wait it out. Four chapters later, she reappeared ready to relate more historic facts.

"It was years and years of oppression," she continued.

Tarian had to refocus his brain to keep up with her.

"Four presidents came and went. We, the Guardians, became neutral observers for many, many years, but we had critical information. Eleanor, she wouldn't get involved. No, no. She was so mad." She rocked some more.

Piper's eyes were not present. She looked at something unseen, a memory, Tarian guessed.

"And …" he coaxed.

"And the United States government had become corrupt. Elections were corrupt. No diversity of ideas. Every aspect of life from education to healthcare to sports was federally controlled. The continent's resources were not being used. Awful, awful, awful." Piper shook her head violently.

"It's okay, Piper. You've told me enough. I can read the books."

She smiled a very mature and un-Piper-like smile. "No, I have to tell you. It's my job. We were making nothing. No industry … this vast land … brilliant people … everything was being imported … inflated prices," she paused, breathless. She looked as if she would explode if she had to say one more word.

Audrey's voice reached the room before she did. "The

government lobbyists had thwarted all rational and profitable uses of our resources. Everything was imported and heavily taxed."

"And it wasn't as if these imports were superior. No, no. Everything was worse than before and cost more money," Piper interjected.

Audrey continued, "Yes, Piper's right. Finally, the states and people had had enough, and an uprising was inevitable. In fear of losing control, the government created a mind control ring. A striking piece of jewelry that had been disguised as a badge of honor and to be worn strictly by the highest-ranking members of all of the United States military branches." Audrey held up the book on the top of Tarian's stack, *The Mind Ring*.

"And the Guardians knew about this ring?" Tarian asked.

"We did," she said, with a sigh of hindsight knowledge.

"We more than knew," Piper said.

"So the government turned its military on its people," Tarian added.

"Yes, but humans are clever. They evolve and adapt and become suspicious. The most brilliant minds of North America fought back. Other nations stepped in and gathered territories. Too many lives were lost and too much progress destroyed before the Guardians finally got involved," Audrey paused, and her gaze dropped to the floor. "The violent deaths I witnessed haunted me for many years."

"It was our fault. We did it." Piper's hand flew to her mouth. She had told him a secret.

Audrey glared at her.

"The Guardians created those rings, didn't they?" Tarian asked.

"And they stole them from us," Piper said.

"Yes, we created the rings, and now we had to destroy them. We had followed this evolution and knew whom we wanted. We knew whose capable minds we needed to put an end to this war."

"An end to the government dictatorship," Piper interrupted.

"Yes, to end the government that had grown too large and uncontrollable and start fresh."

"We closed our borders," Piper once again interrupted.

"We secured our natural resources. We put people back in charge of their lives. We gave them their independence back. We formed the Entente of Nations, creating a solid and united continent. The people owe their prosperity to us, the Guardians."

"But we waited too long," Piper said eyes downcast, voice soft.

"Maybe we did," Audrey agreed.

"What do you mean?" Tarian asked.

"Since we'd waited so long to interfere, the war got severely out of control. It took several more years to retrieve every ring, and we had to kill almost every government official."

"We killed Frankie," Piper said now rocking violently back and forth.

Audrey paused and smiled softly at Piper. Piper's rocking

slowed and Audrey continued. "The rebuilding of the Entente took decades and now to see it threatened. You see, the people have forgotten. The men and women of that generation have either died, or they're way too old to remember. But we can't die, and we don't forget!"

"It's a curse," Tarian whispered.

"No, don't say that," Piper gasped.

"The secrecy and Eleanor's aloofness is concerning," Audrey added. "I went back to the lab, and Eleanor wasn't there. She and Patrick were somewhere else. I just don't know where. They're up to something."

"I've been thinking about what she said about the vials. It's like medicine. It must have to do with Delia's illness. I know it's connected, but how?" Tarian pondered.

"I agree. But Delia is still working with our lead suspect. She's guilty of something."

"She's only eighteen."

"It's the young that are impressionable," Audrey said.

"And recruitable," Piper added.

TWENTY-SIX

WAITING

Audrey and Tarian sat at the breakfast table in Headquarters' charming eatery with stacks of fluffy pancakes, bulging with blueberries and oozing pure maple syrup. Tarian hadn't touched his food. He thumbed through the pages of the book his dad had left for him when he died. He concentrated on the writings in the margins but had come up with no hint of condemnation of Roman, nothing to secure his guilty verdict.

The flashback haunted him. He couldn't shake the feeling that Roman was a good guy, but a good guy wouldn't kiss a girl, fourteen years his junior. He shook his head trying to remain objective, but the beast of rage and jealousy wouldn't tame.

Eleanor hadn't given an exact time for their meeting, but when she showed up, he'd better be well-fed, well-groomed, and ready to meet. Tarian swirled his fork in the sticky syrup, taking few bites. Unfortunately, he couldn't enjoy the fresh fruit or the hearty pancakes. However, the warmth of the coffee satisfied his senses.

Audrey also stirred her food instead of eating it.

An hour and a half later, Eleanor still hadn't arrived, but they'd managed to eat all of the pancakes, lingered over coffee and reminisced about EMA. Tarian wished he had more of a past to share with her. His curiosity about her past grew.

"Are you reading *The American*?" Audrey asked.

"Yes, Dad gave it to me. It was his."

"Where'd you get it?" she asked.

"I sent someone to the Inn to fetch it for me," he said.

"Why didn't you get it yourself?" she questioned.

"I don't know," he sighed. He'd slept in one of the empty rooms at Headquarters. He hadn't found the strength to visit his mother yet.

"I lived it," she said with a chuckle.

"What?"

"The book. It's your father's adventures. Joe was the hero of the story. He's Christopher Newman," she said.

"No way!" Tarian gasped.

"Yes," she laughed.

"Tell me about it."

"Good morning kids. I see you've been here awhile. Did you enjoy breakfast?" Chef Richard boomed after he slapped a friendly hand on Tarian's shoulder.

"Yes, excellent," Tarian and Audrey said in unison.

"You know your dad was a great cook. Use to come in my kitchen, and we'd cook for hours. He made a mean spaghetti sauce.

Would stink up my kitchen with garlic for days. And all without magic."

"Yeah, he did make great spaghetti. Sunday nights were always spaghetti night." Tarian smiled broadly.

"*The American*, oh my goodness," Chef Richard laughed. "Do you know Henry James wrote that book about your father?" He laughed uncontrollably. It was infectious and soon both Audrey and Tarian joined in.

"Ok, I need to know the story," Tarian said.

"You tell him, Audrey."

"Well, Joe had gone gallivanting through Paris, and Henry got wind of the failed marriage proposal by eavesdropping on London gossip. Your dad first read about his horrible misadventures back here in Boston. Articles about 'The American' were being published in the Atlantic Monthly."

"Joe was so angry, salt in his wound," Chef Richard interjected.

"So he went straight to London to put a stop to this Henry James person who was capitalizing on his grief. Before long, Joe was feeding Henry's imagination, and the two were creating a novel together."

"That's unbelievable." Tarian grinned widely.

"We had so much fun that year in London. I hadn't been back since I was born," she reminisced.

"You were all there," he asked.

"No," responded Chef Richard.

"Of course," said Audrey, "Zachary too. We were not about to let Joe go off to Europe alone again. Not after the catastrophe of his first trip."

"So it's all true?" Tarian asked.

"Well, it's exaggerated."

"But the old woman, the mother, she'd rather her daughter go in the nunnery than marry Dad?"

"Yes, she was a horrible woman," Chef Richard added.

"She suffered for it, as she should," Audrey said.

"Died alone," Chef Richard whispered, drawing out the syllables for effect.

"It was rumored her ostentatious eldest son poisoned her just as she'd poisoned her husband. It was a bad time for Joe. She broke his heart. What was her name?" Audrey thought.

"Madame de Cintre," Tarian answered.

"Yes, but that wasn't her real name," she paused in thought, looked at Chef Richard for help but no name came to either of them. "I told him she wasn't the right woman for him. I told him Jeannette Renault was a hell of a lot more fun."

"Who?"

"Miss Noemie, her real name was Jeannette Renault. She had a zest for life but Joe was too proper, and she was too modern for her time."

"Wasn't she a prostitute?" Tarian asked.

"No, is that how you read it?" she asked.

Tarian nodded.

"No, she was a poor, socially ambitious girl that lacked all sense of appropriate behavior for her time," Audrey said, and Chef Richard nodded.

"Oh, I see."

"Excuse me, I can't leave Ralph alone in the kitchen for too long. I think I smell smoke," Chef Richard left the table in a flash.

Tarian and Audrey exchanged a look and a laugh. Tarian had actually relaxed, forgotten Delia, and had an enjoyable breakfast.

"Why do you have it now?" she asked.

"Not sure, really, but it was in my dream, and it seemed important. Luckily, Mom brought it when she was forced to evacuate Salem. She brought all of Dad's mementos." While he spoke, he rolled the book around in his hands and flipped the pages like a magician shuffling cards. "Dad wrote in the margins. I wondered if he left me a clue. I guess he was just sharing a part of his life with me. He probably expected you or the Senator to explain it all," Tarian said with obvious disappointment.

"I'm not sure. What did he write in the margins?"

"Not much. The only thing that may be a clue is a bank account number." He flipped to the page with the *Bank of Boston: 511-6298-2803-37*, written on it.

"Let's check it out," she said beginning to enter the information into her mobile. Then she grabbed his arm and led him out of the kitchen.

He snatched his warm mug of coffee before she whisked him away from the table and into the lounge area. Together they sat in front of a large computer. As she began to speak the banking number, Tarian noticed a large gathering of purple and green suits around the television. A very scared and beat up news reporter broadcast from the center of a city under attack. The reporter's hair pushed back by too many swipes of his hand. Dark red rake marks crossed his face from his mouth to his temple. He was covered in a thick gray ash that could only mean buildings were collapsing.

It took Audrey and Tarian seconds to recognize the city. Boston. Those were the streets they'd walked only yesterday.

Audrey firmly clutched his forearm and jerked him toward the exit. The two of them ran full speed toward the stairs, climbed the flights two steps at a time, raced down the hall, burst through the doors on the left into the reception area, then flung open the solid oak doors without knocking. Eleanor sat behind her computer and looked as if she hadn't slept at all. The stress of dealing with the elusive Prevallers, the emerging war, and the Guardians' mysterious traitor invaded her psyche, withering away her beauty.

"Eleanor!" Audrey yelled. "Oh my God! Thank God you're okay!" she gasped. "I saw the pictures! And you were late! You're never late! And none of this is making sense. What's going on?"

Audrey was the fittest person he knew, so her breathlessness was clearly from fear.

"I'm sorry, Audrey. Tarian. I've had to keep you uninformed because I did not know whom to trust. Yes, it is bad. The Prevallers have attacked the government building in Boston. The city is destroyed, and many of the Entente's Congressmen are missing. I do not know who is dead and who is alive. One thing I do know is Delia and Roman Feng are alive. They have not left the vacant seaport building."

"They must've known about the attack, so they stayed out of the city," Tarian thought aloud.

"Is our team safe?" Audrey asked.

"John, Warren, Sophie, and Keegan are all accounted for, but we still have not had contact with Gabe and Maria. They were surveilling the office buildings. I'm sorry Tarian," Eleanor said.

"What?" Quick, sharp breaths took over Tarian's lungs. He dizzied but his anger strengthened. "No! I can't lose them again!"

Zachary flung the door open in mid-sentence. "There's been another killing. Death Serum. Daniel Silsbury, he's gone." The Senator's coiffed hair askew, dark circles formed under his eyes.

"That means Delia and Feng weren't the assassins," Audrey said, keeping a clear head about her.

Jugular8's dad had been murdered. Delia had stayed with him. There had to be a connection. Tarian's mind wandered.

"Yes." Zachary turned to Audrey.

The Senator gave Audrey an interesting look that Tarian couldn't read. *Was he angry for her lack of concern over Daniel? Was he aware that he'd not thought of his daughter? Do I want to be immortal, to live through years of this turmoil and death, to become callous to the human struggle?*

"Audrey, get them here now," Eleanor ordered.

Audrey left the room. Tarian stood in place awaiting his instructions.

Eleanor yelled, "Go!"

Tarian ran down the hall catching up with Audrey. The two of them leapt up one flight of stairs to the communications room. She linked her secure mobile to the appropriate source and found the location of John, Warren, Sophie, and Keegan. She ordered them to capture Jack Silsbury, Delia, and Feng and return them to Headquarters as soon as possible.

"Do you think Eleanor knows about Jugular8?" Tarian asked.

"I don't know, but his dad's death is no coincidence. All of Joe's closest friends are being murdered. All of the people he entrusted with the secret of your birth. It's not random. Joe was up to something. What?"

Tarian had no answers to give her.

Audrey worked hard at the computer swiping her fingers across the screen and screaming in exasperation when her call to Gabe and Maria failed to connect. The haunting sound of a single dead note was all they heard loud and empty. NO ONE AVAILABLE!

Tarian crumpled into a chair.

Audrey turned toward him, concerned. "Are you going to be alright?"

"I don't really have a choice," he said.

"I know." Her voice softened to sympathetic.

"Do you have another request?" the computer asked.

"Keep searching," Audrey stated.

"As you wish," responded the computer.

They played a game of hurry-up-and-wait. The sterile, gray room glared benevolent, overhead light. Soulless liquid crystal and curved glass screens smudged with dirty fingerprints surrounded them. Misty images danced in the air with maps and places where Gabe and Maria should be, but even the latest tracking technology couldn't find them. They'd simply vanished. Their bodies dead or alive were gone.

The minutes turned to hours, and Tarian's stomach growled.

"You need food. We still have a couple of hours, and then I'm not sure Eleanor will let us interrogate them immediately."

"I know, but if I eat, I'll vomit."

"No you won't unless you want me to give you Sanoxine," she said with a smile.

"Uh no. Never again." He grabbed her into a headlock and gave her a noogie. Finally, his immortal strength matched hers and though she struggled she couldn't elude his teasing touch. For a moment, the chaos surrounding them was forgotten.

TWENTY-SEVEN

THE TRUTH

Audrey sat behind an intricately carved, antique desk in her office while Tarian attempted not to pace the rug in front of her as they catalogued clues they recalled from Delia's blogs. They scoured the pages of *The American,* searching for hidden messages from Joe. The bank account that matched the numbers in the margin of the book belonged to a Christopher Newman and had been closed after Joe's death.

"In my dream, I remembered all the items Dad left us vividly. Especially, the teddy bear he gave to Chloe. The funeral guests were the murdered Guardians. I'm sure of it. I can almost see their faces." Tarian closed his eyes and recounted. Parts of his dream came back in pieces. "Yes, the people hugging Mom were all Guardians." Tarian eyes stayed shut in concentration.

"That's good, Tarian. Focus."

"If all of Dad's confidants were targeted by the traitor, who's next?"

"Me, probably, or Zachary. Maybe even Eleanor." Audrey dropped her head to her desk.

"Why weren't you at the funeral?" Tarian asked.

She lifted her head. "I was. I just kept well hidden. Zachary forbade me to go, said it would interfere with his future plans for you at EMA. I didn't know the plans at the time. He snuck me into the academy that year."

"Of course he did." Tarian wrinkled his brow. "In the dream, I remember being surprised at my father's ill-planning just as I had been on the day of his real funeral. Now that I know he was immortal, I guess he never planned on his death. It just wasn't like him not to plan for the future. He over planned everything."

"He did." She smiled. "Annoyingly organized."

"I don't understand. Where's all of his money?"

"What do you mean?" she asked.

"We were sent to live with the Senator because we had no money."

"That's false," Audrey said.

Shaking his head he continued, "I think Dad and the Senator were in on this together. They were planning something." Tarian's eyes darted with memory. His head throbbed from the constant anxiety and focus.

Margaret stepped into the room and interrupted their conversation.

"They're here. You need to come at once," Margaret ordered.

"Thank you Margaret." Audrey jumped to her feet, hitting her knee on the edge of her desk. "Dammit, ouch!"

Together, they rushed downstairs to the fifth floor into a darkened room that felt more like a closet. They watched Delia from behind a surveillance mirror. She sat alone and clutching her frail body, terrified.

Tarian's heart skipped as it always did when he saw her beautiful face, but he didn't like the look of a trapped dog in her eyes. She shivered, her arms crossed as she rocked back and forth in her chair. Her hair was cropped shorter than it had been when he saw her sedated and strapped to the chair in the warehouse.

He recalled her morning ritual before school. She'd pull up her long straight hair into a ponytail. After what seemed like forever, she emerged from the bathroom, hair down, breathtakingly beautiful. He wasn't sure what she did behind that bathroom door, but her hair would be fuller and bouncier with a slight curl at the end that swayed as she walked. Mesmerized, he'd wanted to stare at the back of her head all day. That luscious hair was gone now.

Her once slender, regal frame downsized to sickly skin on bones. The circles under her eyes matched the circles under his, and he wondered if her sleep had been riddled with nightmares too.

Finally, someone brought Delia a cup of hot coffee and a blanket. She flashed her killer smile, and Tarian found himself smiling back at her. Caught up in his reverie, he'd forgotten the other team members in the room. They were evaluating her movements and appearance, discussing what she'd said and done on the trip to

Headquarters. But, he'd heard only muffled sounds that had no meaning, belonged to no one.

"Tarian!" Audrey said for the fourth time. She shook his shoulders. "Did you hear what Sophie said?"

"No." His eyes refocused and his mind returned to the present.

"Delia is still sick, very sick but she won't talk to anyone. Feng isn't talking either."

Audrey pushed Tarian ten feet over where he could peer into Feng's room. Roman had lost weight as well but carried a healthy complexion and stood strong. He didn't act scared. Instead, he looked defiant and determined.

Eleanor walked into the small room and gestured for Audrey and Tarian to follow her. She escorted them into the elevator where she used a special key to unlock the keypad. After entering a number, and having her face scanned and voice recognized, Tarian felt the elevator jerk and drop further than expected. They stopped far underground. Tarian followed Eleanor and Audrey through the damp cave-like hallway into a windowless room that had strange soundproofing materials on the walls, floor and ceiling. The cushiony floor crushed under his feet. On top of the cushion a haze of fog lingered, hiding his steps inside rippling rings of milky clouds. Tarian had never seen anything like it before.

Eleanor left the room and locked the door.

"She just locked us in here," he said, panic rising up in his throat and evident in his voice.

"It's okay," Audrey said. "This is the only place that's one hundred percent secure, silent, and magic free. We call it the Dead Zone."

"Well, that's comforting," he snapped.

"Look at your mobile." She waited for him as he tapped, swiped, and shook it. "See?"

The device was dead. None of the control functions worked. He'd used the mobile just a half an hour ago in the hopes of receiving information about Gabe and Maria's whereabouts.

"Okay. What does this mean?" he asked.

"I don't know," she answered. "All I know is that I completely trust Eleanor. If she's the traitor behind all of this, then I'd rather be dead."

"I don't think it's her. I know I don't know her very well, but my gut trusts her. It's just a feeling."

"I think she wants us to talk to Delia and Feng in here. I believe Eleanor knows who she can't trust but won't leak that information to anyone yet."

The click of the lock shot through the room like a hollow thump. All sounds harshly flattened by the weird, chevron wallpaper that melted onto the walls. He braced himself for whatever walked through that door. *Delia? Roman? Someone with a Death Serum syringe? We're trapped, vulnerable. No!* He shook away the paranoia and prepared to face the truth.

Tarian first saw the familiar blackberry suit and confident stride of Eleanor Dare. Behind her, barely visible, shuffled a figure with Delia's short dark hair. Delia still had the blanket wrapped around her and hung her head low. Eleanor locked the door behind them, and Delia jumped, glaring distrustfully. Roman didn't accompany them. Tarian's shoulders released the tension that had mounted in anticipation of confronting him.

Delia began to lower her head again, but then looked up. The strength returned to her as she stood taller, straightened her shoulders, and forced her head high. But it was her eyes that broke Tarian. Those giant dark and stormy ocean eyes reflected not evil, but despair, and they pulled him in like the voice of a Siren. His one step forward was enough momentum to drop her blanket. She looked as if she wanted something from him, but what? She teetered on the uneven floor, but she didn't seem unbalanced only unsure. Tarian took another step too nervous and confused to continue. He couldn't comprehend her involvement with Roman, but he saw her suffering.

She slowly walked toward him. Tarian stood still. She kept coming and embraced him. His mind screamed with anger but his body refused to push her away. He breathed in the sweetness of her sweat and began to feel muscle memories from happier days. She burst into tears, her body wracked with sorrow. Instinctively, he held her tighter. His arms had tripled in size since their first intimate hug over two years ago when she'd been the one to comfort him. She'd been the solid rock of security he needed after losing his father. Now it had all changed. He'd become a substantial man, a man that could fight, and a man that could engulf her, protect her.

Eleanor cleared her throat. Tarian glanced up and read her displeasure. He let go of Delia. The release felt more than just physical, it felt personally freeing. Suddenly his love for her had changed, as if the part of his soul she'd kept, but no longer deserved, ripped away when he let her go. She'd always have his past, but she no longer had his future.

"Delia, it's time to talk!" Eleanor stated.

"I don't trust you." Her eyes darted back and forth between Eleanor and Audrey. She turned to Tarian. "They've been spying on us. Testing on us!" Her eyes searched Tarian's for signs of damage.

"No one has been testing on me Delia." Tarian reassured her.

"He has." She sighed and closed her eyes as if she was exhausted.

How dare she think she's tired! They were all tired. Tarian's frustration edged closer to anger. "He who? Roman?"

"No!" She stated firmly, her eyes flew open in surprise.

"Roman killed my father." The words bit into his tongue like acid.

"Is that what she told you?" Delia gestured to Eleanor then turned accusatory eyes upon Audrey. "And you. You're in on it with the Senator."

Delia lunged for Audrey but stopped short when Tarian gripped her arm. Delia sharply looked at him then back at Audrey. She jerked her arm away.

"No Delia, you're confused. Audrey's been with me every

day for the last six weeks, and before that I saw her every day at EMA. You can trust her," he said gently. He needed to convince her to trust them, but Delia's faced paled with more malice. "Tell us what you know about Roman." He urged, surprised by his tranquil tone given her lethal stare. Eleanor smiled encouraging him to press further. "Roman's been making you sick."

"No, no, no!" She grabbed her head and squeezed, then continued in a soft, restricted voice. "You have it all wrong. Roman's trying to make me better. Father …" She couldn't complete the sentence. Her voice deadened and her eyes bulged with tears.

The random puzzle pieces fit together in Tarian's mind. He'd thought it. He and Audrey even spoke of it. But he'd refused to consider the possibility. His mind shut down each time he tried to convict the man that had been like a father to him. But time and excuses had run out and a chill of realization traveled the length of his spine. Little sparks burst and popped at every nerve ending burning his blood and igniting his rage.

"You knew," Tarian growled at Eleanor.

"Yes," Eleanor said.

"How long?" Audrey asked.

"I confirmed my suspicions after the team was established in Boston, but I did not have proof. I still do not know who is conspiring with him. I have told no one."

"You've always been a brick wall, Eleanor." Audrey sighed and shook her head. "So my meeting with him that night, did I screw it up?"

"At first I was devastated by your breach of command. You hadn't broken orders in centuries."

"What was I supposed to do? I couldn't contact you for weeks so I had to make my own plan," Audrey said then caught Tarian's glance and rephrased. "We decided to make our own plan of action. So you sent us communications?"

"Yes, I sent you updates. Zachary must have intercepted them. He was my liaison. I trusted him completely. When there was no word from you, I became suspicious. I waited. I was hoping he would make a mistake, but he didn't. I was so preoccupied in the lab and with other state of affairs that I lost track of time. Time has a different feeling for me. In hindsight, I realize how the waiting for you and Tarian must have been torturous."

"Delia, what's going on?" Tarian wanted concrete facts not feelings and speculation.

She hesitated.

"It's okay. You can trust us, all of us." He tried to mask his fury and convince her.

Eventually, she told her story. "After you left, that first year, I started getting sick. Mom couldn't figure out what was wrong with me, and the doctors said it was just a lingering virus. Over a year I suffered. Healthy one day, sick the next. One day when I was home from school and mom was out, I sneaked into Father's office. I was looking for information about the rumors I'd heard concerning a war, the Prevallers. Instead, I found a syringe and a lot of notebooks filled with scientific studies." She breathed heavily and cast her eyes toward the floor.

"Okay," Tarian coaxed.

"I even found vials of blood, one drawn from Carolyn," Delia paused and looked at Tarian.

He feigned surprise and kept quiet. He couldn't risk her knowing he'd read her secret blogs.

"One night, Father thought I was asleep and injected me with something. At first I assumed it was a medicine to help cure my illness, but then I came to the conclusion that it was what was making me sick in the first place. My own father was testing on me." She let out a wicked laugh. "It was horrible. My plan was to tell you over Christmas. Father's a powerful man. I couldn't just confront him. And I wasn't one hundred percent sure for myself. I needed you. I needed your advice. But then the attack happened." She frowned. "Your name was on a few of the data reports. I think while you were staying with us, he tested on you."

"But I was never ill," Tarian said.

"You wouldn't be if he *took* your blood instead of injecting you with serum," Eleanor said.

"Gary," he murmured.

"Who?" Eleanor asked.

"The physical trainer Zachary hired to get me into shape for EMA. He took my blood once or twice a month. He claimed I had an iron deficiency and gave me pills."

"Your DNA is valuable, Tarian. You are the first of our kind born in over five hundred years. The serum you gave me yesterday, the one that I told you was indeterminate, I decided to test it on the blood I'd gathered from you weeks ago. The results were unimaginable. The serum successfully duplicated your genome."

"What is Roman doing with a serum like that?" Tarian asked.

"He copied it from your dad's notes," Delia said.

"What?" Tarian asked.

"Joe was trying to understand why or how you exist," Eleanor explained.

"Roman was trying to help me," Delia said.

"Zachary is trying to duplicate the process that produced your birth," Eleanor explained.

"We don't need more immortals." Audrey paused glancing at Tarian. "Think of it. An army of immortals would be impossible to fight."

"Unless you had a Death Serum," Tarian said. "Do you think Dad created the Death Serum? Maybe he suspected Zachary."

"Roman found a secret vault with a lot of documents and studies that your dad had kept. He and I have been studying these together. That's when I learned what my father was and what you are." Delia stared at Tarian. "At first I was furious, I couldn't bear the thought of growing old and you remaining young and handsome. The life I dreamed to have with you had vanished. We couldn't get married and have children. How would that work? How did my father do it? He was going to leave us all, maybe divorce, maybe fake death, or maybe he'd just kill us, say it was an accident. What do you people do anyway?" She asked Eleanor and Audrey with the venomous tone returning to her voice.

"We are all free to live the life we choose to live. Some of us never become romantically involved with mortals, some of us do, but murder is not allowed," Eleanor said.

"Where are these papers? Half of Boston has been blown up!" Audrey refocused the conversation.

"They're not in Boston," she said. "There's a safe deposit box at Xia Bank in the Technology District. Roman is from there. He chose to hide the papers there. He wanted them as far away from here as possible."

"What about copies? You must have made copies," Audrey demanded.

"Yes. Some. Your people have everything we kept at the warehouse. We didn't keep anything at the office for fear of—well for fear of exactly what happened. Destruction," Delia said.

A dull thud came from behind the chevron-patterned material on the door. Eleanor answered it and brought in Roman. She also ordered her assistant to arrest Zachary Eastwood.

Roman rushed straight to Delia and wrapped her in his arms. He examined Tarian with a concerned expression. His honey-colored eyes softened and his strong jawline relaxed, but he didn't speak, and Delia lowered her head.

"So, what's this?" Tarian's composure broke. Mad energy coursed through him. "You found out what I am and that wasn't good enough for you." The poison seeped from his words, just as it had from hers. His wound reopened. He ached to see her in his arms.

"I found out what you were and knew we couldn't be together," she spat back at him.

"Thank you for making that decision for us," Tarian snarled.

"You had vanished!" she reminded him. "With her." She pointed at Audrey.

Audrey took the accusation with impenetrable stoicism, Tarian noted, impressed. The only hint that the claim angered her was a slight squint of her crystal blue eyes.

"We are getting off track," Eleanor interrupted. "I'm truly sorry for this abrupt reunion. This should be a private affair, but I'm afraid time does not allow us that luxury. Roman, I need you to tell me what you know. Then we will go upstairs and review the copies that you have. I've studied your counteractant. It isn't working, is it?"

"No. And she's getting worse. Her father's serum is like an agglutinogen, which is a type of antigen. Her cells adhere together but none of the antibodies I've used can repair the agglutination. I thought I was approaching this all wrong and treated it as if it was cystic fibrosis because it shows similarities being that a specific chromosome pair has mutated. But I've exhausted what I know, and I'm out of favors from my physician friends. They're beginning to ask too many questions."

"I'm impressed you've gotten this far, Roman," Eleanor said.

"In my community, our school requirements include two

years of medical training. Most of us are doctors but since I chose law, my medical education is very basic. I took only the required courses that would get me into Harvard Law School. Joe must've been a great scientist. His research was very well-documented. It was like having the best textbook to follow." Roman stroked Delia's back and asked, "You'll help her get better, right?"

"I think I will be able to help her," Eleanor said. "I'm sure those papers will clear up a great deal of confusion. Did any of Joe's studies or papers include a Death Serum?"

"Yes." Roman looked as if he was betraying the confidence of his best friend. "I didn't know what to make of that. I actually wondered if the Joe I knew wasn't who I thought he was. I thought maybe he was murdered because he deserved it."

Roman's words took Tarian off guard. Every day for weeks, Tarian had pondered who killed his father and why? He never once considered that his father deserved to die. Now that he suspected his father to be the developer of the Death Serum, that possibility needed to be addressed. He shivered at the thought.

Audrey placed a gentle hand on his shifting skin then turned her attention on Roman. "How did you know he was murdered? His cause of death was listed as a heart attack."

"I never believed that. In the days before he died, he confided some limited information to me. He left me the key to a safety deposit box at the Entente Bank of Boston listed under the name Chris Newman."

Tarian recognized the name, the hero in the novel *The*

American. He glanced at Audrey. She smiled and nodded. Delia scowled at her.

Roman continued, "I was to retrieve all items from the box and tell no one about them. His instructions were for me to store the items until Tarian graduated college. I wasn't to look at the contents." He focused his attention on Tarian. "I violated his request. I just felt I had to look. It certainly changed everything when I found out he was a member of a secret society of immortals."

"Exactly what is in the box?" Eleanor asked.

"His Last Will and Testament, a sealed note to Tarian, only. No other family member received one, which I assumed meant something. That I did not open." Roman nodded to Tarian with an honest smile. "A ten-page document detailing how to kill an immortal. He explains why his serum works and from what I can gather, he'd been attempting to develop it for a long time. Actually, at first I wondered if he used the serum on himself, committed suicide, but he loved his family too much to do that. It didn't make sense, and all his research seemed to allude to a greater threat. When I looked through the box, all I could sense was fear. Once I found out he was immortal, I realized whatever he had to fear must have been truly horrible."

"Why did you hide?" Eleanor asked.

"I didn't really. I had clients in Los Angeles, but I didn't hide. I did become somewhat of a recluse because of my suspicions. I rarely left my office. There's a hidden room where I spent most of my time. When Delia came to our office in need of an internship, I hired her immediately because I knew her father was a Guardian. The few notes on Senator Eastwood suggested Joe didn't trust him," Roman said.

"Then why did you let me and my brother go live with him?" Tarian asked.

"I didn't open the file for the first year. I tried to respect Joe's wishes, but I couldn't shake the feeling something was wrong," Roman said. "Then it took me another month to decipher all the information I was reading. There's no proof in those papers that Senator Eastwood is Joe's murderer."

"But you suspect him," Tarian stated more than asked.

"Yes, because Joe suspected he was helping the Prevallers, but it wasn't until Delia came to me that I realized the man is evil."

"Evil?" Audrey questioned.

Tarian knew from their previous conversations that deep inside her heart she'd never believe he was truly evil, just influenced by corruption. But Tarian believed. Roman and he now had three things in common: Dad's trust, Delia's love, and abhorrence for Zachary.

"What kind of monster would poison his own daughter?" Roman said bitterly.

"I didn't matter to him, or I wasn't good enough because I'm mortal," Delia spoke again, but this time her words were soft and weak.

Tarian remembered a strong, independent Delia, not a broken girl, but a father's betrayal would break any daughter.

Another knock on the door brought everyone back to reality. The crisis spun outside of the room, and they needed to address it. Delia was taken to the infirmary where Eleanor had given the doctors strict orders to keep her bedridden and full of fluids. Eleanor already had her scientists working on perfecting Roman's antidote. She then ordered Roman and Tarian to retrieve all of Joe's documents from the safety deposit box while she and Audrey interrogated Zachary.

TWENTY-EIGHT

XIA BANK

Tarian and Roman landed on a private landing strip and went directly into an unmarked vehicle courtesy of the Guardians of Dare. The bank wasn't far from the airport. However, the thick traffic moved like sludge through the sewer pipes, taking over an hour to go twenty miles. Stony silence descended upon them.

The Spanish Baroque bank stood only four stories high built over three hundred years earlier during the Wild West days of horse and buggies. The stucco exterior heavily swirled like thick buttercream frosting, and the windows recessed into the arched portals. The Spanish influence extended to the interior as well, with catacomb-like corridors inlaid with Sevillian glazed tiles. It smelled of old clay and fresh coffee, an anachronism among the tall, steel, and glass Xia buildings that surrounded it.

A stout, older woman with a harsh face and a sickly smell of flowers and powder welcomed them with a smile, but her frown lines remained in place. Her many wrinkles made her expressions difficult to read.

"Entente registered license please," the teller said in a rough, monotone. Roman produced the holographic image from his mobile. "That gentleman as well."

This made Tarian uneasy, but he produced his documentation.

Roman filled out the paperwork to allow their joint permission into the vault where the security boxes were stacked and available. If she or anybody else in the bank had any suspicions about them, they hid them well. This was a routine request for this bored teller, who'd probably opened thousands of safe deposit boxes and had asked for identification dozens of times every day.

After the formalities, the elderly teller left her desk and unsteadily led them down a long corridor to a thick vaulted door. Her unbalanced steps on the terra cotta tiled floors caused Tarian to brace for her fall, but she miraculously walked the full distance without a misstep. Tarian watched her arthritic fingers turn the old-fashioned dial to unlock the door. Everything seemed ordinary, but Tarian's nerves wouldn't stop pinging.

Inside floor-to-ceiling rows of small boxes, all with numbers, no names greeted them. Little secure havens for personal and business items, and Tarian wondered exactly what was in all the boxes. *Jewelry? Last Will and Testaments? Drugs? Perhaps something as miniscule as a small figurine, a memento of someone's history to preserve the memory of a lost loved one. Why not?* In a sense, he was there to retrieve a memory of a lost loved one.

His furious joy grew knowing he'd read his dad's letter. He steeled himself to the fact that the note may be intimately personal perhaps bringing tears and sorrow. The last thing he wanted to do was cry in front of Roman.

Roman went to box 428, one of the larger boxes among the many rows. He pulled out a bulky, legal-size file, filled three inches thick, and worn bare. Tarian envisioned Dad flipping through the pages several times, trying to figure out Tarian's existence, trying to keep his family safe from the predators at his door. He must've been ecstatic to find out his son would continue through the years with him. How disappointing it must have been to be slapped with the realization that in the wrong hands, Zachary's hands, birthing immortals could be fatal to the mortal race.

Roman quickly placed the file into his empty briefcase. After the box was obediently returned to its snug rectangular hole like a good schoolboy returning to his line, Roman carried out their mission while Tarian stood immobilized by delight, grief, and anger. Tiny droplets of doubt about his dad's guilt or innocence sneakily multiplied into rivers of uncertainty. *Why did Dad create a lethal serum?*

With a shove to the shoulder, Roman brought Tarian back to reality. He gave Tarian a look of brotherly wisdom. Suddenly Tarian's hatred for him gave way to memories of the old Roman, the fun Roman at the law office that pulled pranks on the staff and made Dad swear. It was hysterical to hear him curse. The graphic words came out stiff and awkward.

As they exited the thick, submarine-like steel door, Tarian

noticed the efficient but precarious teller discussing something with the manager in a hushed voice. The hair on the back of his neck stood up. Something was wrong. *Did Roman feel it too?* A sideways glance of Roman's yellow eyes and a reach into his pocket where his Guardian weapon hid, convinced Tarian they'd need to act.

Tarian's EMA and Guardian training kicked in. The security guard stepped toward them. With one quick move, Tarian disarmed him. Before the scared old teller could press the alarm, Tarian fired a shot. The bullet passed close enough to her hand that she retracted it, giving them enough time to open the exit door. The teller's hasty movement caused her to collapse to the floor. Tarian resisted the temptation to help the poor woman to her feet. No time for chivalry.

The car waited with its alert driver and the untraceable license plate.

"Thank you," Tarian whispered to himself, grateful for Guardian precision.

The bank chaos meant something at Headquarters had gone wrong. Once safely tucked into the back seat of the vehicle, his suspicious instinct reared with such force that he snapped on Roman. "How did they know?"

Before Roman could react, he was pinned against the back of the car seat, weapon taken, arms immovable and Tarian's forearm across his windpipe. Tarian could kill him with a quick thrust of his elbow, but instead he held just short of a life-threatening position.

"I don't know," Roman whispered. The pressure on his vocal cords made his words barely audible. Roman shook his head.

His honey-colored eyes went wide.

Tarian saw his panic and released him. He'd rushed to judgment but wasn't apologetic. He needed to know beyond a shadow of doubt if he could trust him, and it felt good to bully the man who stole Delia.

"Dammit, Tarian!" Roman choked out. "You've made your point." He coughed and rubbed his throat. "Do you think I want to be in this situation? Joe was my mentor. He meant everything to me. He trusted me! Why can't you?"

"It's not you. I don't trust anybody anymore," he said. "Not even my dad's memories are without suspicion."

"Don't forget who he really was, Tarian," Roman encouraged.

"We need to get out of here as fast as possible. Is the plane waiting for us?" Tarian asked the driver, avoiding talk of his father's moral compass.

"Yes," the driver said.

The gridlocked, rush-hour traffic made the trip to the airport unbearable. Cars on all sides trapped them in a mob of vehicles that moved sluggishly, inch by painstaking inch. Tarian felt claustrophobic.

"Can't this thing hover?" Tarian growled.

"Yes, but I have strict orders to remain on the ground," the driver answered.

"Why?" Tarian asked.

"Hovering is illegal on the freeway. Eleanor doesn't want

any unwanted attention brought to you."

"Too late for that. Get this vehicle in the air," Tarian demanded but the wheels remained on the asphalt.

Tarian spoke with Audrey twice. She assured him the aircraft hadn't been compromised, and they should be able to leave without incident. Her tone was too blunt, too much like Cadet Sergeant Gualtiero, and he didn't trust it.

"Is everything good at Headquarters?" he asked for the fourth time.

"I already told you it's fine," she answered quickly, too quickly. She was lying.

What was it? His family? Delia? Gabe and Maria? He hated being on the other side of the Entente.

TWENTY-NINE

THE LETTER

As usual, Audrey was true to her word. Roman and Tarian took off from the private runway without incident. The bank disturbance hadn't flagged them on any travel watch list. *Or maybe, this airport is strictly used by the Guardians of Dare?* Tarian figured if these people had been around for over six hundred years, they probably owned a lot of property.

The aircraft's luxurious interior had twelve oversized chairs, one typical aircraft bathroom, a steward station, and a small conference table. They settled in at the conference table and spread the contents of the file in front of them. The steep incline of the ascent to cruising altitude slid the papers, and they scrambled to contain them.

Roman organized the papers into piles. Scientific studies and lab reports went into one pile, while information about the Guardians went into another pile. Background information and opinions or intuition on government officials made up another pile.

Newspaper clippings from several wars throughout history and printouts from web sites on the looming war created another pile. Bank statements from accounts around the world, some opened hundreds of years ago, stacked up. The rest of the items lay to the left of the stacks: several safe deposit keys that Tarian assumed held treasured possessions collected throughout his dad's long life, along with the letter to Tarian, a paper thin, silver tablet, and finally a copy of the Last Will and Testament which he had seen previously.

"Read it," Roman said. "It's not the same one I read to you on the night of the funeral."

As Tarian skimmed through it, he noticed a life insurance policy. "My dad has a seven-million-dollar life insurance policy?" he asked.

"Yep. Kind of odd for an immortal right?" Roman said.

"Also odd that it would be kept hidden," he said, continuing to think out loud. "Unless the Senator didn't want us to know we had money. He wanted me in his house."

"And who did Eleanor say was the latest Guardian to die?" Roman asked.

"Daniel Silsbury," he recalled.

"Daniel Silsbury," Roman repeated, as he handed Tarian one of the bank statements. It was a joint account for Daniel Silsbury and Joseph Prescott opened four years ago.

"What's on here?" Tarian questioned as he picked up the silver tablet.

"Pictures, a lot of pictures, but nothing more. I don't think your father trusted putting his ideas on anything other than paper." Roman handed the sealed envelope to Tarian. "Read the note, Tarian. Maybe it'll offer more information."

Roman rose from the table and sat in one of the chairs facing the other direction to give Tarian as much privacy as possible in the confined space. Tarian knew he had to do it. He had to open the envelope. Dread and anticipation swirled in his gut like the first day of middle school.

Rip. Out spilled tiny white granules and a silver bracelet. He put the bracelet on and tested the granules. Salt? Then he dove in. The familiar handwriting on three pages sent a stab of longing through his heart. He'd recognize that script anywhere. Millions of individual letters could be scattered about, and Tarian would be able to choose without a doubt the one written by his dad.

Dear Tarian,

First, I must tell you that you are a true miracle. The day Carolyn gave birth to you, I knew you were going to be the one to capture my heart. You were a happy and contented child and grew to be a smart young man. You are truly special. What I'm about to tell you, you may already know because if you are reading this letter, then I have failed. It is my worst fear that I leave this world before you know the truth, and I ask for your forgiveness. You are a Guardian of Dare. You are an immortal just as I am. However, no immortals have been born since 1568. I have prayed for our lives to be forever joined in this impossible immortal madness. I did not want you to go it alone. It saddens me that you are reading this. I remember when I first found out who I was. All the questions I had and no family to guide me. It is a hard journey, but just as I did, you will meet many incredible people and it will be an amazing life for you. After all, I met your mother after only a few hundred years. You will see that you can fall in love and people will leave you. You will wish for death, but it will not come to console you. Life is your gift, enjoy it and use this precious honor wisely. I do believe we are still God's children. We are not evil creatures of darkness or the aftermath of witchcraft, as was believed centuries ago. Luckily, you are in a more accepting time of freedom of religion. A time when science and faith are working together to understand the world we live in. It will be easier for you, I hope. Of course, science is a gift and a curse. For the past few years, I have known you were an immortal. You gave us hope for our kind to develop families, but for some, you gave us hope to populate and gain power and control over mortals. What I saw as a joyous gift, others saw as a future for dictatorship, a future with an army of immortals. I have seen many wars in my time, and I know the quest for control leads to destruction. They will cloak this desire for power under a blanket of false truths of protecting the mortals and state they are only looking out for the better interests of mankind. All wars start with good intentions. There are only 343 of us, and I always believed all 343 wanted to stay in the shadows, wanted to let the mortals live the lives God intended without interruption from us. Few mortals know of our existence, and these people are in extremely powerful positions. They need us for our knowledge and our strength. We help the good, the mortal good, and we never reveal ourselves to the public because they will demand tests and services. It will become a witch-hunt or a malicious scientific experiment. Since we are stronger than mortals and cannot die, the possibilities to use us as weapons are great. We've all known this since the first days, and for that reason most of us disappeared in 1587. Unfortunately, since your birth I have discovered that my beliefs are not that of all of us. Some of us only remained silent because of our limited number. There are few among us who believe we are God-like and should be in control of the weak mortals. We have seen massacres and destruction caused by human ignorance, and these few believe this is mere evolution. We have lived for centuries, gathered phenomenal knowledge and an abundance of wealth. We have evolved further than mortals. Some of us even have special gifts; therefore, we should rule. But that is not what I believe. I fear a genetically created immortal army is not what God intended for us. Through science, I have created a way of killing immortals to counteract our reproduction possibilities, which, by the way, are still a mystery to me. Your birth, as far as I can tell, is a miraculous coincidence. Back in Elizabeth's England, there was a belief that the seventh son of the seventh son would have supernatural powers. I'm a seventh Joseph Prescott and you are my seventh son. These old, silly superstitious beliefs from my past I had dismissed long ago, but life is very strange and people are even stranger. I'm beginning to fear that I put my trust in the wrong individuals. Like I said previously, if you are reading this I have failed; the Death Serum I created has been used against me to silence me. Here is a list of Guardians and mortals I know you can trust:

Eleanor Dare, Daniel Silsbury, Jonathan Ward, Thomas Edwards, Julia Emmerson, David Smythe, Virginia Snow, Audrey Gualtiero, Christine Kershaw, Winston Longhurst, Jake Aston, Lauren Cheshire, Jason Steer, Tracy Smith, Roman Feng, Cameron Tailor, Patrick Wallace

Take care of your mother. She has made this miracle, and she is the love of my life. Take care of Charlie; he is older and on a steady path. I believe he will be fine. Teresa will cling to her mother, and together, they will be a great team. I worry most for Chloe and Joe Jr. Please help them to remember me, but never tell any of them who you really are. As Guardians, we swear an oath of silence and hold a promise for public service. Once you meet Eleanor, you will see why I trust her. She is our Matriarch. She is our punisher. She is the most loyal and dedicated Guardian we have. She is also the strongest person I have ever met. Once you know who you are, you must go to Headquarters. Eleanor will be expecting you.

1192 Rue de la Magie, Quebec District

I wish you good luck. Protect yourself. Even those born to strength must carry weapons.

All my love,
Dad
May 29, 2118

"Do not tell secrets to those whose faith and silence you have not already tested."

—Elizabeth I

Tarian read the letter twice through. He closed his eyes, his nostrils stung, his brow creased and his eyes watered. He caved into his empty chest and silently suffered the loss of his dad all over again. He was tired, but sleep was a luxury he couldn't afford. He cleared his throat, put on a brave face, and welcomed Roman back to the table.

"Well, Dad has a list of people I should be able to trust and you're on it. In fact, you're the only mortal on it as far as I can tell," he stated.

"Who else is on it?" Roman asked.

"Not Zachary Eastwood," he said.

"Well, that solidifies my beliefs," Roman said.

"Yes but, you, Patrick, Eleanor, and Audrey are the only ones left alive. Somebody's wiping out my dad's confidants." Tarian held up the paper with the list of names on it.

"That sucks. I'm on some sort of immortal hit list."

"Yeah," Tarian chuckled. "There was salt in the letter and a silver bracelet." Tarian raised his voice alluding to a question and showed Roman the fine, yet masculine, bracelet hanging from his wrist.

"Superstitions from the past. My people have some too. We believe if a dog howls for a long time late at night, someone has died, or if you cut your toenails late at night, you'll invite ghosts." Roman shook his head and laughed.

Laughing felt good. Tarian had a few answers now, and the slime of suspicion began to clear.

"Unfortunately, Dad doesn't implicate Zachary in his murder. I mean, he doesn't list him as a possible suspect, but he's not on the people-to-trust list either. We know Zachary must have changed Dad's will and hid the life insurance policy. I'll confront him at Headquarters, and he better have given up several names of the conspirators," Tarian said. He wondered just how many Guardians Eleanor would lose to Zachary's collaboration with the Prevallers.

They spent the remaining hours of flight reading and analyzing the file. Eventually, the steward served a plate of roasted chicken and mashed potatoes. It tasted better than most restaurants. Neither mentioned Roman's relationship with Delia. Tarian checked his phone repeatedly for any transmission from Gabe and Maria. Still nothing, and his dread returned. He tried Audrey, but she kept stalling and stating they'd talk once he was back inside the security of Headquarters. She sounded frantic.

THIRTY

SILVER BRACELET

Tarian found Audrey trapped deep in concentration at her lion-footed desk. Her office cluttered with old and new objects. Her two worlds knitted together: immortal/mortal, old/new, magical/ordinary. He wondered how many years this had been her space. She peeked at him from behind her paper-thin screen before he called her name. She looked as if she'd aged ten years.

"Tell me now! Don't dick me around," he ordered, more harshly than he intended.

"Zachary escaped." She put her face in her hands then ran them through her hair and dislodged her ponytail. She looked up and he knew that wasn't all. "They have Charlie, Gabe and Maria."

"Charlie?" The horror speared his insides so hard he jerked. "What about Mom and Chloe and—"

"They're all fine. I told you the village is impenetrable," she said with confidence.

He felt a nudge of relief as if one life replaced the other, but it only lasted for a second.

"Do you have the file?" she asked.

"Yes, I do, but we've to go. We have to go now. We have to get Charlie and Gabe and Maria. We have to go." Tarian barked and paced, but she wasn't moving.

She still sat in that damn chair. No hint of going anywhere. He craved action. He pushed the chair, shoved it harder than he had meant to. The wheels whirled the chair across the room. Audrey hit the far wall. Her neck jerked back, then snapped forward. He rushed to her.

"I'm sorry, I'm sorry." He caressed her neck trying to take the pain away. Then he fell to his knees, and his head slumped into her lap.

She gently stroked his hair, and he let it go. The torture of the past two and a half years spread into her lap. She cradled his pain, made it easier to release his brave exterior. Tears drizzled out and onto her thighs.

"It's okay," she said.

"Nothing's okay," he corrected.

"I mean I'm okay. You didn't hurt me. Yes, we'll leave. We'll find them, but first things first."

"I know. What's first?" he asked, still desperately anxious for a task.

"What's this?" She looped her finger through the bracelet. Her eyes glinted knowingly.

"It was in the note from Dad. What does it mean?"

"Joe," she said, with a tender smile attached to his name. Her mind drifted far away, to a distant memory of his father many years ago. "He was always so superstitious. Silver brings good luck and I recognize this piece. It's very old. He wore that for many years when we first came to America, but then he put it away. We all have trinkets like that stashed in safe deposit boxes scattered around the world. You can collect a lot of treasures in six hundred years, but it's the things we had at the beginning that mean the most, usually because back then we were all poor, uneducated, scared. These antiques are precious things we clung to so that they became a part of our soul. You have your dad's soul. Right there." She gently trailed her finger around his wrist and the silver bracelet.

Tarian shivered at her touch. He liked her gentle side and felt privileged that she shared it with him—only him, it seemed. Her attention warmed him from head to toe, tickling the lining of his stomach and tingling his senses. His vision tunneled straight to her, and he couldn't look away. They both sat, she in the chair and he on the floor, knowing that once they stood up, this special moment would disappear like smoke, and poof, in its place chaos and fear would return. But they had to carry on, and Audrey released herself first from their emotional trance.

THIRTY-ONE

THE HIGH COUNCIL

Eleanor stood in the back of her enormous room next to the giant monitors arguing with four other purple people while her two green-clad assistants stood next to her holding remote controls. Tarian recognized these four people. Their pictures were mounted on the wall in front of the library. Under their faces hung plaques stating their numerous achievements and awards in a range of different sciences.

"This is the High Council," Audrey whispered.

Tarian nodded, but he'd already figured that one out.

The three gentlemen and one woman dressed in flowing blackberry coats studied the screens. They were infinitely paler and thinner than Eleanor. Tarian suspected their ghostly pallor was the by-product of a life spent indoors. At least he hoped it due to a lack of sunlight and not to a weird demonic explanation.

"Come in, come in." Eleanor waved her hand hastily.

Audrey and Tarian entered the rear of the room followed

by one last guest, Margaret Davenport. The eight of them gathered around a conference table. All eyes upon him, he froze

"The file, Tarian?" Eleanor asked.

"Oh. Yes." He organized the file papers into groups just as Roman had done on the plane.

"Here's the letter from my father. He explains someone is trying to create an immortal army. There's a list of people, and they're all dead except for Eleanor, Audrey and Roman …" Tarian began to read the list of names, but one of the gentlemen interrupted.

"No, no, no, son. The data on Death Serum development that's what we need. Where is it?" The gentleman began to jumble Tarian's piles of papers.

"That's enough George, let the boy continue," the woman councilor said.

"Here." Tarian slid the stack of papers that included all the pertinent information on creating a Death Serum.

George snatched the papers. The woman chastised him for his rude behavior. Soon the pages tossed around like plucked feathers. Eleanor and all four councilors speculated over Joe's theories. Tarian and Audrey no longer seemed relevant to the discussion.

Tarian watched the feeding frenzy. Dad's list didn't include any of the high council members except Eleanor, and Tarian understood why. The councilors were nothing more than giant brains devouring their scientific candy. Tarian hoped he'd done the right thing giving them his dad's work. But someone needed to create an antidote.

Eleanor and Margaret pulled Audrey and Tarian aside to talk.

"Zachary gave us a few names before he escaped. It wasn't a total failure," Eleanor said.

"What happened? How could he slip away?" Tarian asked.

"He got violently ill, and I sent Gregory Lycott to escort him to the infirmary while Audrey and I spoke to the President. It was a mistake. Gregory was helping Zachary all along," Eleanor admitted.

"The President's phone call was urgent and couldn't be ignored, Eleanor. You did the right thing. He informed us of vital intelligence concerning Zachary's suspected treasonous activities and the current negotiations being established with the leaders of the Prevallers." Audrey defended.

Eleanor sighed and nodded reluctantly. "They poisoned the guards then disappeared. Both these men were extremely familiar with the building. They knew where the cameras were and where they weren't. They knew where each hall led and what was behind each door. It wasn't that difficult for them to escape, especially since everyone was dealing with a multitude of issues."

"Now what?" Tarian asked.

"At least Gregory's betrayal gave us insight as to how the fifteen Guardian's had been murdered. Gregory is capable of invisibility," Margaret stated.

"So he can sneak up on people and inject them?" Tarian asked.

"Yes, but to another gifted immortal he can be seen as a shadow that is why he has not attempted to kill Eleanor or Audrey," Margaret added.

"This is him." Audrey showed him a picture.

Tarian recognized his face as the rumpled meditating man in the corner of the conference room that he entered on his first day at Headquarters. He remembered the disturbing qualities of the man, and the fact that no one else seemed to notice his presence.

"Gregory is a precious weapon and now he's gone," Audrey stated.

"I've seen him," Tarian said.

"Where?" Audrey asked.

"The first day, when you brought me into the room with Margaret." Tarian turned to Margaret, but she looked puzzled.

"I don't remember seeing his shadow," Audrey said.

"I saw him clearly, not as a shadow," Tarian said.

"You are very gifted, Tarian." Eleanor smiled proudly.

"What about Charlie? How are we getting my brother, Gabe and Maria?"

"They're being held at an old Coast Guard base on Mount Desert Island," Audrey said.

"The Entente base that was recently shut down?" Tarian questioned.

"Yes, ten of our bases are now being used by the Prevallers

to house prisoners and provide shelter," Eleanor explained.

"Of course, shutting down those fifty bases was a stupid idea. You can't deplete your military during a time of peace. Peace isn't free." Tarian threw his hands up and began pacing.

This was one of many hot-topic issues he and Delia disagreed on. During high school, he'd followed the congressional decision to close bases and voiced his opposition on several social outlets. Of course, Delia argued the opposite. Their verbal sparring sometimes lasted days.

"I understand you are upset. Many people are. I am now dealing with violent protests breaking out all over the nation. But the President and I have rescue teams in place for those captured," Eleanor said.

"In place?" Tarian yelled loud enough to be heard by the councilors in the distance.

"Tarian, I assure you we are doing everything in our power to get our men and women home safely. This is a delicate house of cards. In less than twenty-four hours, many cards have been put in place. We are dealing with numerous threats. The Prevallers have destroyed our drones and penetrated the closed borders. They are making demands and threatening war. They have an impressive army stationed and ready to attack. It's now an intense standoff with the President and Congress. Negotiations have begun, but …" Eleanor paused and glanced at the High Council.

"But what?" Tarian barked.

Audrey concluded Eleanor's explanation, "But the High

Council is considering the history of events leading to this war. And the history before that. The High Council's reluctance is due to the Entente's continued dismissal of the Guardians' warnings. None of the advice given to the Entente has been acted upon, and now the Entente is in a vulnerable predicament just like the past."

"But they have to consider Zachary's role in all of this. He and his group of traitors may have been diluting the Guardian's advice," Tarian suggested.

"Yes they do," Eleanor said.

"Who does the Senator have?" Tarian asked.

"About 45 members of congress and several other influential people," Eleanor answered.

"He also has his immortal army!" Tarian's hands balled into fists.

"That's preposterous," George yelled back.

"What do you mean? It's in my dad's papers," Tarian returned, walking back to the table.

"Nothing has been proven. These are simply theories of mind control or cloning," George countered.

"Well, the mind control ring was invented," Tarian hissed.

"Yes … well … We have taken all precautions to prevent that from ever happening again," George said.

"What about cloning? He took my DNA. He's tested on Delia!"

"Hosh Posh! Zachary's attempt to alter Delia's DNA was unsuccessful. He has done nothing but damage her beyond cure. She is far from immortal," another gentleman councilor added.

"Beyond cure?" Terror twisted Tarian's gut.

"We have not given up, Tarian. I'm still working on a few alternative medical experiments," Eleanor said, and she looked confident. "But I agree with the Council, cloning is impossible. We have tried in the past with nothing close to success."

"Zachary is conspiring with the Prevallers. We know this. He is not creating any army. He already has one, a bunch of Wastelanders," George spat.

"We will work on the concrete evidence, not the speculation. Joe's creation of Death Serum is our top priority. We must find an antidote. And if Zachary has done the impossible then we will be forever grateful to your father for this weapon," the female councilor explained.

Tarian left the briefing with the puzzle still unfinished. Haunted by the fact that he knew his dad wouldn't have developed a Death Serum simply to prevent the Guardians defection to a new and different world leader. The High Council may not be interested in speculation, but Tarian wanted very much to hypothesize with Audrey, conjure their plans of their own. However, having been awake for over twenty-four hours, he couldn't think straight. He needed a few hours of sleep before he could do anything.

THIRTY-TWO

CHLOE

Tarian stared at the swirls in the wood on the door before working up the nerve to knock on it. Now his family knew Delia was sick, the Senator was a traitor, and Charlie had been kidnapped. And the biggest secret remained untold.

Tarian's mom swung the door open and put her arms around him. He felt the wetness of her tears as she buried her head into his chest. The burden of responsibility lifted from his shoulders as he sank into his mother's arms, defeated and vulnerable. They stood in the doorway hugging for seconds as he let her love engulf him until Teresa pulled her off and gave him her version of a bear hug. She was sixteen, short, and skinny. He gathered her into his arms and lifted her off the floor. She and Tarian had never been able to converse easily, but all the awkwardness disappeared with one loving embrace. They were blood, a connection that could never be broken.

Joe Jr. paid zero attention to him because the Guardians had provided him with brand new toys that were much more important to a six-year-old than hugging his big brother. Joe Jr. gave his brother a glance, a nod, and a smile, as if Tarian had been in the living room for many days. It was actually the perfect greeting. Anything else would've concerned him.

Chloe broke his heart and took the normalcy away again. She and Tarian had always been the closest, but she shied away like he had a disease that she didn't want to catch.

"Hi Chloe." Tarian stepped over the threshold and into the apartment that smelled of cinnamon and warm bread. When he closed the door behind him, Chloe grabbed their mother's skirt and hid behind her.

"She knows Charlie's missing," Mom whispered.

"Are you frightened that I'll get taken away like Charlie?" Tarian knelt to be at her eye level.

She nodded and a tear rolled down her cheek. His heart crumbled.

"It's okay Chloe. I know where Charlie is and I'm going to go get him. Will that make it all better?"

She nodded again, still no words. Normally a talkative child with many questions and lots of enthusiasm, her timid muteness a painful reminder of what Zachary had done to his family. But he couldn't let the rage show.

"Hey! Look at this Chloe." He pulled the egg out of his pocket. Tarian had on a Guardian uniform designed to look like a business suit, and several interesting gadgets hid in the folds. Hoping to win her trust, he offered it to her.

She slowly inched away from Mom's hip, still nervous and quiet, but curious.

"You know, I'm pretty important around here," Tarian teased, touching the fancy pockets on his shirt with the Guardian emblem.

"I know. Mom said so," Chloe said.

"Are you proud of me, Chloe?"

"Yes!" she said, coming out of her aloofness.

"Then come give me a hug."

She ran into his arms, and he squeezed her tightly. He needed her approval more than anyone else. She smelled of sugary vanilla, and he sniffed her hair.

She giggled. "What are you doing, Silly?"

"You smell good enough to eat. Gobble, gobble, gobble." He tickled her and pretended to eat her up.

The sound of her laughter trailed on in his brain. Echoes of satisfaction filled his soul. His little sister had to be happy and safe at all times, in order for him to move forward.

The warm and cozy suite at the Inn sprawled to include a spacious living room with a separate office, a quaint dining area, and an overly equipped kitchen. Mom assured him over and over she was very happy here, but he saw her vacancy. This wasn't her home, but then again, no place would seem like home until Charlie was safe. He had to get Charlie back as soon as possible.

"Thank you for staying here, Mom," he said as he guided

her into the kitchen away from the children.

"Of course, I want to be here." Carolyn poured hot water for coffee.

"No, you don't," he said, and watched her gaze drop. "It helps me to know you're safe. I can concentrate on bringing Charlie home if I don't have to worry about them kidnapping you or Chloe, Joe or Teresa. I need to know you are secure."

"We are. We are safe and secure. Joe Jr. is ecstatic with all of his new toys. Chloe is scared since the news of Charlie. She has to be next to me every minute. Most nights she sleeps in my bed instead of with her sister. Teresa loves it here, thankfully. Eleanor has taken an interest in her. Said she's very bright. Teresa wants to go to the lab every day. I'm actually quite proud of her. She's matured greatly in this adverse environment. I never knew how strong she was until now."

"Really? I didn't know. I haven't seen Teresa around the lab." Tarian paused to comb his memory. "And what about you?"

"I'm fine." She smiled but her hands shook.

"Come on Mom. This is so much for you."

The rattle of the delicate china cup on its saucer told a tale of quiet suffering. Tarian wanted to reveal his secret now since his three siblings had settled in the other room with toys and television, but would the truth bring more pain than peace. Telling his family went against his father's wishes, but so much had changed since Dad's death. He'd discussed this possibility with Audrey and her thoughts were divided. Together they hadn't come to a conclusion on the better option—truth or well-intended deception.

"I know. It doesn't seem real. I mean, how is any of this possible? I've been reading their history, and now I guess your history. It's a fascinating, magical phenomenon. I'm happy for you, Tarian, I really am. This is a gift. You'll have a unique journey ahead of you." Carolyn's eyes filled with unshed tears, and she moved her shaking hands to her lap.

"What? You know the truth?" Tarian asked, not yet willing to say the word 'immortal' for fear she meant something altogether different.

"Yes. I know you're an immortal and so does Teresa."

"Who told you?" He felt betrayed. *Who had the right to give away his secrets?*

"Teresa found out at the lab. Like I said, she's a very bright girl. No one told her. She became suspicious and inquisitive. Of course, at first the two of us thought it was absurd, but the innkeeper downstairs isn't very good at hiding her magic."

"How can a sixteen-year-old comprehend such a thing?"

"Actually, she's taking it very well. Our little life here was going along splendidly until Delia arrived. What Teresa doesn't understand is Delia's illness. You know how close she and Delia are. She wants to help Eleanor find a cure. What upsets her is the two women she admires most don't seem to like each other."

"Delia doesn't trust immortals. I can't imagine she's representing us in a very nice light."

"No, she's very hurt by her father. Teresa has a mind of her own, though. Like I said, she figured it all out on her own before she shared it with me. After she convinced me her crazy idea was true, we started our research. After Chloe falls asleep, she and I sneak down to talk with Ms. Emma. She's the innkeeper, very sweet lady. She also has taken a liking to Teresa. She knew Joe, and of course she knows Zachary and Audrey. They seem to be a big, happy family."

"They were until the Senator decided to murder them."

Mom winced, concerned for his older brother. Tarian wished he could take back his horrible choice of words.

"Yes, true, but Zachary is the exception. They are a very close community. They care deeply for one another. I'm glad you have them for the rest of your long life. I just wish I could be there to see it."

He grabbed her hand and squeezed it. "Me too."

"I can't imagine what your poor father went through. I wish he would've told me. I wish I could've helped him."

"He was hoping for a different ending."

Tarian slipped the letter from his father across the table and watched his mom read her husband's words. She smiled with tear-filled eyes but didn't speak. After a long pause, she spoke of Delia. He knew she couldn't bring herself to discuss Joe.

"When I went to visit Delia, she told me about Roman. I'm sorry, honey."

"It's okay. I just hope she gets better," he said, wondering if he'd ever go visit his ex-girlfriend.

"She didn't look healthy, but Patrick seems to think she'll recover. I hope so," she said, and then paused.

"What is it Mom?" he asked.

"Whom are they sending to rescue Charlie?" she asked.

"That's still to be determined. I don't care what they decide. I'm going to go find him."

"I want you to stay here," she said, with steady hands on her cup. "Delia needs you. We all need you."

"No," he said.

Her shaky hands and slumped shoulders evaporated, replaced by her fierce protective instinct. She wouldn't have it.

"Chloe needs you. For the sake of your family, Tarian! What if she loses two brothers?" she asked, then lowered her head. "I don't want to lose two of my babies." The stranglehold of sobs audible under her breath.

"Don't worry. They won't send me." He weighed his words.

He wanted to obey his mother's wishes, but he couldn't stay in the village while his brother and friends suffered as prisoners. How selfish of him to take off into enemy territory, but how selfish of him to stay here to be coddled by his mother. She'd already lost her husband and her son was missing, but he couldn't stay. He was of no use to anybody here.

What am I going to tell her? He had to lie or avoid the topic.

But she wouldn't drop it. "Promise me." Carolyn grasped his face, forcing him to look at her.

"I promise." Tarian looked straight into her eyes, so she'd

believe him.

The lie tore him apart, but EMA and Guardian soldiers fought. They didn't sit around kitchen tables drinking coffee. Every cell in his body pulled him toward combat. He'd also been trained to lie if ever taken as a prisoner of war. He never imagined he'd use his training on his own family.

"Thank you," Carolyn said.

"I'm going to go visit Delia now. See how she's doing," Tarian lied again and stood. He wanted to separate himself from the family that relied on him and go to the one he now needed, Audrey.

THIRTY-THREE

OR ELSE

Audrey stood in the doorway as Tarian opened it to leave the apartment.

"What are you doing here?" he asked then noticed Eleanor stood behind her.

"May we come in?" Eleanor asked.

Tarian didn't step aside. He didn't like the look in Eleanor's eyes. To his dread, Mom welcomed them inside.

They gathered around the breakfast table. Tarian sat back in the same spot, and his mother warmed his cup with hot coffee. Both Audrey and Eleanor refused any beverages or food. Once the niceties concluded, Eleanor handed her small tablet over to Tarian.

"You need to see this," Eleanor said. "This broadcast has been transmitted to all immortals via their Guardian issued tablets."

The Senator's smug face appeared. Tarian's stomach churned.

"Watch." Audrey tilted her head toward him with

determined eyes.

"My fellow Guardians I have set a plan in motion." The Senator spoke in a voice that didn't belong to him. He attempted to be likable, but he came across like a man who had a very indecent proposal to make. "I have a vision for the future. A future without war, with only peace, a future where everyone will be safe and will be cared for by my new government, my new military."

"Lies," Tarian growled but kept listening.

The Senator spun accusations in his eloquent speech. He charged Eleanor and the High Council with a lack of dedication to the mortals, putting Guardian needs first. He described a lack of empathy for mortal suffering while the immortals lived lavishly in the village and spoke of government incompetence, resulting in an inefficient and vulnerable Entente.

"None of this is true!" Tarian yelled. Under the Senator's well-manicured nails and powdered face lay an evil dictator trying to take all mortals' freedoms away.

"We know. It's pure propaganda but he has managed to persuade some of us. With this speech maybe more will follow. We need you to speak on our behalf. The Guardians need to hear from you, from Joe's immortal-born son. We need to give them a positive message of hope and erase this lie from their thoughts," Eleanor explained.

"He has to hear the rest, Eleanor," Audrey said.

Eleanor reluctantly hit play.

"You have 48 hours to surrender the First Born."

The screen went black.

"Or else what? What are his demands?" Tarian asked.

"Tarian won't go," Carolyn ordered. "He will not go!"

Tarian slid his chair closer to his mother and held her hand.

"Or else he kills Charlie, then Gabe, and then Maria," Audrey stated.

She stared into Tarian's eyes with a look of defiance. *She had a plan.* He saw it. He also knew she was only willing to share her plan with him.

"No!" Carolyn barked, causing Chloe and Teresa to run into the kitchen.

"What's going on? Why is everyone here?" Teresa demanded.

"Hello, Teresa," Eleanor said. "Everything is going to be okay. Please take Chloe back into the living room."

Teresa didn't move. She focused on her mentor.

"Please, when we are done, I need you in the lab. I have new data for our cure for your friend," Eleanor said.

With this, Teresa left with notable unhappiness.

"I'm going to get my brother and my friends," Tarian stated.

"We need you here. We cannot risk your life at this vulnerable time. Zachary has injected a poison into our community, and you are the only antidote. I've already assembled a team to extract your brother and your friends. Without them as leverage, Zachary has nothing," Eleanor said.

"Do you have an execution team assembled? Because that's

the only way to stop this man," Tarian said.

"Yes," Eleanor said.

Eleanor wanted to create her own propaganda, a simulated take down of Zachary and his traitors by the First Born. Tarian didn't appreciate this fake portrayal. He wanted to fight in reality, not in some sort of commercial. He protested but Audrey shot him another fierce glare so he shut up.

Once Eleanor left with Teresa, Tarian's anxiety to leave with Audrey swelled. He politely lingered at the table to console his mom, but he didn't want to venture into a discussion about his *First Born* persona. She deserved better than lies but the truth was too uncertain and death still a possibility. He pretended to be content with Eleanor's plan.

The conversation kept circling and skirting Tarian's and Audrey's true intentions. Tarian broke out in a guilt-ridden sweat.

"Let's go, Tarian." Audrey tugged on his sleeve impatiently.

Mom's hands still shook, but she seemed mentally stable or as stable as she could be until Charlie returned safe and sound. She looked from Tarian to Audrey then let go of Tarian's hand. Without a word, she stood up from the table. Her regal face bore the wrinkles of a woman whose forty-eight years of life had given her wisdom and courage. She would ask no more questions of Audrey, nor would she make any more demands of Tarian. She simply grasped Audrey's hands and shook them fervently, then kissed her son's cheek. A whispered *I love you* grazed his ear. Then Carolyn left the kitchen to sit in the living room with her two youngest children.

Once out of the apartment and in the hallway, Tarian turned Audrey toward him and asked, "The tablet went black. How do you know his demands?"

"All Guardian tablets went blank except Eleanor's. Her message had a photo at the end, a picture of a piece of paper with the execution information on it. It happened unexpectedly. We saw the photo; then it was gone. Luckily, Eleanor wasn't alone. I witnessed this along with four other Guardians, but we didn't think fast enough to save it," she said.

"Execution," he murmured. "I never thought the word execution would exist in my life." He stared once again at the swirled wood on the closed door of the apartment and prayed for the safety of his family inside.

"You can't cling to things, Tarian." Audrey placed her hand upon his shoulder and pulled him around.

"These aren't things. This is my family," he rebuffed, his stare incendiary.

"I meant ideas. As an immortal you have to accept change even when it's excruciatingly painful. Clinging to people only makes it hurt worse and devours productive energy. You must learn to just be and to let your loved ones just be. Do you understand?" she asked.

"I get it. Believe me, I've done a lot of soul searching. Being immortal has made me very possessive of my family and even Delia. I realize that. But I can't stop. They'll be gone from my life forever, how can I not cling to them? Seeing Delia in Roman's arms was like having my best … I don't know … my best car stolen." He paced struggling to find the words to describe the indescribable. "I've never felt like this before. I used to be carefree and happy."

"Reality check, most teenagers are carefree and happy, then they get older and wiser and more troubled. It's not just an immortal problem. It's a human problem." Her kind tone was gone.

THIRTY-FOUR

ROGUE

"Ready?" Audrey asked.

Tarian took her in as he walked toward her. She looked like a glorious and fearless predator, and he felt like a meager field mouse.

"No," he confessed, in a miserable tone still haunted by his mother's last kiss.

"Sucks for you," she said with a mocking smile.

They left during Eleanor's meeting with President Lloyd of the Entente. Their absence would go unnoticed long enough for them to be well into enemy territory. Once Eleanor found out what they were up to, she'd either offer them assistance or not.

They'd begged Eleanor for the rescue mission, but she'd denied them even after Tarian starred in her humiliating propaganda commercial. Luckily for Tarian, Audrey had a soldier's heart and wanted to help him. She understood his need to save Charlie and his friends, and had the resources and contacts needed to conduct the mission without Eleanor's support or approval.

He buckled into the Guardian hoverbike, a far more advanced and deadly version of the one he'd flown at EMA. He was basically strapped to a titanium death gun, but it flew with dauntless precision. Soon the thrill of speed engulfed and rejuvenated him as he raced alongside Audrey.

Their plan was to land on an aircraft carrier stationed off the coast but close enough to the Coast Guard base for them to approach underwater. However, the weather wasn't cooperating. Gusty winds drove the torrential rains in their faces, and formed white capped fifteen-foot swells on the water below. As they approached for landing, Audrey turned to Tarian, giving him a wide grin and cocked, cheeky eyebrow before she dove.

He offered a weak smile back, but his palms were sweaty and his grip on the controls slipped several times. His heart pounded, and breathing inside his helmet became almost impossible. He mustered his courage and dropped his bike down for a fast landing but failed.

On the third landing attempt, they received orders in their headsets to abort, but they refused to give up. Tarian's mind reeled. He imagined the unbearable pain to survive a fiery crash. Survival would take days of healing, time they couldn't afford to lose.

Tarian took one last loop around for a better angle then looked at Audrey. "Let's do it!"

"Yeeaahh!" Audrey yelled and nosedived.

The city-sized, floating craft swayed so drastically. Tarian feared he'd end up in the hostile ocean. The bow and stern rocked like a carnival seesaw, threatening to jam the front end of the bike. Audrey landed perfectly. Tarian and the bike rolled then skidded before stopping in a heap of embarrassment.

"Smooth," Audrey teased.

"I told you to abort!" the Captain of the craft yelled. "Look at this bike."

"Sorry Captain. Don't worry, I'll take all the blame," Audrey said.

"Damn right you will. This must be Tarian Prescott."

"Yes sir," Tarian said.

"Welcome aboard."

"Thank you, sir."

Incessant pellets of rain pounded their backs as Captain Jeffrey escorted them under cover. Jeffrey didn't stop scolding until they stood in front of a massive map.

"Are you sure about this Audrey?" Captain Jeffrey looked long and hard at her.

Tarian got the impression they'd worked together in the past. He must have owed her a favor.

"Why wouldn't I be?" Audrey smirked.

With an exhausted sigh, Captain Jeffrey briefed them on the area and his latest intelligence. Audrey had asked him to run his own surveillance operation, independent from the Guardians. She didn't trust anyone.

"My men didn't find your prisoners on the base with the rest. They're three and a half miles north in an underground bunker."

Captain Jeffrey pointed to a spot on the map.

Audrey glanced at Tarian with raised eyebrows and a nod of her head. They'd expected changes but didn't like it.

Coordinates were established, and they suited up in the Entente's best SEAL suits, courtesy of Captain Jeffrey. The SEAL suit was like nothing Tarian had ever seen and would never have known existed. The material could be worn in and out of the water without compromise, designed to go from wet to dry in a matter of seconds. The aerodynamic suit held a multitude of waterproof secret compartments. A walking/swimming toolbox as weightless as a feather.

Enormous waves thrashed cruelly against the vessel, rocking it uneasily and making their every movement a struggle. Audrey lost her balance while attempting to pocket a syringe with Death Serum and nearly jabbed her thigh with the point. Tarian rushed to help her up.

She rejected him. "I've got it."

He grunted at her stubbornness. "If you fall again, I'm taking it."

With assistance from Joe's notes, Eleanor had finally succeeded in duplicating the lethal serum, and now Audrey carried it. Who carried the weapon had been an ongoing argument, but Audrey'd won. He was still her underling and ironically, this both infuriated and consoled him.

They plunged into the freezing waters of the Atlantic. Once submerged, he felt more secure. The power of the propulsion devices kept them stable in the crosscurrents. Time was the prevalent enemy. Luckily, their special suits and state-of-the-art equipment were built for speed. The accuracy of their landing location was critical. Captain Jeffrey did his best to educate them in their short time together. He'd been stationed in this area for several years and knew the terrain and waters well.

The location took some delicate maneuvering to get to. He'd programmed the propulsion devices with the coordinates and route that took them from the violent sea, through the narrows, and up the Somes Sound, where they emerged in an empty boathouse. The unpopulated area of land was quiet. They borrowed time from the official attack, theorizing that Zachary would be so preoccupied fighting Eleanor's team that they could slip through unnoticed. But the attack force was headed to the old base, not the hidden bunker, and no one knew where Zachary lay in wait.

After trudging through the mountainous land for two hours, they hit upon the earth monster Captain Jeffrey had told them about. The building had been swallowed whole by dirt, ice, and snow, leaving very little steel and concrete visible. Three well-armed, massive men stood alert in front of the mouth of the beast. Tarian blanched.

"It's okay, Tarian." Audrey said. "We knew your brother and friends were the well-guarded bait."

"They're your friends too," he said.

"Yes, they are my friends too," she corrected softly.

He didn't appreciate her patronizing tone.

"I'm fine," he spat, but his frozen hands could barely grip his gun.

"Okay, that's all I needed to hear."

"Can't you warm this place up?" His wicked sideways glance expressed his annoyance.

She didn't respond, but he felt a blast of warm air.

The three thugs wouldn't fall easily. Audrey and Tarian had to take the guards before they had time to contact Zachary. Tarian and Audrey had the advantage since they hadn't yet been seen.

Their weapons fired simultaneously, silently hitting both targets. Audrey swooped in on the third mark as graceful and quick as a lethal cheetah. Her opponent analyzed the situation instantly and reacted with experience. He slammed his forearm into her chest, causing her neck to snap disturbingly backward. She fell onto the unforgiving ground and lay motionless.

The kill-move shocked Tarian. He froze. His Realm training to think like an immortal vanished. He saw Audrey dead on the ground and fierce rage burned through him. He rushed the enemy with too much noise and commotion. His ridiculously obvious, civilian-like attack startled the thuggish guard. Maybe he looked so absurdly incapable that the guard took him for granted. Fortunately, the guard neglected to call for backup and while Tarian thrashed about causing a diversion, Audrey awakened from her semiconscious state, cleared her head, and threw her steel blade into the center of the guard's back. He went down with a thud. She snapped his neck without hesitation. It was vicious and primal, and Tarian admired her for it.

"Seriously, Tarian," she said exasperatedly. "You have to think like an immortal. Can you handle this? This is only round one, and you've failed."

"I know, I know. I'm fine now. Just a little on edge. I got it now," he said, but she didn't move. "I do, I do. Honest!"

"Grab all communication devices and weapons! When the other two wake up, we don't want them having access to anything."

"How long have we got?" he asked

"Probably an hour until the stunners wear off."

It took several minutes to strip the two soldiers of their clothes and weapons. They pulled on the uniforms to fool the surveillance inside the bunker. The entrance hid under thick avocado green moss, thorny shrubbery, and a layer of snow. Nature had gone out of its way to warn them off and Tarian expected furry spider legs to curl around his fingers as he fumbled for a keyhole or doorframe.

Finally, Audrey found the opening. She gently put the key into the hole while he kept his back to her and his eyes toward the path. No one approached. The door opened smoothly. With so much damp dirt and decay, he expected loud creaking. They were soon inside without anyone seeming to notice.

Upon entering, blinding darkness surrounded them until their eyes adjusted. Every several feet a soft yellow glow illuminated the steel hallway. The familiar strangle of an oxygen dump squeezed his throat. He grabbed his neck and gasped for breath.

"Are you okay?" Audrey asked.

Once again, he proved to be a cadet not a soldier. "Yes." He forced his breath to slow, but he wasn't okay. Nausea twisted his gut and and his head ached.

"Are you sure? You don't look good?"

"I'll be fine. Just having a little trouble breathing."

"It's just like in the game. Remember?"

"Yes." His voice struggled to release words.

"Zachary has set this trap up specifically for you. Calm yourself."

"I'm going to pass out."

"It's okay, relax your breathing. You must put mind over matter. Concentrate." She looked into his panicked eyes and gently rubbed his shoulders.

Her touch worked, so did the blanket of cool air she created. As he gazed into her stalwart eyes, his strength grew. His breathing steadied, his head cleared, and the nausea in his stomach subsided.

"Thanks."

She smiled affably, the smile he loved. Her eyes were brilliant, clear-cut diamonds layered with varying shades of blue and a hint of silver that sparkled and comforted him. They could glare icily. He'd been at the receiving end of those fearsome eyes way too many times. Yet, they could dazzle and invite. The latter softened her angular face, and when combined, her icy stare became even more intriguing.

The hallway gradually sloped and morphed into an open space again, still resembling a submarine. Screens monitored inmates. The young technician watching the screens didn't see the trespassers until it was too late. The needle from Tarian's syringe plunged into the kid's arm before he could do anything about it. He'd sleep for a while and then not remember a thing once he awoke.

"Found 'em," Audrey said after scavenging through a clipboard with a meal log on it. "They're scattered down different hallways."

"Charlie first," Tarian said.

"No, Maria and Gabe, they can help us fight off the guards. Your brother's training for the courtroom not the battlefield."

"Fine." He knew she was right.

Strangely, they didn't find a guard stationed at any of the three cell doors. It was as easy as getting three dogs out of the kennel. This baffling lack of security made them uneasy. After the ecstatic reunions filled with embraces, tears, and laughter, they sat perplexed next to the young technician lying crumpled on the floor.

"What the hell, guys!" Maria unfolded the young man's legs.

Tarian had missed her brashness.

"You could at least lay this poor kid down nicely." Maria turned the young man gently onto his back, cradling his head so it wouldn't fall to the hard surface. Her coarse speech and body language contrasted with her tender actions, but at heart she was a very nurturing person.

"Happy?" Audrey jeered at Maria after the young man lay more comfortably.

"Yes!" she said.

"They're not with the Prevallers," Charlie flatly stated. "I figured that out when they let me outside into the yard for some sunlight. Senator Eastwood took me to another building, a giant compound."

"What?" Audrey's head snapped around to examine Charlie.

"The Coast Guard base?" Tarian asked.

"No. At first I thought I was a political prisoner. I was manhandled, and when I fought back I got the crap beat out of me—three against one. They rarely fed me. I assume you were too." Charlie gestured to Gabe and Maria.

When they nodded in agreement, vomit hit the back of Tarian's throat, but he managed to swallow it back down and cover up his guilt-ridden disgust.

"Then the constant attention toward me stopped abruptly. Suddenly, I was like last year's Christmas toy. They no longer had any reason to play with me, so obviously, a new toy came into town." Charlie said.

Gabe and Maria nodded in agreement.

"That still doesn't imply that they're not the Prevallers," Audrey said.

"No, but that along with the fact that most of these people are not military soldiers. Don't get me wrong, there're a few thugs around here, but I get the feeling most of them are scientists. I also believe that they're not as numerous as they want us to think. I've noticed a very limited number of guards. Always the same people. No new faces," Charlie said.

"Maybe the Prevallers don't have as many followers as they'd like us to believe," Audrey said.

Charlie shrugged. "The Prevallers' movement is huge. No doubt about it. I'm pro-Entente, but I do understand their motives. The outside world has suffered, and they want to reestablish trade. Knowledge of the Wastelands and their horrible living conditions is spreading. They're gaining sympathy and rallying allies."

"How do you know all of this?" Tarian asked.

"I'm going to Harvard. Do you know how many Senators' kids attend this school? It's rife with influence."

"It doesn't matter." Audrey shot to her feet. "We need to get you all back to Headquarters."

"Wait a minute." Tarian stood to face Audrey. "We need to find out what's really going on here."

"No," Audrey countered.

Tarian didn't like her tone of voice. "You can't order me, Audrey."

"You wanted to secure your brother's and friends' safety. That's our mission. Nothing more. I can't guarantee their safety if we go AWOL on a mission without proper channels and information." With a rigid jaw, she growled the words at him.

Despite her harshness, Tarian saw her concern. She worried another mission would get them killed. He couldn't have their deaths on his hands. He had to bring his brother home to Mom.

"You're right. Let's get them home safely." Tarian gathered supplies and readied to leave.

"What?" Maria said. "I'm nobody's fricking Christmas toy. I want to know what the hell's going on."

"Me too, Tarian," Gabe said earnestly.

"I'd like to get some revenge." Charlie grit his teeth.

Audrey paced the floor like an Alpha dog whose pack was challenging her. "What do you know of this other facility?" She directed the question to Charlie.

"Well, I know this is just a mound of dirt where they hold prisoners, nothing more," he said. "I believe the main building is a few miles north. He took me to it, but I was blindfolded. I've been closely listening to the conversations. He has visited me several times, and I've observed him closely. I honestly think he assumed I'd cooperate with his cause. Screw that. I spit in his face. SOB has some balls to think after he's beaten me, that I'd follow him. If Dad only knew what his friend was capable of!"

The hatred in his brother's words stung Tarian to the core. Charlie didn't even know the half of it. After all of this craziness, Tarian would have to tell him that Zachary murdered their father and that he was immortal. How was he going to accept all of that?

"What have you heard Zachary say exactly?" Audrey's eyes narrowed.

"I don't remember … but his eyes were different. They were infinitely black. He wore sunglasses the entire time I was with him, but when he took them off to wipe the sweat from his nose, I saw his eyes, strange and fascinating. Then," Charlie hesitated. "It sounds stupid, but I think he was talking about babies."

"Babies?" Audrey's brow furrowed and her head twitched to one side. "Like children?"

"No, like newborns," he answered.

"Tarian!" Audrey gasped, horrified.

Audrey stumbled as she reached for Tarian. He braced to catch her if necessary. Her relentless strength faltered. There was beauty in her vulnerability but also fear. His fear. Could he help lead? Could he help shoulder the burden Audrey carried? Is that what she wanted? Her eyes weighed upon his as if she in fact did want him to step up, to be an equal.

He stepped up.

THIRTY-FIVE

SUCKER PUNCH

After Tarian re-injected the technician so he'd sleep longer, Charlie led them down the long, dungeon-like tunnel to exit the facility. The crisp, chilly air hit Tarian's face refreshing him, but the hard, closed-fist sucker punch that followed derailed him. Charlie caught him before his face slammed the ground, while Gabe landed a convincing punch squarely on the man's temple, knocking him out cold. Unfortunately, another guard had enough time to contact a superior before the bullet took his life. They didn't know how much information he was able to convey about their presence at the facility.

Audrey lowered her head. The bullet had pierced his heart. He looked to be about twenty-five, someone's son or grandson. She was a trained assassin and didn't miss.

"We can't get caught," Audrey said in a ragged voice.

A stunned Charlie whispered so only Tarian could hear, "She's charming."

Tarian glared at him. "Do you want to live or die?"

"Touché little brother!"

Tarian staggered back to his feet while Gabe, Maria, and Audrey gathered the guard's transmitter. The aged and tarnished machine had definitely transmitted an electromagnetic wave to someone.

"How did he have this communication device? We took all of their equipment," Tarian asked Audrey.

"I don't know. He must've left here to retrieve it or he had it hidden somewhere. He has no weapons, so my guess is that they had the emergency back-up radio hidden somewhere."

"Let's move, Audrey," Maria said impatiently. "If we've been made, we need to get the hell out of here."

"Lead the way Charlie," Tarian said.

Charlie marched north with confidence. It was evident he had the most knowledge of Zachary's operation.

Audrey distributed guns to Gabe and Maria. Tarian quietly slipped his brother a sharp, steel blade. His brother may not be EMA but he could fight. He doubted his brother could shoot. A knife would be helpful in a fight, and if he came up against a gunfight, he'd be at the disadvantage with or without a gun.

Given the extensive training and weaponry on hand, they should've been at an advantage, but the lack of proper footwear for Gabe, Maria and Charlie crippled the escape. The icy, jagged rocks and uneven pathways sliced their prison slippers. Luckily, just enough material remained to prevent serious injury, but now that it was compromised, there was nothing between skin and freezing cold ground. Audrey worked her gift, but their fragile feet succumbed to hypothermia. In true EMA fashion, this drawback didn't deter them, but it slowed them down considerably.

The dense, wicked terrain reminded Tarian of the game and the Realm. He saw shadows and a monkey and feared they were being tracked. No one else witnessed these creatures because everyone else gazed downward, hoping to avoid more injury to their feet. Audrey had the front, careful to guide them through areas with less ice and snow. Tarian had the rear. It was his job to keep all of them safe. But he couldn't shake the uneasy feeling that something unwanted followed behind him. Fear tightened his abdomen and heightened his senses. Several glances backward found only an empty path, but this fact didn't settle his prickly nerves.

The frailty of their plan sank into Tarian's thoughts. His suspicions were confirmed once they reached the vast facility and heard the whirling blades of many tiltrotors. Dozens of men with machine guns walking the perimeter made Tarian feel foolish. At the sight of such an intricately designed, lethal compound, Tarian knew this place held something extremely precious to Zachary. Something he'd viciously protect. Looking at his motley crew, he felt the weight of inadequacy. They were undersupplied. Audrey knew it too. Her shifting skin, hawk-like stare, and taut mouth mirrored his.

"What the hell kind of Christmas present is in there?" Maria's eyes opened wide as she viewed the ceremony of weapons displayed around the building.

They all stood hidden by the shadows of the forest looking down onto the building from the sizable hill they'd just surmounted. The tan, sharp-edged erection of concrete that sat at the bottom of the bowl-like valley looked as deadly as a scorpion in the bottom a glass container. The large hills encircling the building provided the ultimate security and conquering this place on foot would be impossible. The inner slopes of the hills were intentionally bare to make intruders highly visible. A person could easily be seen from the ground, trekking down the snow-covered slope to get in or climbing up to get out. Either way, the person would be an easy target. Another scan of the facility and then a glance at Audrey convinced Tarian that they needed a new plan of action. He needed a private conversation with her, but first he had to get Gabe, Maria, and Charlie someplace safe and warm.

"What do we do now?" Gabe asked.

"We can't go down there," Maria said.

"Is there a tunnel?" Audrey asked Charlie.

"I don't know. He's definitely upped his game. I don't remember armed tiltrotors." Charlie eyed the swirling blades closing in on their location.

"Get down!" Tarian ordered.

They all fell flat to the ground. The pulsating wind of the deadly bladed bird swept past them then traveled out-of-sight.

"We have to wait for nightfall." Audrey slowly stood up and wiped the dirt and snow from the front of her uniform.

"I'm about to catch frost bite and I'm starving," Maria said.

"We haven't eaten since breakfast, and not only is the food crap, but there's barely a mouthful of the mystery cuisine. They want to keep us weak and it's working."

"That looks like a cabin over there." Gabe pointed to a heap of logs that had been thrown together by unskilled laborers long gone.

They trudged the small distance to the cabin. It stood dwarfish, vacant, and nonthreatening. Tarian ducked severely to squeeze his tall body inside, but Audrey walked through the threshold unchallenged. Together they swept the area before the rest staggered inside.

"It'll have to do," Audrey said. "But I doubt there's any food in here."

"We have rations in our suits, Audrey, remember?" Tarian told her.

Captain Jeffrey had gone over all the compartments of the land and sea combat suits, and one compartment had packages of food.

"Oh, that's right." Audrey smiled at him. She peeled off the guard's clothing covering her SEAL suit and looked down at her outfit with all its secret compartments. She fumbled through the different pockets without success.

"This one." Tarian reached out and opened the pocket on her left thigh. He felt Maria's interrogating stare.

"Thanks," Audrey said, but didn't look at him.

"You're welcome." He enjoyed knowing something she

didn't.

Again, he admired her state of amenability. A creature of fierce beauty when she was strong and fighting, but the allure of her true, vulnerable self entrapped him. Knowing she'd find the remark sexist, he only smiled inside. It was a nice feeling to be able to help her. He didn't get the opportunity very often.

"Okay, I have a package of dried something and two protein bars. What do you have?" She met Tarian's stare.

"The same." Tarian handed her his meager rations.

Audrey distributed the food evenly. She added a few extra pieces of protein bar to Gabe's, Maria's, and Charlie's portions.

The cabin's moldy smell proved it'd sat empty of human life for years. Veins of black ran horizontally through the faded wood walls. The dark cracks throbbed with life as millions of creepy critters crawled along. Tarian felt the belly of the cabin consume him. He couldn't shake off the sensation that tiny bugs burrowed into his skin. The urge to scratch every inch of his body overwhelmed him, but he suppressed it until miniscule flying black specs invaded. They'd stirred a nest of tiny, flying gnats that promptly proceeded to devour Maria's and Tarian's blood. They jerked and kicked their arms and legs to deter the small but incredibly irritating pests.

Clearly annoyed by their noise, Audrey gave Maria her shoes and ordered, "Go get water."

"I'll go. You stay here," Tarian advised Maria looking at the borrowed shoes that were a size too small.

"No, I'll go too." Maria looked at her feet as well. "Really,

I'm okay now. All that flapping around raised my body temperature."

Audrey's gift raised her temperature, but Tarian bit his tongue. Uncertain which Guardian secrets mortals were allowed to know.

"You have on a survival kit. Isn't there something to repel bugs?" Maria barked.

"Yes." Tarian remembered seeing a small aerosol spray bottle. He savagely ripped at his suit. He pulled the bottle out of its compartment with satisfaction and pushed it into Maria's face.

"That's sunscreen you idiot," she said.

"What?" he looked at the label, SPF 55. "Ahhhh," he sighed loudly, and Maria laughed. "Oh, I'm funny, am I?" He wrestled her like his little sister then riffled some more through his survival suit. He found it. They lathered every square inch of their bodies.

"So what's up with you and Audrey," Maria queried.

"Nothing," he said, surprised by her question. But he welcomed this brief distraction from their dire circumstances.

"Do I look like I'm stupid?"

"Yes," he teased.

"You're about to get slapped."

"Nothing. She's my …" But words failed him. She was his everything, but how could he explain that without sounding like he was in love with her.

"Exactly," Maria said with satisfaction.

"No, it's just that she's been there before. She knows what

it's like to go from mortal to immortal. She's helped me a lot."

Maria nodded in understanding. "I get it. I feel like Gabe gets me because we're both from the mines. Our families know each other. It's comforting to have an equal."

Her words were meant to be supportive, but in actuality the words highlighted the inequality of his relationship to Audrey. Actually, he knew very little of her background.

Heavy silence lingered for a while. Tarian fidgeted uneasily as a sense of urgency washed over him, but nightfall remained an hour away. He could indulge a little longer in conversation and felt a confession on his tongue.

"I like her." Tarian started to tell her how he'd dreamt about Audrey during the game, and how the dream had overheated him with angst. But he bit the words back.

"I know." Maria smiled a huge, toothy grin at him that warmed his soul. "I'm glad for you."

"Is it that obvious?"

"It's obvious that she likes you too."

"It is?"

"Yes, fool!" Maria slapped the side of his head.

"She looks at me and sees Joe's son. I know it. I can feel it. I'm too young. She is, after all, hundreds of years older than me."

"Yes, technically she's a lot older, but physically you're very close in age and physically you're a hot ass man!"

"Do you think I'm sexy?" He said in a funny accent placing his hands on his waist like a silly schoolgirl.

They both burst out in raucous laughter and forgot about the irritating insect bites and their duty to get water. They forgot about the fact that they were about to delve into an intricate labyrinth created by a treacherous immortal, who may very well take any future they were dreaming about away from them.

"What about Delia?" Maria moved in the direction of the water.

"She doesn't understand or like the whole immortal thing and she's in love with Roman Feng." His bitter, dry words sounded like a jealous boyfriend. He guessed he was a jealous ex-boyfriend. He didn't mention the severity of her illness. Voicing it aloud made it too real.

"Oh, I get it. She's afraid she's going to get old, and you aren't." Maria knelt to scoop the running stream of water into her bottle.

"Maybe, but I think her hatred for immortals stems more from her father's abuse. He's the reason she's sick," Tarian said. Even though Maria looked stunned by his confession, he didn't go into the details of how Delia's father had betrayed her. "Let's just say, Delia had plenty of time to analyze her father's bad intentions. Whether all her accusations are true or false doesn't matter. What matters is how she feels as a daughter of a horrible father. She said things to me like 'How was he going to leave us?' 'Fake his death?' 'Murder us?' 'Disappear?' She seemed pretty hurt by the reality of an immortal parenting a mortal, and I have to agree with her."

"This whole situation is messed up." Maria tightened the

cap on the bottle.

"We better get the water back before Audrey hunts us down," he said.

"When are you going to tell Charlie?"

Tarian shrugged. He couldn't worry about that. His mind stretched paper thin already.

THIRTY-SIX

LIVING GARDEN

At precisely three o'clock in the morning, Audrey and Tarian snuck down the hillside leaving behind a heavily sedated Maria, Gabe, and Charlie. They wouldn't wake until the mission was completed. Audrey and Tarian had come to this agreement earlier that evening. The others were still very weak from their incarceration—plus five people entering the facility would be too noticeable. Also they lacked the support of Headquarters and had no links to the outside world, which meant a very slim chance for success. Tarian wouldn't risk his brother's life, nor the lives of his mortal friends.

The darkness hid them, but the silence was tricky, every footstep had to be calculated or else they'd be heard. They treaded carefully to avoid trampling fallen tree branches and miniscule twigs. The snow blanketed the trail, hindered their speed, but also muffled their rustling.

They met the fringe of brightness radiating from security floodlights. They'd reached the concrete monstrosity unnoticed.

Tarian's heart sank with relief.

They approached what they believed to be the correct door based on Charlie's vague recollection of the layout of the building. Audrey silently prowled up to the guard and took him down before he knew what was happening. She stripped the guard of his weapons, then hog-tied and gagged him in a matter of seconds. Being the middle of the night, the halls were devoid of people but not from the watchful eyes of cameras. Audrey and Tarian had their guard uniforms on from earlier that day and strode confidently down the long, narrow corridor as if they belonged there.

Once past the entrance, Tarian could not rid the cancerous fear and uncertainty that spread inside him. Sweat rolled down his neck despite the frosty air. Everything about this place seemed wrong and horrible.

Wrong. He inhaled.

Horrible. He exhaled.

The corridors were a labyrinth that snared them in its twisted halls and disorienting turns. They found several rooms empty of people, spotlessly clean in appearance, and filled with medical equipment, military weaponry, and the latest information tracking systems. None of it was set up yet, but new home anticipation hung in the air. The moving boxes piled high and waiting, but for what? What did the new homeowners have in mind for such an elaborate house? They rounded the last corner and found the heart of the facility—the precious jewel Zachary coveted.

The horror surpassed Tarian's wildest imagination. Tiny

hospital beds lined up in rows upon rows and filled with infants. Crying, sleeping and curious infants were everywhere connected to strange, brand-new machines. He recognized the heart monitors but not the other machines. Data clicked out. Click. Click-click. Click. Tarian shuddered with every beep or twitch on the screens.

The Senator had his army right here in this room. Charlie was correct. The Prevallers weren't involved in this madness. The threat of impending war had been a perfectly orchestrated distraction, an ideal cover to hide the truly terrorizing operation. The Senator was a magician, and like all great magic tricks misdirection and sleight of hand scammed the audience.

Tarian touched one of the tiny hands as it reached upward out of its plastic container toward nothing. Instinctively, the five little fingers curled around his one digit with amazing strength. The need for human touch and interaction began at days, possibly hours old. But the touch electrified Tarian. It coursed through his veins and immobilized him. Images of Delia and himself vividly broadcast through the touch of this newborn clone. And then, he also saw his mother.

Why are you showing this to me? He asked through touch. The little being twitched and kicked impulsively as all newborns do. It was impossible for Tarian to distinguish a reflex from an intentional movement.

A serene composition of symphony music filtered through the air, but it wasn't calming this little one. He smelled of fresh laundry and sour milk, and his eyes spread wide like a night owl. The infant looked haunted and familiar.

Tarian turned to Audrey. His confused face stared into her horrified eyes and parted lips.

"We have to destroy them," she said, slowly and deliberately.

"What? No!" He scowled, petrified at the idea of killing newborns.

"Tarian, these aren't human babies. These are genetically mutated, immortal clones."

"No, he spoke to me," Tarian said.

Audrey's head snapped around. "Another gift. What happened?" Her expression filled with delicate intrigue.

"When I touched him, I felt a shock or a sensation. It was weird. I don't know. Then I saw Mom's face." He explained as best he could, but there were no words to describe what he'd experienced.

"Hello, kids." A recognizable voice fell over them.

"Zachary! Have you gone completely insane?" Audrey's voice was guttural, and her eyes bulged from their sockets.

The Senator stood in front of a dozen armed guards. He wore a liar's face, and his eyes were no longer hazel. What had changed them to oil black?

They'd been naïve to assume they could waltz in there undetected. An operation of this magnitude was too valuable to be left unguarded.

"Audrey, you have lived as long as I have. You have seen

the destruction these mortals favor year after year. They continue to repeat history. They never learn. They need to be controlled and now we have the numbers to keep world peace," Zachary said.

The Senator drew out each syllable making it maddening for Tarian to listen to him. His words reflected pure madness, yet he looked like a charming, educated congressman.

"At the expense of people's freedom of choice," Audrey argued with quick, clipped words.

"And what do they do with this freedom of choice? Dictators under the guise of whatever idea of the century is popular. Threatening freedom, killing innocents. Then governments with good intentions end up in a useless war, accomplishing nothing. Religious crusaders will murder an entire race for their own beliefs without any scientific data to substantiate their truths. Nothing changes. This repeats again and again and again. A cyclical pattern of ignorance. I'd like to live out the rest of my immortal years in peace, wouldn't you?" Zachary's lack of anger or emotion was more frightening than anything else.

"Your ideals sound just like the 'good intentions' you just spoke of," Audrey snarled, refusing to take the arm he offered.

"No," he spit back at her, finally raising his voice and sounding a little more human.

The Senator shook with anger, and she bit back another retort. Her blues darted to Tarian. He tried to mentally communicate to just go along with whatever crazy adventure he wanted to lead them on. When they got a chance to escape, they'd take it. He hoped his strained eyes relayed the message.

"Come, let me show you the product." Zachary put his arm around Tarian and guided him forward.

The Senator spoke in an eerily calm and saccharine voice as he strolled further into the room. His anger had subsided. They were soon surrounded with the cloned infants and their disturbing noises. It felt like they passed over the threshold into hell. The acrid smells of human waste inside full diapers combined with lavender scented cleaning fluids created an intoxicating potion. Innocence mixed with evil swirled and dissolved inside the room and Tarian understood Audrey's point. The little beings looked pure and harmless but were an alchemy of corrupt ingenuity designed for mass destruction.

"Your father admired my vision. His accident was a pure shame." Zachary continued the tour of his hidden netherworld.

"Accident?" Tarian asked. Zachary wasn't making any sense.

"Yes, of course, Tarian. You didn't think I killed him on purpose? I loved him like a brother." The words flowed from Zachary's tongue like honey.

The Senator spoke with conviction and his eyes didn't betray him, but his grip on Tarian's shoulder tightened as he lied. It took all of Tarian's willpower to smile and nod at his demented captor.

"Zachary, these are just newborns. You won't have soldiers for several years," Audrey said. Her eyes scanned the entire facility, mapping out all persons and objects.

"That's the beauty, Audrey. I will mold them. I will train them. I can guarantee Eleanor; they will embody good values and fight for the Guardians' cause. Together we can accomplish great things with these tiny marvels. Where is Eleanor?"

"What do you mean?" Tarian asked.

"She's late. That's not like her." Zachary still possessed his serpent sway and strange cadence.

Was he expecting her? Did she know about this facility? How long had she known? Tarian's heart skipped.

As if she could read his thoughts, Audrey glanced at him with a lined forehead. This development had to be handled delicately, for they didn't know what could be believed.

Zachary strolled him arm in arm through the madness inhaling deeply and gazing proudly at his work as if they were amongst rows of beautiful roses. The magnitude of what Tarian was witnessing finally struck him. He struggled to breathe, and his knees weakened to buckle. He fought the urge to collapse and forced himself to stand tall. He wouldn't give Zachary the satisfaction, but feared he already had.

"Hold on, Tarian, just a few more steps. It's all right, son. You are home now." Zachary smiled.

"I'm not your son," Tarian growled, as the venom in his veins rose to the surface, breaking through his composure of false amiability.

He couldn't go along with this façade any longer, but Audrey came to his side and pulled him close to her, stopping a further outburst. She wanted his silence, and he gave it to her hoping she had a plan to get them out of the freak show alive.

"Audrey, you are so fond of him. Isn't that wonderful?" Zachary's oily black eyes narrowed, and his posture stiffened. "Here we are."

Zachary opened a shiny, white door that loomed before them at the end of the neat rows of cloned newborns. The door led to an apartment. Floor-to-ceiling stark white walls illuminated the room. White tiled floors, white leather couches, and the kitchen held white cabinets and countertops, and finally, a chair with white upholstery sat in front of a window. Tarian envisioned toddling clones with dirty hands covering the pristine whiteness with smudges of browns, reds, and yellows, and it satisfied his desire to shove this false heaven in Zachary's face. The Senator was trying to sterilize his contaminated vision, but Tarian knew it would never work.

The view from the single white chair didn't look upon the outside world, but on Zachary's obscene, living garden. He gestured for Tarian to sit and gaze upon his masterpiece. It was more than sick.

"What do you expect me to do?" Tarian asked.

"Nothing, son. You've done so much already. I can't thank you enough. I want you to sit here and watch your children grow. You were the first. We will need to continue to monitor you in order to secure the accuracy of our children. Sit," he commanded.

Tarian didn't move. He would never sit in that devil's throne. They glared at one another for several seconds.

"Sit!" Zachary bellowed.

The calm facade Zachary had displayed vanished. Irritated by Tarian's refusal, he stalked over to Audrey, fastened his arm around her neck. "Audrey Darling, tell him to sit down now."

Tarian quickly sat and Zachary released her, returning to Tarian's side. With one swipe of the device in Zachary's hand, solid steel cuffs encircled Tarian's wrists and ankles. Once the chair had completed the binding, he prepped Tarian for an intravenous needle.

"What are you doing to him?" Audrey asked in a rough voice loaded with exhaustion and helplessness.

"He is dehydrated. He needs fluids and nutrition," Zachary said.

Audrey released a sigh of anxiety that echoed throughout the room. Her momentary relief depleted her energy, and she collapsed into the couch and crumpled. She put her head in her hands and cried, and that's when Tarian knew they'd been beat. Zachary had won.

"Audrey, I would never hurt you or Tarian. You must know that. You are safe now."

If Zachary intended to create a haven, he had done a poor job. The symphonic music meant to put them at peace only sounded ominous, and his syrupy sweet voice pushed them further into the depths of despair.

"Okay, okay, I know, I know," she mumbled repeatedly, trying to muffle the sounds of his voice and music. She had the Death Serum inside her pocket, but Zachary was well armed. The serum might as well have been miles away since she couldn't inject it.

Tarian's mind fervently thought, but everywhere he looked men and women with guns stood guard. He couldn't reach his gun and Audrey could not risk using hers. The rows of cloned newborns seemed endless, like looking into an infinite carnival mirror. If they started a gunfight, the newborn clones would surely get caught in the crossfire. Audrey said they had to destroy them, but he felt conflicted. He couldn't murder newborns, not even cloned ones.

As Tarian gazed out the glass at the little stringy hands, skinny fingers, tiny plump feet, and pudgy toes, he knew he couldn't eliminate them. Suddenly, he looked more closely at their petite round faces and gasped. These were boys *and* girls. He'd assumed they were all males. No, that's not true, before he hadn't thought about their gender at all. They were just strange little things. Now they had a familiarity that tapped his soul. Once the recognition hit his brain, the monitor he was hooked up to beeped loudly and the needle erratically swooped across the page in violent skips and leaps.

"What did you do?" Audrey screamed at Zachary.

"Nothing, he is stressed,"

Tears rolled down Tarian's face in voluminous streams of agony and his body convulsed, seizing in a horrific display of his inner nightmares.

"Liar! What are you doing?" she howled, as she watched his body thrash against the tethers that held him.

It was visually horrific, but he felt no pain, just rage and fear.

Audrey shot to his side and gently wiped the tears from his reddened face. One of her delicate but strong hands placed on his chest extinguished his writhing.

Electricity flowed between their two bodies. He opened his soul to her, and he saw into hers. Flashes of visions of Joe crossed between them. Distant memories from centuries ago flooded into Tarian's mind, while Audrey saw such things as Tarian's birth and the horrible school bus accident that should've taken his life. Her true feelings for him as his for her crossed over in this unique gift of communication that Tarian possessed. Suddenly, the flush of pleasure pivoted, turning into torment. Audrey jerked her hand away as if she'd been stung.

She bent her head and whispered into his ear, "What is it, Tarian?"

"The clones." He looked into her soothing blue, silver eyes.

She turned to study them from his vantage point, and he saw the flash of his realization cross over her face.

"They're me and Delia," he stated in a surprisingly restrained voice.

Zachary ignored Tarian's words. He was busy sterilizing equipment and marking notes down on a chart as if everything was normal.

"Aren't they?" The words flew from Tarian's mouth in a masculine deep scream.

"Yes," Zachary said again without emotion or reaction to his outburst. "Isn't it magnificent? They are not clones. That's the beauty of it. They are your offspring. Yours and Delia's."

"And my mother's." Tarian's body went limp.

Zachary didn't verify this fact, but Tarian knew it was true. The newborn had showed him in his touch. Zachary had created immortals concocted out of a powerful alchemical blood mixture.

Audrey spoke no words of comfort to Tarian, and no words of disgust to Zachary. It simply was too unbelievable. She slid her hand into Tarian's, and they both gazed out the window at the absurdity of his offspring, rows and rows of offspring.

As they surveyed the nursery once more, a figure came into view. It entered from the door at the other end, the same door Audrey and Tarian had entered over an hour ago. Her face quickly came into view. Eleanor. She was alone. This meant she was either working with Zachary or trapped as they were. Zachary and his guards left the room and locked the door.

THIRTY-SEVEN

POINT OF THE NEEDLE

"Get me out of here," Tarian said.

Audrey scavenged the chair and all of its gadgets for the control that released the implacable steel cuffs.

"He's taken it," Audrey said, and they both looked out the window to see Zachary holding a flat square pad, the control panel for his torture chair.

"You don't think Eleanor's going to negotiate with him?" he asked.

"No," she said, but offered no other explanation. "He's changed. His eyes."

Tarian nodded. He didn't need further explanation. They'd both seen the strange otherness that possessed Zachary.

"He's stronger now too," she stated in words barely a whisper.

Tarian and Audrey watched as Zachary and Eleanor conversed for what dragged by like hours. The walls were soundproof so they couldn't hear a word, but visually it looked as if they were making an ordinary business deal. Zachary's wicked grin never shifted, and Eleanor's green eyes never tensed. The conversation seemed civilized until Eleanor suddenly, with one unexpected move, stabbed Zachary in the heart.

"Oh my God! Did you see that?" Tarian's head jolted forward but the steel straps kept his body in place.

"She has Death Serum!" Audrey ran to the window.

Eleanor and Zachary tangled on the floor. In unison, the men and women surrounding the perimeter began the emergency procedures they'd been trained to execute. Half of them remained in place and raised their weapons, while the other half rescued the offspring. The guards quickly removed the crib-like, plastic containers and stacked them one on top of the other. They wheeled them at rapid speed toward an exit on the west wall. This escape route had clearly been meticulously practiced and well organized.

Audrey rushed to the exit, pulling and pushing, but it wouldn't open. She kicked the door and banged the lock, but still, it didn't budge. Her immortal strength fell short against Zachary's modified steel and security-controlled lock. She shot it with her gun and destroyed the lock, but the door remained sealed.

Outside, Guardians and military swarmed the nursery while Audrey and Tarian were forced to sit helplessly inside the white room and watch the bloody massacre unfold. They couldn't hear the gunfire, the screams of the people, or the cries of the offspring, but they could watch and almost feel the events transpire, like a silent horror movie. Smoke, blood, bullets exploded in the space in front of their faces. They shut their eyes trying to unsee the death and destruction.

"There's Lycott!" Tarian attempted to lift his arm and point, but it was immobile. His frustration built as she looked in the opposite direction and he couldn't fix it. "Over there, to the left, escaping."

Audrey scanned the room rapidly searching for a shadowy figure. "I see him."

"We can't let him get away." Tarian thrashed pointlessly in his entrapment.

Audrey bombarded the door with bullets. It remained stubbornly closed. She rummaged through the many pockets in her SEAL suit and guard uniform to find a small explosive device. She quickly detonated it. The door opened. She ran headlong into the gunfire.

Tarian sat helpless. He watched as she rushed to Zachary's body. She wasn't trying to seize Lycott or save the offspring. She wasn't fighting at all. She wanted the control pad. She grabbed it and ran back toward the room. As she ran with a grin of accomplishment, Eleanor swiped the control pad out of her hands. The two women stumbled into the room.

"Eleanor, what are you doing?" Audrey asked, stunned at her maneuver.

"What has to be done," Eleanor said. "I'm sorry Audrey. Immortal DNA cannot be replicated. Zachary and I have been attempting to clone it for years."

"You knew about this operation?" Audrey asked.

"No. I gave up the cloning idea long ago when I found it was impossible to replicate our chromosome sequence and cell division. My attempts did not include taking over the world, but now I see the true evil that will come from our reproduction. I realize this cannot go any further. Zachary may be dead, but he is not the only Guardian or mortal who may attempt this ill-fated mission."

Eleanor's words came together in Tarian's head. He was the missing link to the reproduction puzzle. He had to be terminated. He squirmed against the restraints, but it wouldn't release. All he accomplished was bloody, bruised wrists and ankles. He stopped and prepared himself for death. His mind drifted away from this life and to his dad who would be waiting for him in the next. He'd be able to experience what his dad had gone through. He'd see him soon. He tried to hold onto these thoughts in order to stay positive, but his will to survive fought against this delusion and forced him to consider those left behind. They needed him: Chloe, Joe Jr., Teresa, Audrey, Mom. *Would Eleanor kill Mom too?* He fought again for his mother, but the solid steel of the cuffs was unbreakable.

He transferred his attention to Audrey. She could change his fate. Frustration and confusion tainted her face as she listened to Eleanor. Eleanor—her leader, her chancellor, her sister. Audrey would never go against Eleanor's orders. His life was over. He prayed for his mother's safety.

Eleanor placed the chair's control pad on the counter and

removed another Death Serum syringe from her pocket. Her emerald eyes locked onto Tarian's but she didn't speak. In fact, she didn't look apologetic at all.

Tarian refused to speak as well. He glared at her and offered no excuses. His eyes stung and itched from dried tears, but he wouldn't blink or look away. The two of them had an unspoken understanding. His immortality had been a natural phenomenon that provided a genetic gateway into the new scientific world. Unfortunately, mortals and Guardians couldn't be trusted with this power. Zachary had corrupted Tarian's existence. His dad had known this. He'd known not to trust outsiders, never imagining an insider would betray him. He'd died to save his life, to save many lives.

Wait!

"No!" Tarian roared. His epiphany erupted inside him. He wasn't finished. He'd fight! His dad wouldn't have died in vain.

His protest thrust life back into Audrey, wrenching her out of limbo. It was just enough of a distraction to allow Audrey to knock down Eleanor with a swift kick to the knees. She grabbed the control pad and pressed the release. Tarian sprung out of the horrible chair. Two against one, but Eleanor held the lethal syringe.

She treaded toward them, and he saw her calculating eyes dart around the room, examining her options. Eleanor could move objects at will, and Tarian feared her next move could come from any direction. Tarian instinctively pushed Audrey behind him to protect her. Audrey was his equal in strength and probably a superior fighter, but he wanted desperately to protect her from the point of the needle. Surprisingly, she accepted his safeguard, yet her role was still vital. She had a gun in one hand, raised shoulder height around the side of his body, and aimed at Eleanor. With her other hand, she maneuvered her guard uniform to find her Death Serum tucked deep inside a protective pocket of her SEAL suit. Her shaking hands were unable to locate the serum, and her grip on the gun slipped. Her eyes teared and Tarian couldn't rely on her shot to be accurate, not this time.

Unable to grab a weapon, Tarian prepared to round kick Eleanor's hand that held the syringe. He'd destroy the serum, not Eleanor. She was out of line and too hasty, attempting to salvage a bad situation. If he could save everyone in this room, together they could arrive at a conclusion that didn't involve death.

Eleanor looked into his eyes and read his thoughts. Tarian reacted too late to Eleanor's swift move. She stabbed herself with the needle. It took a second to process that she'd taken her own life instead of his, but Audrey was already by her side pulling the needle out of her body.

"No, Eleanor. No!" Audrey cried, as she knelt beside her friend. "Why?"

"It's okay, Audrey. I'm ready. I'm tired," Eleanor said, with tear-filled eyes. "I've lived far too long. I was willing to take the life of an innocent man to help the greater good. I've become what I hate."

"No you haven't. It's just all new and different."

"Yes, and I'm too old to do my job. I failed you. I failed Joe. I can't do it anymore." Eleanor closed her eyes and rested.

"It's not your fault," Audrey pleaded and hugged her friend.

"Virginia? Honey?" Eleanor's faded voice called out.

Eleanor opened her eyes. Her gaze transfixed on someone in the distance they couldn't see. Slowly she drifted away from their reality. She had a content smile on her face as her eyes became still. The weight of her body substantiated and her breathing gradually silenced.

Audrey sat on the floor cradling her friend's lifeless body and sobbed.

Tarian watched patiently as Audrey grieved and prayed for her friend, but he couldn't allow the grieving to continue after he heard the explosion.

"Get up Audrey!" he ordered brutally, trying to snap her out of her despair.

There's no time to mourn. She looked at him startled as if she didn't remember the massive attack going on outside of the room.

"Take off the uniform." Tarian stripped down to his original SEAL suit. "We need to leave the building immediately. We have to find Gabe, Maria, and Charlie."

She followed his orders like a veteran soldier, quick and precise. She then picked up Eleanor's body. He almost ordered her to leave it behind but then remembered Audrey's immortal strength. As much as he admired Eleanor and wanted to take appropriate measures, his priority was Audrey's safety. His goal was to get them out of there alive and return safely to their home and their families. He was Audrey's family now, and he'd make sure nothing happened to her.

He bolted for the door when he heard another explosion in the nursery. Metal, plastic, flesh, and blood flew from savage, ardent flames. Thick smoke seeped into the apartment billowing above the floor. He turned and searched for another exit. There had to be another way in and out of this place. He frantically opened two closet doors and a bathroom entrance, before at last finding a back door. He and Audrey exited into the hall.

They ran. Every couple of seconds, he glanced back to ensure Audrey was still following him. Her silence disheartened him, but she ran resolutely, determined to stay alive. That was all he wanted from her right now. Death seemed to be a gift for Eleanor, and it scared him. Cognitively, he understood why after centuries and the loss of her daughter and loved ones, she'd welcome death; but emotionally, he didn't understand her desire to exit a wondrous world filled with so many admirers and friends.

Once again, he looked back at Audrey. She still ran. He loved her. He had to destroy all the Death Serum. Selfish or not, he wouldn't let Audrey leave him. If he was going to get through several hundred years, he needed her by his side.

"Faster, you're slowing down!" Audrey sprinted passed him.

The sound of walls caving in around them propelled them faster. With a jolt, they burst through an exterior door.

Bright morning sunshine hit their faces. The light blinded them, but they kept running until a whirling wind sucked them still. Several tiltrotors hovered overhead. Tarian aimed his weapon upward until his eyes adjusted. The familiar Guardians of Dare emblem illuminated on the aircrafts. At once, Tarian felt the tackling embrace of Gabe, Maria, and Charlie. Gabe retrieved Eleanor's body, but Audrey couldn't let go. Tarian placed a hand on the lower part of her back, and she released her long-time friend.

When the heavy burden was physically and emotionally lifted from her, she looked as if she might float away. Tarian vowed he wouldn't let her disconnect from him, not now, not ever. He'd lost one love. He wouldn't let another slip away. Aggressively and passionately, he grabbed her and pulled her into his arms as if his life depended on it. She returned his kiss with a hard, needy mouth. All of his doubts disappeared as their bodies melted into one. He'd never be without her.

Maria yelled, "Let's go!" Her voice was harsh and authoritative, but she gave them both an enormous smile.

The eight tiltrotors, loaded with Guardians and Entente military, lifted in uniform grace toward the orange sky. A handful of men and women dressed in the black uniforms of Zachary's army ran from the burning building and began to fire at them, but they were already too high in the air for their bullets to reach the craft.

Tarian swore. None of Zachary's army could be left alive. He was not only thinking like a soldier, but he was also thinking like a man in love. The need to protect overpowered any of his guilt at the loss of life he was about to administer.

"We have to shoot them!" he yelled at the pilot. "Where's your gunman?"

"Look Tarian." Gabe pointed to the attack aircraft quickly flying into view.

Soon air-to-surface tactical missiles were launched, destroying everything in sight on the ground. As far as he could see, nothing, nor anyone would survive. The lifeless facility's blood red, bright orange, and ink black colors slowly faded. As the distance grew, the vast evergreen forests and snow-covered mountains of the region swallowed the colors. Quickly, it became invisible, however, his mind held the image. How had his birth turned into a massive evolution of an immortal army? Eleanor was right. If his DNA sequence could reproduce unlike the other Guardians, this could happen again.

For once, he was eager to see Roman. He needed answers. Those newborns weren't just a part of him. They were a part of Delia and his mother too. He'd never tell them the whole truth. He'd have to convince Roman to keep his secret. If Delia knew hundreds of her offspring had been destroyed in the name of science, she'd snap out of control. She'd hate immortals even more than she already did. And her father, how was she going to feel about his death? Relieved? Sad? Or would she rejoice?

Audrey's fingers intertwined in his, snatching him from the depths of his inner unrest. She looked exhausted and miserable, but she consoled him with her silvery eyes and gentle touch. She kissed him again then laid her head on his shoulder. As long as he held her, he was happy to forget everything during the flight back to the village.

THIRTY-EIGHT

THE FUNERAL

The dense drapery of clouds hung against the dark slate sky making for a gloomy February day, as if Nature herself mourned Eleanor White Dare's death.

Tarian sat in the plush leather seat of a bulletproof, unmarked, dark green sedan in a line of thirty identical vehicles with Audrey by his side. Charlie sat in the front passenger seat with Guardian Warren Edwards at the wheel driving to Eleanor's prestigious farewell. Charlie now knew the entire absurd truth about Tarian's life and the life of their father. He took it quite well and offered his complete support to all the Guardians and Tarian.

Carolyn and Teresa also attended Eleanor's funeral. They rode in the car ahead of Tarian with Eleanor's trusted lab partner, Patrick Wallace. When Teresa became a fixture at Eleanor's side in the lab, Patrick had welcomed and encouraged her participation. He promised he'd continue Eleanor's work and insisted she continue to help him as she had Eleanor. Teresa promised him she'd try her best, her grief too raw to fully commit.

Tarian gazed out the car window as the many shops of the village rolled past. Usually, major political figures' funerals were held in the Entente's National Cemetery in the Government District, but with the unstable atmosphere, Audrey insisted on Quebec. The village was Eleanor's home, and the villagers would want to be a part of her funeral. Her actual resting place would be in Roanoke, next to her daughter and husband, however, that wasn't common knowledge.

"It's not the same." Tarian regarded the village streets.

"I know," Audrey agreed.

The village had been magically expanded to accommodate the multitude of guests. The guests would never realize the true wonder of the village and the mortal villagers were accustomed to strangeness, having lived through it for generations.

"It's not just the size. It's … it's …" He had no words.

Audrey looked at him with grief-stricken eyes and squeezed his hand.

The guests, villagers, and Guardians wore black, stripping the streets of its colorful movement. Every aspect had dulled from the aromas escaping the bakery to the chiming of the bells on the doors. The magic and beauty of the cobblestone streets Tarian had enjoyed at Christmas time were now dismally idle. Tarian feared the exceptional enchantment had vanished with Eleanor's spirit.

The sedan stopped at the top of the hill. Tarian exited and held the door open for Audrey. She teetered a little on her heel highs and adjusted her tailored skirt. Together they paraded through the mass of political heavyweights to their designated seats in the first row. As Tarian glanced around to view the extensive audience that included the president of the Entente, all Entente congressmen, heads of districts, and chancellors of justice from across the nation, apprehension overwhelmed him. He turned to look at his beautiful girlfriend and tried to exude confidence.

"What are you so nervous about," Audrey asked, still fiddling with her skirt.

"I'm not nervous," he lied.

She smiled at him, placed a calm hand on his bouncing knee, but said nothing.

He forced his knee to stop bouncing. He wanted to shield her, not the other way around. He wondered how she could be so strong. In minutes, she'd be giving the eulogy for the woman known around the world as the Entente's Secretary of Border Affairs, but who was actually the Chancellor of the Guardians of Dare, who had led and inspired the immortals since her journey to the new world in 1587. It was her daughter, Virginia, that had provided the first glimpse of hope to immortal procreation and her father, John White, had been the colony's governor. Simply by association, she'd become the Guardian's leader and matriarch but then remained in power for hundreds of years due to her brilliant mind for politics and instinct for public service. How could Audrey give Eleanor the eulogy she so rightly deserved?

"I can't do it." Audrey wiped the sweat from her palms and

gritted her teeth.

"What?" Tarian asked. Terror struck him as he was just thinking the same thing. He gathered himself together. He wouldn't let her down in her time of need. He had to say something encouraging. "Yes, you can. Of all the people I know, you are by far the most qualified to speak for Eleanor. She'd want you to speak for her."

"I know," she sighed. "But Eleanor was charismatic, never apologetic, always fair, admired by all. She was a natural born leader. How can I explain that? How?"

"Just like that." He touched her face gently. "You have rehearsed your speech to me a hundred times. It's perfect. You're perfect."

Silence fell upon the audience in anticipation of Audrey's speech. She took one long look at Tarian then stood. She left his side and walked on stage alone. Standing tall behind the podium, she spoke with grace and truth.

"She's wonderful," said a familiar voice.

Tarian turned. Piper perched next to him, sitting in the chair Audrey left moments earlier. Piper smiled wide as a tear rolled down her youthful face. She turned and cast her lavender eyes upon him. Her usual hyperactivity replaced with calm wisdom.

"Never doubt her love for you," Piper said.

"I wouldn't," he said.

It seemed like a strange thing to say, and he wanted to question Piper, but he didn't want to miss any of Audrey's eulogy.

He returned his full attention back to the stage.

Audrey was applauded for her speech. Tarian scanned the sea of people dressed in the color of shadows roaring in appreciation, Piper still next to him bubbling over with affection. He'd never been prouder of Audrey and realized at that moment, she may accede as Chancellor.

As he watched her at the podium eloquently accepting the audience's praise, he imagined kissing her again. Amazed by her poise, style and beauty, he'd never been happier. Once the ceremony was over, he selfishly pried her away from the publicity piranhas.

"Finally." He tucked her warm, petite body into his.

It was midnight, and the two of them lay, entwined in her bed. He'd been sleeping in her room ever since they returned, seven days ago. "Your speech was exceptional."

"It was?" she asked, surprised.

"Yes," he replied with a gentle kiss.

"I miss her. I miss all of them."

"I know." Tarian ran his hands down her body, caressing the softness of her abdomen and outlining the edges of her hips with his fingers. "You have me now." He kissed her again and forced his hands to stay in place. He wanted to run them all over her, to touch every inch of her, but he didn't know if her desires were the same.

"Six hundred years is a long time to live," she said, and the words sounded frightening.

Confused, he pulled away so he could look into her eyes. "Are you okay? Are you happy with me?"

It sounded like an immature question, but fifteen people over six-hundred-years-old had just died, and he needed to know that she wasn't considering the option of death.

"Yes, I've never been happier." She reassured him with a passionate kiss. "I meant, it's a long time. I wonder what's going to happen next. I thought I had seen and done everything, but now life is new again. It's both exciting and frightening."

"I'm looking forward to the next six hundred years." He slid his hands down her body once more, reigniting the desire.

Her skin stirred, and her voice moaned with delight, evidence that she hungered for him too. She pulled him into her tightly, their bodies touching from chest to toes, her head nestled into his chest, his arms wrapped tightly around her. They fell asleep as one.

THIRTY-NINE

AND YOU CRUMBLE

Several weeks had passed since the funeral, and the halls of Headquarters gradually adjusted to Eleanor's absence. In a few days Audrey would be inaugurated Chancellor, and Tarian wouldn't return to EMA with Maria and Gabe.

As Tarian strolled the familiar halls, he pondered visiting Delia. He'd avoided her. He'd gone so far as to not walk anywhere near the infirmary. His last visit ended with Roman escorting him out of the room with Delia yelling and her blood pressure rising.

"Tarian!" Roman's voiced echoed in the hall.

"Roman?" Tarian questioned the running body coming closer toward him.

"Delia needs to see you right away," Roman said in a rough, ragged voice. He looked agitated, as if being away from Delia for any length of time was toxic.

Tarian understood this feeling. He felt the aching void whenever Audrey wasn't within sight. "Is she okay?"

"No." Roman rushed Tarian down the hallway.

Dried tears stained Roman's cheeks. Tarian's heart sank. The gleeful butterflies that had fluttered inside Tarian's stomach every hour of his days with Audrey since surviving Zachary's inferno vanished. A hollow, hurtful pit dwelled in its place.

Tarian had been so busy. The funeral arrangements, the paperwork, the lab work had all taken precedence. He'd been consumed with planning an immortal future with Audrey. The last notion he wanted to address was a past pain. The girlfriend that left him, that hated what he was. He couldn't hide anymore, and he was scared to look into her eyes and be held accountable for his absence. His life exceeded his expectations and hers slipped away.

"I'm sorry, Roman. I know I should've come to see her sooner." Tarian confessed while standing face to face on the elevator.

Roman's pale skin and swollen yellow eyes looked as if he hadn't seen the sun in weeks. "I don't expect her to make it through the night."

The words made it real. It shocked Tarian even though his mom and Teresa had kept him up to date on her decline. He'd stubbornly refused to believe she'd succumb to death. The Delia he knew had the will of a bull. Tarian had convinced himself she'd live and when she got better, he'd visit her. To face her now, on her deathbed, terrified him.

Roman looked back at him. He still lingered in the elevator. "She's asking for *you*." He accentuated the word 'you' to insure

Tarian wouldn't retreat. "She's made peace with herself, her mother and brother, but she needs to see you before she can move on."

Tarian searched Roman's bloodshot eyes. If Tarian refused, she'd keep fighting for life. She was that stubborn, he thought, and a smile flashed across his face as he remembered the old days of their courtship. Glimpses of the past rushed before him. He saw her when she was only sixteen, when they studied in her father's library, and they walked through her vegetable gardens. He remembered their awkward first kiss. It had happened too quickly, and he didn't even remember how he'd approached her lips with his. He was sure he'd done it all wrong and that she'd never kiss him again, when her lips touched his once more. The second kiss was one he never forgot, a passionate verification that she was his. She was the first girl who loved *him* and not his better looking, overly charming, older brother.

The buzzer on the elevator door shook Tarian out of the past. Roman had held the door open for too long. The protesting door and Roman's stern glare forced him to move forward.

"If you don't go in there now, you'll miss your chance to say goodbye," Roman said. "She can't fight it off any longer."

Tarian exited the elevator but halted at the door leading into her room. He tried but couldn't keep the watery tears from building and slipping onto his cheeks. He hurriedly stroked them away with the back of his hand, raised his head, and straightened his shoulders. He had no right to cry. He had no right to feel bad. She was the victim. He had to be strong for her. He had to give her the best of him. She deserved the best of him. With that thought, Tarian flung open the door.

He saw a hint of Delia trapped inside a pathetic body of bones: sunken eye sockets, piercing jawline, and limp hair. The best of him that he tried to give her fell apart. He turned around and almost ran from the room, but instead, he pulled himself together and pivoted to face her.

Her conspicuous eyes enjoyed watching him suffer but not in a vicious way. It was more the way an older sister feels when she has the upper hand or final word over her little brother. "Hi, Tarian." Delia's voice was strong.

"Hi Delia," he said.

The room felt like an ice chest. Shivers took over his skin at the thought of being trapped inside a human refrigerator that attempted to preserve the lives of the already deceased. Panic set in as the silence lengthened between them. He took in the surroundings, tried to focus on anything but the awkward quiet. The cracks in the walls. The fingerprints of the many doctors, scientists and loved ones that visited. The medicinal products spread everywhere. This wasn't a room he would want to spend his last hours in.

He needed to get her out of here, outside into the crisp, winter air. The sun shone, and a few birds had returned home in the hopes of an early spring. Sweet melodies floated outside, and she was stuck in this sterile freezer. He opened his mouth to suggest it, but Delia spoke first.

"Is it true?" she whispered.

He could barely hear her. Her strong voice had faded. He moved close to listen.

"There were babies, innocent babies?"

"Yes," Tarian confessed, angered that she'd found out. But he couldn't lie to her. He owed her the truth. Lying would not make her passing any easier. It may relieve him, but he didn't have the right to deny her the truth for his own satisfaction, his own feelings.

"Tell me Tarian." Delia forced herself to sit up in her bed.

He told her most of the horrible truth. "Yes, they were cloned offspring. They looked like you and me." Tarian debated whether to reveal how the single newborn communicated with him. How he had the gift of transferring memories through touch, how he had seen his mother's contribution to these offspring. He resisted the urge to utilize his gift and release the terrorizing memories upon her. He protected her from the obscene knowledge that repeatedly haunted his dreams. "I believe your father found a way to combine our genes to produce cloned offspring. In the process he destroyed your cells. It's still unclear how he made it successful, but I assure you I'll study it. I'll find out and never let it happen again. Why he did it? We'll never know. He went delusional with self-righteous power." He refused to mention her father's infinitely black eyes, increased strength, or otherworldliness.

"That's all Father cared about was power. He only cared about his precious immortals," she snarled, her jealous rage giving strength to her voice again.

"That's not true, Delia," he said, defying her.

She looked deeply wounded by his betrayal. Maybe he should just let her vent, but he couldn't.

"Delia, don't you remember how he used to be when we were kids? How he took us so many places. We were little and Dad was alive, and we went together to amusement parks and ice cream stores and the park. Remember?"

She nodded but didn't speak.

"And Audrey has told me—"

A primal cry escaped her. "Don't mention her name! Don't mention any of their horrible, immortal names to me!"

Her words were meant to hurt him. She was in pain and didn't want her misery to be lonely.

She recoiled back into her pitiful self. She continued in a less venomous tone, but her true intentions were clear. "Tarian, I know that you are an immortal. I know that you're the first hope. You will be different, but I don't trust the father I thought I had. He was always evil. You don't just discard people decade after decade if you're not evil. A mortal human couldn't do that. It's an immortal trait."

Tarian refused to humor her. He turned to face Roman. "We're taking her outside. Unhook her from all of this."

"No, she's too weak. She's connected to these machines because they're keeping her alive," Roman said.

"I don't want to be kept alive, Roman. If I can't live independently, then I'm not living."

"But darling." Roman reached for her hand.

"Tarian's right. I may only have a few moments left. I don't want to spend them in here." Her voice quivered. Tears filled her eyes, but she held her head up high and faced Roman with dignity. "Do it! If I die after just one breath of fresh air, it'll be worth it."

They placed her gingerly in a wheelchair and wrapped a cozy blanket around her. She smiled up at Tarian and reached for his hand. They walked hands connected, as Roman pushed the wheelchair. They passed a few Guardians, some strangers and some friends. People looked at the threesome with bewilderment and then sympathy, no doubt wondering what they were doing with such a sick woman out of the infirmary.

Tarian glared sternly at each of them, knowing pity was an emotion Delia despised. He noticed she pulled her shoulders back and held up her chin as people passed. She flashed her radiant smile. She would forever hold a place in his heart.

The sun shone warmth onto their faces the instant the doors opened to the exterior. It was the warmest day in months.

Delia exhaled a precious, joyful sigh. "Thank you, Tarian. Thank you for the suggestion that we go outside." She coughed a deep guttural cough.

Tarian panicked. "Is it okay? Do you feel okay? We can go back inside."

The questions skidded off of Tarian's tongue like slippery nails. He worried about his actions as Roman gave him a distressed glare. He'd stripped her from those horrid machines, her life force.

The fear in Roman's eyes registered with Delia too.

"Roman, I'm fine." She looked into his eyes as calm and peaceful as if she were a healthy, immortal woman. "I know you're sad and confused, but I'm not anymore. Thank you for giving me a couple extra months of happiness. Thank you for being there when I had no one and no answers. You gave me hope. You loved me," she said, but her words gave out as her voice wavered. She paused to breathe and swallow.

Tarian fidgeted as she confessed her love and appreciation to Roman. Yet, Roman had been there when Tarian couldn't be, and for this, Tarian would be forever grateful.

She continued, "But I'm not going to survive any longer. I'm going to die. I'm going to die out here. Outside in this beautiful sunshine with the two men I love most. The two men that have given me so much in such a short time. You've made my life full and definitely interesting." She grinned.

"Interesting." Tarian nodded.

They walked the path, strolling away from Headquarters towards the vibrant hustle and bustle of the vendors and cafes in the village. Soon the cobbled street curved toward a quaint community park where Roman pulled the wheelchair up onto a small bluff. Here they watched the children play and listened to the birds chirp. They kept silent for at least ten minutes.

Tarian hoped she was enjoying the beauty of what surrounded her, dismissing thoughts of all she was leaving behind. He didn't want her mind filled with worries about immortals, the Prevallers, the betrayal of her father. He hoped for those brief ten minutes, peace found her.

All of a sudden, a sharp pain grabbed Delia, and snapped her body forward. The poke of death, the pain of the inevitable, came to steal her away from them. She clasped her chest and looked at Tarian with fearful eyes. She had something to tell him.

"What is it, my love?" Roman knelt down by her side.

She didn't respond. Instead, she wrapped her arms around him and kissed him for several seconds.

Tarian turned his eyes away.

"I love you," she finally said softly but adamantly, as if she never wanted there to be any doubt that he was her chosen one. Then she turned to look at Tarian and told him she loved him too.

"Please forgive me. I beg you. You must forgive me." The apologetic words flew from Tarian's mouth without hesitation or consideration. He'd known and loved her all of his life. He couldn't bear her suffering.

"I don't forgive you my sweet Tarian." She wore a mocking smile. "But everything happens for a reason. You've been thrown into a life you didn't choose. Both of our fates were chosen for us, and we had to make the best of it."

The pain gripped her again and she doubled over in agony. Roman and Tarian both embraced her, trying to ease her suffering. Tarian thought she was gone this time. He didn't expect to hear another word from her lips, but she looked at him deliberately. She appeared desperate to tell him something. Her focus aimed at him, and her posture straightened to that of a strong, lethal woman.

Roman and Tarian pulled away from her fearing the look of determination in her eyes. Passionately, she clutched Tarian's arm and drew his face to hers so he could hear her last words while making sure Roman could not.

"Don't trust her." She exhaled her last words with confidence but with a lack of strength, her voice forced and airy. Death's grip held her shoulders until her lifeless body doubled over and died in a pitiful lump of human frailty.

Roman quickly unfolded her to place her in a more dignified position.

Tarian felt his pain. His need to position her properly eased his distress. Tarian reflected on the absurdity of man continually 'fixing' reality. The reality was she died with words of hatred on her lips in a cold, metal chair in the awkward position that comes when death slaps you hard on the back and you crumble. Roman and Tarian, acting humanely, had tried to bring peace to her death but she knew better. Peace may have held her momentarily, but the cruel reality of her mortality had seized her. Only a fortunate few are genuinely ready to die. The rest fight death until the bitter end.

"I'm going to take her back now," Roman said in an admirably sturdy voice.

"Okay. Do you mind if I stay here?"

"No. I'd rather be alone."

Tarian felt the same. He remained at the spot where her life had ceased. He sat against a tree, folded one knee up to his chest, and reclined back onto its trunk.

For an hour he sat alone in sober contemplation. Delia's last words haunted him. He focused on the children playing in the park and listened to their joyful laughter in the hopes that it would reassure him of the goodness in people. He found amusement as the kids stubbornly refused their mother's orders. He sympathized with the mother's plight, but secretly relished the kid's defiance. The children were resilient. They fell but got back up with even more energy and determination than before. Tarian smiled to himself.

A familiar, gentle caress startled him out of his reflection. Tarian glanced up to see Audrey. She sat next to him and entwined her warm arms around his. Then she laid her head on his shoulder. He welcomed her company.

"I'm sorry Tarian," she said, as they both looked straight away.

"Me too, beautiful." He drew her closer.

He would never leave her, and he would never repeat Delia's last words. He loved Audrey, and he trusted her with all his being.

FORTY

SLEEPERS

As Audrey stood alone and cold inside the dark, cavernous room, she examined the chocolate brown eyes of Joe Prescott and thought, they would not look so different when they changed to black. She fooled herself. It wasn't the color of the eyes. It was the infinite depth of nothingness. The awakened eyes weren't just black they were empty.

Joe's milky colored, frigid body rested on one of the many beds inside the crypt. It was four o'clock in the morning, Audrey's usual working hour for this exclusive project, when she jerked wildly at the thud of the door shutting behind Patrick. His entrance always startled her even though his presence was expected.

"Audrey, come on! Maybe if you allowed yourself a little heat you wouldn't be so freaked out all the time," Patrick argued.

"I can't. They need the cold to survive." She snugly wrapped the lab coat around her narrow torso.

"*If* they survive." He corrected her.

She hung her head suffering from her own inability to conquer the Awakening Serum. She and Patrick had been clandestinely working inside Eleanor's hidden, stone chamber laboratory for four months to no avail. They had no idea as to how long a Death Serum injected immortal could sleep. This was uncharted scientific territory for the Guardians.

As she meandered around the beds, shuffling her wool-lined boots she gently touched each corpse-like body. She desperately wished they would rise and scare the living hell out of her. She'd spent endless hours inside the village church at the feet of an intricately sculpted Christ praying for answers, for help, for enlightenment, but only received the permanent stare of his sympathetic eyes chiseled out of wood. He offered her no help. She wasn't faithless, but she wasn't without doubt either. And she hadn't stepped foot inside a church for decades. At all her recent church visits, she vowed to be a better person, she promised to believe, and she did believe. She'd seen the Devil, so she knew there had to be a God as well.

Eleanor had had the unquestionable faith and the brilliant scientific mind, but even she had not mastered this problem. Zachary had though. Zachary had somehow awakened himself from the grips of the Death Serum. Audrey had Eleanor's notes listing theories to explain many mysteries of Death Serum and its counterpart, but Eleanor's ingredients and equations were not producing the serum. Or maybe it was the amalgamation. Audrey was simply failing to apply all the parts correctly.

Audrey's horrible drop into the rabbit hole had begun when she journeyed alongside Eleanor's corpse to the remote Roanoke burial site. Eleanor had left something for her to find. It had been buried under the dirt at the gravesite. The buried object was a formally sealed letter addressed to Audrey informing her of the secret underground laboratory where several sleeping immortals lie. The letter read like a fairy tale—sprinkle special awakening fairy dust over eternal, sleeping immortals, and they'll miraculously spring to life again.

In this particularly wicked fairytale, Eleanor told that the eyes of those having been awakened would be of the blackest black. Eleanor sadly admitted she'd failed in her attempts to produce such an awakening. The fairytale was just that, a fictional tale. Only Eleanor confessed that it wasn't fiction, that Zachary had been successful at producing the power. As with all good fairy tales there was a horrible warning. Death cheating immortals strolled the halls of Headquarters wearing colored lenses to mask their transformation, a reality that made Audrey uneasy around all of her trusted Guardians.

At the gravesite, after reading the last line, she had crumpled the letter and thrust it as far away as she could. *Do not wake me! Let me rest in peace next to my family!*

Audrey shook off her memory and the guilt it brought, as she placed the thin white cloth back over Eleanor's still face.

Audrey turned sharply to face Patrick. "Give me the bear."

"Please," Patrick teased.

"Please," Audrey added more docile. Her heart hardened inside the walls of this morgue, making it easy for her to snap at her trusted friend. She'd loved each sleeping immortal inside this refrigerated meat locker. Seeing them serenely resting with stunning magnificence of peace on their frozen faces was too fascinatingly wicked for Audrey to handle.

Patrick handed Audrey Chloe's teddy bear. Audrey gently sliced it open at the seam so as to leave no evidence once she restitched the bear. Placing her slender fingers inside the fluff of its belly, Audrey felt for the letter she expected to find. Cautiously she pulled out the folded paper, taking care not to harm Chloe's bear. To Audrey's surprise she felt another object inside the spun cotton candy filling. She pulled the object out carefully. It was a miniscule vial surrounded by a clear protective box. She'd never seen such an encasement before and had no way of opening it. Audrey resisted the urged to slam it onto the ground hoping to break it into tiny pieces, but she knew this action might destroy its contents.

Joe Prescott's note that was cleverly hidden inside the teddy bear provided detailed chemical equations that Patrick understood far better than Audrey. The arduously imprisoned vial was a sample of the Awakening Serum, she was sure of it. Another warning scrolled in ink on the paper. This horrible fairy tale kept getting worse, and she hadn't had the heart to involve Tarian. He already struggled with vividly, gruesome nightmares. How could she possibly tell him his father was a sleeping corpse in the basement?

The final paragraph of Joe's note read:

This is new and imperfect biochemistry. As should be expected, death comes to immortals in a form of sleep. The body does not die, it hibernates and once awakened, it transforms. This transformation produces a stronger, less human immortal. Proceed with great caution!

FIRST BORN TRILOGY

WHO HELPED AND WHAT HAPPENED?

First Born has been a unique journey along a very bumpy road. One I began several years ago. Book 1, *First Born,* was first self-published in December of 2015 with *First Awakened* launching soon after in March of 2016. The third and last book in the trilogy manifested slowly and in pieces that proved difficult to organize. Also, another book idea took root in my head. It was loud and wouldn't yield so the *First Born* trilogy got placed on the back burner. I wrote *Dog Girl*, my debut young adult contemporary romance. *Dog Girl* found an agent and a publisher. If you're interested it's out in the world under my pen name, Gabi Justice.

Meanwhile, the third book, *Last Chance*, began to come together. Before releasing *Last Chance*, I decided to query a few independent publishing houses that accepted self-published books. One loved it and offered to publish in 2022. So, in 2019, *First Born* and *First Awakened* were shelved and the waiting game began. Then the pandemic hit. The said publishing house went out of business. It was difficult and discouraging but all three books were complete, never published with said publisher, and I had my rights back, so what was I to do—relaunch the trilogy myself!

I'd learned a few things since 2015. The wild ride had brought me knowledge and industry friends. I am forever grateful to those who have helped shape the *First Born Trilogy*.

A big thank you to my SCBWI critique group: Jill Watson, Andrea Tripke, and Ann Marie Meyers for reading lengthy, monthly experts of *Last Chance* and other stories. Thank you to my friends at the Tampa Writer's Alliance critique group—over twenty-five fellow writers who thickened my skin. Special thanks to my agent Sharon Belcastro for constantly believing in me. You may not have played a key role in these books but within my writing marathon you take the lead.

Thank you to Allison Newell, Tarian Prescott's first fan; to Sandy McCain who helped edit my first drafts; Jim Robertson for my eye-catching covers; to Diane and Jenny at BookRhythm for the fabulous support and promotion. I will be forever thankful to have sat next to Tasha Vincent at the On Point Book Fair in Tampa. Your editorial input lifted my writing to a greater level. Thank you, April Schlee for your keen proofreading eye. Thank you to my insightful friends and beta readers Mark Charest and Darrel Polsley for finding those pesky typos and errors that slipped past, for letting me know when something was out of place, and for your constant encouragement and input. To Emcat designs for former book covers and beautiful map designs. To Marina Charalambides for bringing the characters to life with your drawings. Also, to the beta readers who probably wondered if this trilogy was ever going to be completely published: Mattea Carberry, Valerie Senske, Susan VanNort, Julie Carrigan, Mimi Daniels, and the Book Gremlins.

Since this journey has been a long and winding path, I've probably forgotten to mention someone. If I have, I'm truly sorry. Every little bit counts and I'm grateful.

Lastly, a giant thanks to my readers and fans that have written reviews, joined my newsletter, and parties, all in support of Tarian and Audrey. You have brought my characters and world to life.

JANELLE GABAY

Janelle lives with her husband, three dogs, and a cat in Florida. Two of her three children are out of college and in the workforce. The third is close behind. They are her pride and joy. She was born in Nebraska and grew up in the Philippines, Virginia, Alabama, Maine, and Florida as an Air Force Brat. *First Born* is her debut novel. She spends her time writing, taking care of her animals, going to hockey games or tennis matches, and traveling with her family. She is a graduate from the University of South Florida.

You can visit her online at www.janellegabaybooks.com
Twitter @JanelleGabay
Instagram @janellegabaybooks
janellegabaybooks@gmail.com
Follow on Goodreads
Facebook page Author Janelle Gabay @authorjanellegabay

Made in the USA
Columbia, SC
02 October 2023

23778671R00217